The LOST CROWN of APOLLO

by

SUZANNE CORDATOS

With luck
and a prayer !

Suzanne Cordatos

SUNBERRY BOOKS
Sunpenny Publishing Group

THE LOST CROWN OF APOLLO

ISBN # 978-1-907984-50-1

First published in Great Britain in 2015 by Sunberry Books, a children's imprint from Sunpenny Limited www.sunpenny.com (Sunpenny Publishing Group)

Dedicated to the Yiazlas and Kordatos
families for sharing many sunny adventures
in the amazing country of Greece

Author's Note

One hot and sleepy August afternoon in Greece, the ferry was pulling a load of tourists away from the island of Delos when our small boat arrived. In the company of a few fast lizards, we felt we were first to discover the headless statues and marble remains of temples built to worship ancient gods and goddesses. Who had lived there? What had happened to make the white city and proud lions crumble?

Acknowledgments

Laurel crowns to my first readers and writing friends: Kristi Rhodes, David and Gloria Cournoyer, Rachel Blakely, Debbie Austin, Sherry Auger, Brenda, Sean and Annika Sturmer, Gretchen Evan, Louise Fleck. A special thank you for the constant support and encouragement of my parents, siblings Jackie and Jon, extended family and beautiful daughters, Jessica and Erica and to my twin sister and writing soulmate, Sunpenny author Sonja Anderson. Heartfelt thanks to Jo Holloway for Sunpenny's faith in this story and her expert attention to detail and quality. Another laurel crown to my husband, Haralambos, for his constant support and love of adventure, and for sharing his wonderful family and friends with me. Characterizations are fictional; special thanks to his extremely fine buddies who allowed their names to be used for the bad guys. In bringing contemporary characters into contact with ancient history and Greek mythology, bumps with historical accuracy are not intentional, and any mistakes remaining are mine.

ABOVE:

A BOAT VERY SIMILAR TO "SARGOS", 23 FEET LONG AND WITH A 200 HORSE-POWER ENGINE, AND A SMALL CABIN AT THE FRONT (IN THE BOW).

LEFT:

THE MYKONOS PELICAN, PETROS (YES, HE DOES REALLY EXIST!)

PART ONE

For the sun rises with its scorching heat
and withers the field;
its flower falls
and its beauty perishes.

James 1:11

1

THE BAD LUCK MAGNET

With the speed of a glacier, the classroom clock ticked the final minutes to summer vacation. Forty-two and a half, according to the restless eyes of Elias Tantalos.

"Class, you are fifth graders for a little longer," announced Mrs. Struggles. "Time for one final essay."

The almost-middle-schoolers groaned at their teacher, but Mrs. Struggles ignored the complaints.

"Write an essay on what you learned in fifth grade. It won't be graded, but I want to see your best work. The assignment is important for your self-reflection."

"Old bat," muttered Elias, but he had *plenty* to write about. P-L-E-N-T-Y.

Did it matter if the stuff he learned had nothing to do with lessons?

Chewing on the end of his pencil, he was ready to air out the rotten truth:

What I Learned in Fifth Grade
By Elias Tantalos

No offense, Mrs. Struggles, you are my favorite teacher OF ALL TIME (and I'm not saying that just so you'll like my essay) but do you have to make us work in the last hour of the worst school year of my life? Torture!

You've tried hard to teach us math and science and history and stuff, but in fifth grade I learned that the world has two kinds of people in it: lucky ones and the kind that bad luck sticks to like a magnet. Guess which kind I am?

Exhibit A
Lucky People

1. Kennedy Anderson is the luckiest person on Earth. Her grandma never remembers her birthday. Lucky? Listen. Kennedy gets a birthday card on the third day of every month, not just November. With money in it. Every month! That grandma never misses!

2. Kennedy Anderson was the first person at Evamere School to get a cell phone, because she paid for it herself. I don't have money to buy

one, and even if I did my mother thinks I don't need one. (When Mom makes a decision, it takes an earthquake or tsunami or tornado to change her mind. All three at once might do it.)

3. Kincaid is lucky because his blonde hair goes straight. Plus, he gets Brandon to do his dirty work for him.

4. Brandon hit puberty way early. Between fourth and fifth grade he turned into Brandon the Gorilla Boy. Strong hairy arms. Lucky? Yes, see #5.

5. Nobody messes with Brandon.

6. Kincaid and Brandon are lucky because they never get caught doing mean stuff. Teachers don't notice. (Not even you, Mrs. Struggles.)

Exhibit B
Bad Luck Magnet
Me, Elias Tantalos

I am the fastest runner on the Evamere Wings soccer team. Lucky? Sadly, no. Last November, I ran super-fast during the Fall Soccer State Cup Championship. Nobody could catch me, and I kicked the ball past the goalie's shoulder smack into the net—but I was running THE WRONG WAY and kicked the ball past OUR OWN GOALIE and WON

THE STUPID CHAMPIONSHIP FOR THE WRONG STUPID TEAM. (Later, Kennedy Anderson said it was an awesome kick and there was no way she could've stopped it, and she's the greatest goalie Evamere Wings ever had.)

Kennedy Anderson is the only person who still talks to me. No idea why. I'm skinny and have brown eyes and boring brown hair that won't go straight, and I'm the worst bad luck magnet in the world. Kennedy Anderson should be afraid my bad luck will rub off on her good luck—if it was the other way around, I would avoid me like a rat-infested bubonic plague. Remember the Fall of Rome you were teaching us about, Mrs. Struggles? My life after the State Cup game was just like ancient Rome: it fell to ruins.

More Examples of the Bad Luck Magnetism of Elias Tantalos

1. My (former) best friends Kincaid and Brandon changed my nickname from "Fireball" to "Wrong-Way."
2. My (former) best friends Kincaid and Brandon tried to MEASURE THE CIRCUMFERENCE OF MY HEAD WITH A RULER, because if it is

regulation size they want to use it for the GAME BALL next season in middle school—to make sure it heads down the field the right way.

3. My (former) best friends Kincaid and Brandon are not my friends.

4. When they stopped being my friends, everybody stopped. Almost everybody. See Exhibit B reference to Kennedy Anderson.

5. My homework started to look like it had been in sword fights. Bleeding red ink.

6. My back is breaking from homework papers stuffed in the bottom of my backpack that I don't want my parents to see.

7. After summer vacation it's Middle School. HEL-LLLOOO, see number 2 above. Kind of terrifying.

In conclusion, I learned that I can't wait to get out of Evamere School, the state of Connecticut and the United States of America. I NEED TO GET OUT OF THE COUNTRY. My family is flying over the ocean to a country called Greece. People might think boating in the Greek islands is a lucky vacation, but how lucky can it be for a bad luck magnet like me?

It will take all night to fly to Greece. We are

borrowing my aunt and uncle's boat, which must be an old tub because it is the same boat my dad used in the olden days. With me on board it will probably sink to the bottom of the Aegean Sea on our way to the middle of nowhere to some island called Mykonos.

My dad is from Greece, but I never learned to speak Greek and that's the only language they talk there. Plus, I hear they don't eat ketchup or peanut butter. What kind of country doesn't eat peanut butt—

"Time's up!" Mrs. Struggles glanced at the clock over the door. "The final bell will ring in a few minutes."

Elias fist-punched the air. "*Yesss!*"

As if they shared one giant eyeball, his classmates turned to stare.

"Not so fast. We have time to hear a few essays."

Mrs. Struggles held out the classroom microphone. It usually made them feel like rock stars to give reports over the mic—except when Elias's stomach twisted and felt like throwing up. Like now, for example.

"Nobody?" Mrs. Struggles waited.

Elias stared out the window at summer vacation, teasing him. He willed the clock to speed up—but the teacher looked straight at him.

"You seem anxious to be done with fifth grade, Mr. Tantalos. Am I interrupting a daydream?" She smiled and handed him the microphone.

The sick feeling wormed around in his stomach.

"Please join us. What did you learn this year?"

Exhibit C
I rest my case
The End

WAIT—

P.S. What will I eat in Greece? I'll die of starvation over there.

P.P.S. I'm not coming back. EVER. Even if I don't die from starvation. Which I'm sort of counting on.

P.P.P.S. Can I leave my little sister on THIS side of the Atlantic Ocean? Second graders can be very, very, VERY annoying, and LILY IS THE WORST. I'd explain, but that would take another essay. And I am out of here. Seriously.

2

KING OF THE WORLD

After a long, *long*, LONG flight, Elias looked out on a morning that held nothing but blue sky and promises as far as his eyes could see. In spite of the early hour at the marina in a small port town near Athens, hot sunshine beat down on his bare back while the bluest sky he'd ever seen made a canopy over the bluest sea.

"Happy early birthday, Elias!" Standing next to a battered-looking boat docked at the marina, the burly Greek uncle he'd just met handed him a brown paper package. Uncle Costas, or *'Theo'* as the word for 'uncle' was here, scratched the black hair curling out the open neck of his shirt. "Your *Thea* Katerina and I thought you might like it ahead of time to read on your trip."

"*Efharisto, Theo.*" Read? The gift under the boring paper was a boring book? Elias faked politeness but promised himself he would never open it. This was vacation. Not school!

His uncle leaned down and kissed him on both cheeks. "Whaaat?" His face turned hot. Elias wiped away the kisses with the back of his hand.

"Better get used to it, son." Dad teasingly rubbed the top of his head and laughed. "Ways of doing things are different in Greece."

Deep in his gut, Elias felt the familiar tug to get away. Back home that feeling spurred him to run, but taking off on foot today wasn't an option.

"I packed a cooler on board with some cheese pies, juice and water bottles," said *Theo* Costas, "but you will arrive on Mykonos this afternoon. This boat may look old, but her engine is powerful. She's twenty-three feet long, with a two hundred horsepower outboard."

"You're not coming with us?" Lily piped up.

His uncle laughed and swept Elias' small sister off her feet with double-cheek-kisses. She giggled and her short blonde curls bounced in the bright morning sunshine.

"If we have your boat, how will you get there?" Lily asked. "Will you fly?"

Theo Costas laughed again. "I'll take a ferry, *koukla*. Your *Thea* Katerina is already at our summer apartment, working on her Sunny Days Camp plans." He turned to speak to Elias' father, who was also his brother. "Give her a call when you near Mykonos Harbor. I will finish my work here in Athens and join you in a few weeks. I should be there in time for Elias' birthday."

They cast off the lines and the boat motored away from the marina. Once at sea, they picked up speed and left land far behind, and the Tantalos family waved at passing water traffic. Elias tested out his sea legs, balancing on the moving deck and shading his eyes with his hand. They soon zipped past one after another of the windswept islands of the Aegean Sea, some not much more than floating boulders. The islands had a burnt look, as if the relentless sun never gave them a break. These were not white-sandy-beach, palm-tree-swaying, postcard kind of islands; the Greek islands had a lonely kind of beauty that suited Elias just fine. After the school year he'd just finished, he would much rather spend time with rocks than people.

The boat's engine rumbled in his bones, salty air filled his lungs, and Elias marveled at his lungs expanding, shoulders melting under the sun. He stretched out his fingers and rubbed the deck railing, breathing deeply. How long had his hands been clenched into fists?

The wind whipped more waves into his hair than usual, and he tried finger-combing it straight but quickly gave up. Seabirds wailed overhead, begging for breakfast. Elias tore small chunks of bread and tossed them overboard, watching the terns dive and fly off with the soggy pieces. Like the seabirds, he had flown to get here, too. Can one airplane ride take you to a place this different from home? Was it far enough?

Like a swimmer with water in his ear, Elias tried to shake out the bad memories of fifth grade. *Summer vacation!* Time to forget! Time for adventure!

Mom rubbed sunscreen on her arms, then on Lily's back. "Elias, would you like to drive the boat? Be co-captain?"

"Are you kidding? *YESSS!*"

As excited as a kid on Christmas morning with the biggest pile of presents under the tree, Dad stood at the captain's wheel and smiled. After handing Elias the key to the ignition, he placed a navy and white captain's cap on his head. Its gold braid twinkled in the sunlight.

"Ready for your first lesson, Captain Elias?"

Elias adjusted the cap and grinned.

"*Bravo.*" Whenever Dad was especially happy or proud (or on rare occasion angry) he slipped from English to his native Greek language. "Picture the wheel like a clock and keep your hands at nine and three o'clock. Hold her steady."

"*Her?*" Curled up to Mom on the boat's comfortable back bench, Lily dug into her bag—a fake-gem-studded *Dazzle It!* bedazzled pink bomb of her own creation—and pulled out her doll and its matching bathing suit. "A boat's not a girl or boy."

"Technically, you are correct, but it is a tradition," said Dad. "Something done the same way for generations is a tradition."

"In the old days, sea captains left home for months and years at a time. No cell phones or internet," Mom reminded them. "Captains often named boats after their wives left behind during long voyages, as a way to let them know they would be remembered. Calling boats 'she' stuck."

Driving was easy with no other boats in sight.

"Keep the bow pointed to the right of the island ahead. The bow is the front of the boat, remember?"

Elias nodded and turned the wheel slightly right. "Bow, front. Port, left. Starboard, right. The back is the 'stern', right?"

"*Bravo.* Once you're past the island, keep left of the next one. We should arrive at Mykonos in a few hours."

Near the high captain's chair was the large plastic cooler. It was multi-purpose, serving as their refrigerator, a dining table, and with a cushion on top an excellent seat. Dad sat down on it and closed his eyes, turning his face to the Greek sun. "You're a born driver, son. I can relax!"

A warm glow spread through Elias' chest, and the powerboat was flying. *"I'm king of the world!"*

3

THE FIRST FLAW

The ancient Greek gods must have felt this way—in control of the universe. Or they would have, if the ancient rulers had existed. When he was a kid, Elias used to wish mythology was real. Thousands of years ago, Greeks explained ordinary things in interesting ways. Take electricity. If an ancient Greek stepped into our world, would he think Zeus was controlling his lightning bolts from on/off light switches?

A sun-drenched sleepiness came over him, and Elias had trouble staying focused. His fingers left their clock positions on the wheel to punch buttons on the Marine GPS and depth monitor. *Wow.* Below *Sargos,* the sea was eight hundred meters deep. Which was longer, a meter or a yard? Elias could never remember, but the Aegean Sea under the boat had to be over two thousand feet deep!

The screen went black. What had happened to the boat's electrical system? He jiggled the buttons, but nothing happened. Should he tell Dad? What if he'd broken it? He could sure use some of Zeus' lightning power right now to zap it back into action!

Elias whacked the side of the GPS, and it came back on. *Phew!*

Mom peered over the top of her sunglasses. "Everything all right up there, Captain Elias?"

"Aye, aye, Matey Mom."

"Bubbles!" Lily knelt on the back bench and pointed off the stern. The propeller blades under the engine were decorating the flat blue sea with a trail of white-water ruffles.

Elias held the captain's wheel with one hand and turned to look. He was about to give her a thumbs-up but instead he pointed at her hair. The wind whipped her curly blonde strands so they danced straight up like crazed, wriggling snakes.

"Lil, you should see your hair!" The captain's area was protected by a window, so he didn't feel the wind from the speeding boat as much as the others. Mom's hair was kept neatly pulled back, but Lily looked ridiculous. "You look like Medusa!"

For reasons Elias could not fathom, the ratty doll on Lily's lap was her favorite. Its hair, yellow and snarled from dozens of baths, reminded him of the ancient Greek tale of the magical woman with snakes for hair who could turn people to stone with one look. Sort of like Lily when she was angry over things like her dumb doll.

Lily hugged the doll close. "Don't call her Medusa. She's not a monster."

"She's not real—" Elias protested.

"Someone better pay attention to their boat driving or lose the privilege," said Mom.

Dad came to his rescue and cut the engine. "Who wants to cool off with a swim? Then we can have a contest to see who will notice the famous windmills of Mykonos first. We must be getting close." Dad studied the GPS (which seemed to be working fine, much to Elias' secret relief), then the horizon, then the navigation system again, and scratched his head. Elias could have sworn he heard his father mutter, "We seem to have gotten off course."

His sister did not get up to swim, but instead got very busy twisting a length of white nautical rope like a pretzel. "Pull it tight, Marina," Lily instructed her doll.

"You know Medusa can't hear you." Elias teased.

"It's *Marina*! Anyway, teaching Marina how to tie boating knots helps me remember them."

"I've got a better idea. Let's tie Medusa to a line and drop her overboard. C'mon, Lil—make her swim!"

"MOM!" Lily's squeaky voice cut through the wind. The line fell off her lap to the deck and she protected the doll with both hands.

"That's enough out of you, Mister Sassy Pants." Mom's blue-gray eyes looked like the Atlantic again. "Don't think I can't enforce house rules because this is a boat instead of a house. Any Tantalos with stinky behavior can have a turn cleaning out the Port-o-Potty."

"Ha!" Lily danced with her doll. "You'll be the Pooper Scooper!"

"No, I won't! Get away from me! All of you!" He took off the captain's cap and flung it onto the deck, feeling trapped. His legs itched to run, and the first flaw in his plan for a perfect summer vacation became as clear as the crystal water beneath them. He was on the far side of the world from the mean kids at school, yes—but how could he escape his annoying family on an old boat not much bigger than the minivan they'd left behind in the long-term parking lot at JFK International Airport?

4

AN OLYMPIC CHAMPION

The boat came to a rocking stop on the blue sea. Father and son took careful footsteps along the narrow ledge following the railing to the bow.

Elias lifted onto his toes, shifting his weight to balance. "Last one in is a rotten hunk of spinach pie!"

He sprang off the front end in a neat dive, the water cooling his sweating body. Plans for the perfect summer vacation flooded his mind.

What to do first?

The options suddenly seemed as endless as the Greek sky:

1. Snorkel to look at sea creatures
2. Explore an island
3. Find a hidden cave
4. Discover the lost city of Atlantis
5. Dive off the boat
6. Go fishing

Refreshed in body and soul, his daydreams grew bigger with every deep stroke of his arms. When Elias came up for air, water cascaded over his head; he pushed the brown mass of hair sticking to his eyes and licked sea salt from his lips. It tasted of summer. Sweet freedom. With a little luck, on a day like this anything could happen.

"It doesn't stay blue."

Lily leaned over the side of the boat, her perky chin pointed down to the sea with a frown clouding her blue eyes. She dipped an empty jar, scooping water, only to pour it right back out.

"What are you doing, Brainless?" Second grade girls! Elias couldn't understand his little sister. Like why did she prefer to stay in the boat, bone dry? "I promised my friends a souvenir to show them what Greece is like," Lily complained. "The ocean at home isn't this blue. I want to bring some A-jeen Sea water back for them."

"It's Aegean. Pronounced UH-GEE-UN."

But Lily was right. The Aegean Sea was like swimming in a vat of Mom's blue window cleaner. The water in Lily's jar, however, kept coming up clear. Dad explained how the sea's depth, mineral content and clarity impacted the color.

Not in the mood for a science lesson, Elias hugged his knees and did a back roll. Anything that reminded of him of school was *not* allowed.

"Son—are you listening?" Dad treaded water near him, pointing to worn-off letters in silver paint on the back of the boat. "*S-A-R-G-O-S*," he explained. "The boat was named for the small, silver-bellied fish that live in these waters. Small fish," Dad said, "but fast!" He floated by on his back with hands behind his head as if he were relaxing on their couch back in Connecticut. "Ahhh... sun, sea, family. This is what a Greek vacation is all about. When I was your age—"

"No growing-up-in-Greece stories, Daddy," said Lily.

Elias was in full agreement with his eight year old sister. He already knew those stories by heart, like how Dad had moved to the United States for college and met Mom. And how Dad changed his name from *Michalis* to *Mike* because he said American tongues tripped over it too much. (People never got *his* name right either, saying 'E-*lie*-us' when it was 'E-*lee*-us', but Mom refused to let him change it.)

When he and his sister were small they'd heard Dad's bedtime stories of how ancient Greeks thought the gods and goddesses ruled the planet. Elias liked myths about the sea god, Poseidon, best.

Spear fishing like Poseidon! *That's* what he wanted to do, if he could talk his parents into letting him try it. Just like Poseidon with a pointy trident, Elias wanted to swim into a school of fish and *POW*—nab the biggest one before it could blink its fishy eyeballs. *Well, not real blinking of course; fish don't have eyelids,* he thought.

Elias decided to have a private chat with Dad to ask about spear fishing (without Mom's supersonic ears nearby), but Dad was back on board, cupping his hands like a megaphone. "INTRODUCING THE TANTALOS FAMILY GREEK OLYMPICS!"

At once, Mom and Lily protested. "Not us!"

"Have it your way," said Dad. "ANNOUNCING THE TANTALOS MEN'S OLYMPICS!"

Elias grinned. "You're on!" Time for spear fishing later.

"First up: Cannonball Competition!" Dad leaped off the front of *Sargos* hugging his knees to his chest. The boat tilted steeply and a titanic splash rose over the side.

Mom and Lily shrilled in unison, "We're getting wet back here!"

Girls. They didn't make any sense—getting wet was the whole point of a vacation. For a little girl, Lily was normally fearless, but she was afraid of water. How could she be such a baby about an activity he loved as much as running and soccer?

Correction. His passion for that sport had died on the State Cup field when he scored for the wrong team.

Elias climbed up the ladder and jumped off the bow like his father, grabbing his knees. He plopped into the sea with an unimpressive, nearly splash-free *kerplunk.*

"Next up: Most Creative Jump—go!" Dad jumped off backward and twisted around like a screwdriver.

Elias tried to flip with a twist, but halfway through changed his mind. Belly smacker!

"Ooh, impressive. Willing to suffer for the sake of the Olympic Games."

"Very funny!"

Elias rubbed at the stinging red mark on his chest. "Let's try a less painful contest. Treading Water?"

"I've got an idea. Wait here." Dad climbed up the boat's ladder and disappeared into the cabin, coming out a moment later with a small package in his hand. Dad whispered something to Mom. She nodded and unwrapped it, since Elias' hands were wet. It turned out to be an underwater watch—another early present!

"It has a stopwatch feature," Dad explained. "We can use it to time ourselves treading water."

"Wow, thanks!" Elias pushed a button. "Begin!"

Father and son swished their hands and kicked their legs bicycle-style through the blue sea, but when it became obvious both could tread water pretty much forever, they called a tie. After a Lap-Around-The-Boat contest, which Elias won by two strokes, he handed the new watch to Dad. "Breath-Holding. Time me."

"Are you sure, son?"

Elias filled his lungs with deep practice breaths.

"Don't stay under too long."

Elias took a huge breath and ducked under. Several long moments later he came up gasping for air.

"A whopping minute!" Dad handed back the watch. "Here. Hop on the boat—it's getting late."

"Do we have to stop already? It was your turn."

"Time's up. But you're the champion!"

A string of green seaweed was stuck to the underside of the boat, and Dad plucked it off *Sargos'* hull. With a ceremonial flourish, his father draped the seaweed around Elias' forehead. "In ancient Olympia, the Greeks adorned the victors with crowns made from evergreen leaves," Dad said. "Laurel leaves, not seaweed!"

"Ew. I hope laurel leaves aren't as slimy!" Elias laughed and pulled the clinging vine off his head. He dropped it into the sea, where it floated on the surface for a few seconds before spiraling slowly through the blue depths. "I want to keep racing."

"Plenty of time for more Olympic Games on our vacation, but if we arrive late to Mykonos, we may find restaurants closed. People enjoy a long afternoon siesta on hot summer afternoons. We men can't miss our lunch and nap!" Dad rubbed Elias' wet head playfully.

"I'm not a baby. No nap for me. But I'm starving!"

The ancient Agora (Market place) of Delos

5

PINDAR THE RAIDER BOY

Back on board, Mom passed out beach towels, but Elias let his dangle from his fingertips as if it were diseased. Blue, with a red-and-yellow Superman's shield. His favorite towel, back in first grade. Parents! All right one minute and then *WHAM,* they embarrass you.

Elias let the sun dry his skin and then he crawled on hands and knees through the low doorway into the cabin to stash his unwanted towel someplace. The door latched shut behind him, and a tight feeling clutched his chest. Closed-in spaces bothered him, but a shaft of yellow sunlight poured in through the round porthole, casting the cabin in a comfortable glow.

Hoping to catch the first glimpse of the Mykonos windmills, he checked the view from the porthole and realized the boat was not moving yet. He opened random storage compartments along the cabin walls and found a surprise that Mom must have brought for him. "Fireballs!" A new bag of the hard candies was stuffed in a space behind the brown package from his *Theo* Costas.

Bored, Elias popped a hard candy from its crinkly plastic wrapper, rolled the atomic fireball around his tongue and without thinking ripped open the gift.

With nothing else to do, Elias flopped onto his stomach and ran a finger on raised golden letters spelling out the title: *Myths and Legends of Ancient Greece*. Pictured on the cover was a boy about his own age standing in the prow of an old-fashioned ship. Its sails were square, not triangles like sailboats he'd seen. Dozens of oars poked out from holes below deck stroking water as blue as the Aegean Sea under *Sargos.*

The boy on the book cover was tall and strong with large dark eyes and dark hair curling from underneath a helmet. Dressed for battle, he seemed too young. His sword was nearly as long as his leg. A warm breeze puffed out the ship's sails, and his eyes were set wide apart. Eager for adventure.

The red-hot fireball flared like fire in Elias' mouth, but he didn't spit it out. He dared himself to keep it going as long as possible. That was the best part of fireballs, seeing how long he could take the heat.

Flipping to the book's Table of Contents, Elias saw it was divided into two sections. Under *Greek Mythology* was a list of many stories he'd heard from Dad: stories about Poseidon, Zeus, Cyclops, Apollo, Medusa, and more. He found the cover story in the other section, *Legends from the Past.*

Pindar the Raider
and the Lost Crown of Apollo
88 B.C.E.

Elias did quick math in his head. 88 years 'Before the Christian Era' was over two thousand years ago. About twenty-one centuries.

He turned back to read Pindar's chapter:

The raider's bad breath seeps over my shoulder, and I shiver in the heat. We set sail across the sea with orders from King Mithridates to find Apollo's treasure. What the treasure is, nobody will tell me, but gold lingers on the minds and lips of everyone. Now that we are arriving in a small bay hidden from the island's citizens, I'm heaving down the sails as rowers pull on the oars to bring the ship quietly close to shore without scraping bottom. As far as I can see, this island is a rocky, barren place with no houses in sight. A bad omen. No treasure in these hot rocks, if you ask me.

"Come with me. Special task for you. Orders of the King!" His rough, calloused hands grasp my shoulders, and he pulls me away from my job at the sails. Spitting over the rail, he watches his spittle make a white wad on the blue water. He leads me to a small boat ready to be lowered over the side and shoves me at it. "Get in!"

Another raider—one of the white-haired old soldiers —takes over. "I'll row the boy over. Get back to the oars." I throw him a grateful glance but I am leery. I am excited for the raid as are all the men, but why am I singled out? What would the great King of Pontus have me do?

Elias concentrated on the fireball scorching his tongue. It burned, but he liked the way they made his eyes water. Whenever the red-hot candy's heat grew too much, Elias shifted the fireball to the inside of his cheek and felt tough enough to handle anything.

The small boat scrapes up a pebble beach, while from the ship I hear shouts. The men were ordered to dress for war. We disembark, my feet finding the solid ground strange to walk on after a month at sea, but the old raider gives me no time for my legs to become accustomed to the rolling of the land underfoot.

We leave the beach and walk a few paces on dry ground. "Where are we going? What must I do?"

With his finger, the old raider sketches a shape in the dusty earth—round, but like a fried egg with jagged edges and a hump in the middle. He points at the northwest. "We are here. Low mountain in the middle."

I study the man. Old, over forty, with much experience, like my father. I listen. He scratches a line across the dust further southwest and then east. I pay attention. My life depends on it.

I trust him. He befriended me on the voyage from the Black Sea and, in rare moments of free time when the god of the wind bestowed gusts strong enough to pull our sails without the aid of the oarsmen, he taught me swordplay. I trust him—but what secret mission does the King of Pontus have in store for me? If this is a joke of the gods, I do not find it amusing!

"The marble city is not far for one with the swift reputation that follows your fast feet!" The man gives a satisfied snort and tests the sharpness of his sword blade on a thick stand of weeds. They slice easily. "The islanders are preoccupied with the coming of their evening meal," the old raider says, his eyes glinting with lust for the coming battle. "When the islanders see us, it will be too late!"

"Is the city so white it is blinding to look upon its many buildings?" Questions are spinning in my head. Excitement and wonder jostle with fear.

"Greek quarries produce the finest marble. You will judge the whiteness with your own eyes!" The old raider snorts again. "Enough talk. This is what you must do. Run until you see a lake." He makes a circle in the dust with his finger and taps his earthy map. "Here. Then, Pindar, run past the lions. Go through the marketplace and you will see the Temples of Apollo."

"Did you say—LIONS?"

To be bold and brave like Pindar! Without warning, thoughts of Evamere Middle School reared up in Elias' imagination. Like a great beast, middle school—sixth grade—lurked in the shadows, waiting for him at the opposite end of summer. Saliva dripping, sharp jaws yawning open, classmates panting for his next screw-up. How would Pindar handle a pack of lions? Elias needed to know! He kept reading:

"Worry not, young Pindar, but do exactly as I say." A most serious expression dented the old raider's brow. "Our success depends on how swiftly you do this: Run to the Temple of Apollo and find his Crown of Victory—and bring the god of the sun to our side of the fight! You MUST do this."

Not worry? I hardly know which problem to worry about first—getting past lions, stealing the crown of a revered deity, or surviving the battle sure to follow! The hilt of my sword slides out of my hand from sweat. I grip tighter.

"How will I know which grand temple to enter? Can a god be so great he needs more than one house to store the gifts offered to him? How will I move unseen?" My questions tumble over each other, and his eyes twinkle at me.

"Apollo has three temples on this island. Boreas, the North Wind, will guide your feet to the grandest one." The raider pulls his sword and strokes its eager blade. "I make you this promise: We will keep the citizens of Delos busy while you search its store of treasure. "If you can find the sun god's Crown of Victory the battle will be ours. You are the smallest and swiftest among us, least likely to be noticed. You, Pindar, are our secret weapon. Off with you! Run!"

Running toward the heart of the white marble city I fight against my fear. Like my old raider friend, the other warriors for the great King Mithridates of Pontus seem fearless. My father's sword is long and heavy and smacks uncomfortably against my leg. With each step, I pray to every god whose name I can remember.

Entering battle like Pindar the Raider Boy would be much easier than facing middle school, thought Elias, closing the book. The raider boy had a sword, but there wasn't a weapon in the world that could swack away at the bad luck magnetism of Elias Tantalos.

6

MYKONOS TOWN

argos had not moved. Elias slid out of the cabin to find Dad lying on his back under the captain's wheel, fiddling with equipment. By the frustrated look on Dad's face, Elias hoped to learn some Greek swear words soon.

"Nothing wrong with the old girl this morning," Dad grunted. "Elias, what did you do?"

"Why does everyone blame me?" Secretly, however, Elias worried. Could bad luck magnetism follow him halfway around the world?

"Mike? This is not a good place to get stuck." Mom looked worried, her forehead scrunched behind her large black sunglasses. Only one island was in the distance, and it looked as barren as the rest.

The engine suddenly roared to life and soon the incident was forgotten. The propeller churned through the sea and Elias watched the white foam making a trail through the blue water. Soon a different island bumped out of the blue horizon. White boxes dotted the landscape like dozens of sugar cubes. As *Sargos* motored closer, he could see that the boxes were actually houses: small and square, with flat rooftops.

Poised on a low hill on the far right end of the island, three huge circles rose in the air like spokes of bicycle wheels belonging to giants. Elias had a good guess what they were. "The Mykonos windmills!"

The Tantalos family cheered. "We're here!"

From up close, the houses were not pure white as they appeared from a distance. Blue-painted doors and blue-painted window frames looked as if the sea itself had splashed its color onto the buildings. Flowers crammed their reds and pinks into blue-painted vases that marched up crooked blue-painted staircases and spilled over blue-painted balconies.

"What beautiful colors," Mom said, taking in the sights with wide eyes.

"What beautiful *smells,* you mean!" Dad slowed the boat engine, and *Sargos* putt-putted into the busy harbor where innumerable aromas greeted them, teasing their noses. Grilled chicken and pork mingled with the scents of oregano and lemon, making Elias' mouth water well before they reached the crowded dock. Umbrellas cast shade over people sitting at outdoor restaurant tables; these *tavernas* were positioned around a horseshoe-shaped harbor and competed for hungry tourists. Loud music sounded from instruments Elias did not recognize, and the fast-paced, cheerful sound lured people to the tables. T-shirts and inflatable water toys crammed the doors of souvenir shops and filled sidewalk racks with fun.

"I'm *starving,*" Elias informed his parents.

"Lunch after boat business," said Mom. "We're all hungry. If everybody pitches in with the work we'll eat sooner."

An awful amount of scrubbing salt water from the

boat's seats and every other visible surface is what Mom meant; after wiping everything down with fresh water, she insisted they change into fresh clothes before they could eat lunch.

There was little privacy on a boat. Each member of the Tantalos family went one by one into the little cabin to change out of their swimsuits. Last in line, Elias kicked the low door. "What's taking so long, Lily?"

Lily poked her face out. "Almost done. Can you hand me my bag?"

It wasn't as heavy as his backpack, but her *Dazzle It!* bag was a large, 'bottomless-pit' tote from which his sister pulled handfuls of chunky plastic beaded bracelets representing every color of the rainbow, and more shades of pink than Elias thought should be allowed to exist. She stacked each arm to the elbows. "Mom said people dress fancy on Mykonos."

"My turn." Elias pushed past her and latched the cabin door behind him, glad for the golden sunshine still streaming through the porthole. He rolled over and felt into the corners of the compartment for a set of clean clothes. In the cramped space, the pointed end of his elbow whacked against its brass latch. A flame shot down his arm and tears sprang into his eyes at the unexpected pain. Moving around on a boat was going to take some getting used to.

It had not occurred to him that they might sleep on the boat; he had assumed they'd stay at his aunt and uncle's island apartment—or perhaps one of those white boxes he'd seen would turn out to be a hotel? He hoped he did *not* have to sleep in the cabin that night!

He rubbed his elbow, squirmed into a clean shirt and pants, and crawled out; he and Lily asked their parents for permission to explore the dock area while the adults finished tending to the boat.

Tethered on lines to the dock in Mykonos Harbor, boats of all shapes and sizes curtsied in rhythm with the gentle movement of the sea. Sailboats with tall masts and varnished wood railings gleamed under the Greek sun, and shiny new powerboats with twin engines bobbed gently next to fishing boats smaller and older than *Sargos*. Traditional Greek fishing boats, *caicque*, as his father pointed out, were made of wood and painted with stripes of red, yellow and blue. Orange fishing nets spilled out of *caicque*, and proudly flying high over nearly every boat were the blue and white stripes of the Greek flag. Elias recognized flags from other countries, too.

"Look, Lil!"

At the end of the dock, standing patiently as if waiting just for them was a tall, bright-eyed pink and white pelican.

"What's your name, Mr. Pelican?" Lily squatted at eye level with the pelican. She had a knack for making animals feel comfortable around her, and this bird was no different from animals back home. A flabby yellow pouch hung from its pink foot-long bill, the color of shrimp. Creamy white feathers covered the jumbo-sized bird's body.

An old fisherman tipped back the blue cap shading his eyes. "Hey ho! *Yassou*, kids! This isn't your ordinary, everyday sort of pelican, no! Mykonos' finest bird. Introducing Petros. Best friend to Christos the fisherman and a fine-feathered welcoming committee!"

Lily was enchanted. "Really?" she piped breathlessly,

The fisherman winked at her, encouraged to continue. His ancient-looking *caicque* was squeezed between the dock and an elegant, modern white fiberglass sailboat. His rough hands were untangling his net. His bushy moustache moved up and down on his upper lip in a funny way as he talked to them about how the pelican came to Mykonos.

"Many years ago, a pelican got injured in the sea, nobody knows how exactly, but that pelican was found by a local fisherman—my own *papous, yessir!*—all the men in my family have been fishermen and my grandfather was no different." The fisherman took a deep breath and kept talking.

"That pelican was hurt, and my *papous* saw that he could not fly away. He brought that sad pelican back to Mykonos and nursed him back to health with tender loving care. Named him 'Petros' and set him free. Free as a bird."

The elderly man—Christos, as he had introduced himself—took off his cap to scratch his head, and his bushy hair made a kind of halo around a balding top. He waggled his eyebrows at Elias and Lily and spoke in a rumbling voice. "This is the best part."

They were impressive, the fisherman's eyebrows. Elias had never seen anything like them—or *it*, as it appeared to be one thick, salt-and-pepper-gray hairy line. Beneath its curve, and sparkling like the sea in sunshine, the old man's eyes were a brilliant shade of blue. Elias was surprised, because the only Greeks he knew (Dad and *Theo* Costas) had dark eyes.

"Now, Petros was a funny bird. Had other ideas, he did!" Christos said. "Flew around, but he came back. Made his home near my family on Mykonos Island ever since, him and his offspring. Most of 'em get called the same name. Petros."

The fisherman reached into a cooler on the deck of his *caicque* and tossed a fresh fish to the famous pelican. "Here you are, Petros. Trust Christos to bring you the best fish from his daily catch."

The large bird caught the fish and gulped it down in a single bite. A small crowd of tourists gathered near Elias and Lily to watch the pelican eat. Christos tossed another fish. Petros ate it quickly, and Elias clapped along with the crowd. The pelican scratched his back feathers with his long pink bill as if to say, 'Thank you, it was nothing'.

Hand in hand, Mom and Dad walked down the dock.

"This is Petros," Lily told them. "Isn't he beautiful?"

Petros waddled over to Elias and pecked at his birthday watch. "And hungry!" Elias pulled back in alarm. "My arm is not a snack!"

"Petros won't hurt you," Christos laughed. "He likes things that shine in the sun," he said to the crowd, and Elias was mesmerized by the fisherman's belly-laugh that seemed to shake his whole self with joy. "Tourists become part of his family, see? Where are you from?"

Elias answered, "the United States", but many others called out places in Europe. Exotic-sounding places like Naples, Italy and Lyon, France. Most were from Athens, the largest city in Greece.

The travel-weary Tantalos family wandered away from Petros and his crowd of fans while they telephoned Aunt Kat.

"Strange. No answer from Aunt Kat." Mom's face got that worried look again. "I thought she was expecting us."

Dad shrugged. "Let's go find a *taverna*. I'm with Elias—we Tantalos men are starving!"

The straw seat creaked as Elias slumped into the chair, faint from too much sun and too much good-smelling food being delivered to neighboring tables. A waiter covered their table with a paper cloth, and within a few minutes their own table was weighed down with food.

Elias ate and ate and ate until his stomach could not hold another morsel, while his father called his brother back in Athens. "That explains it," said Dad, turning off his cell phone. "*Thea* Katerina owns Sunny Days Camp and is away for an overnight camping trip. Costas insists that the *pedia* go to day camp one of these days. Would you kids enjoy meeting other children?"

Lily chirped "YES!", while the idea of day camp made Elias feel two years old. But with his belly happily stretched with grilled lemony chicken and pork pieces on skewers, he would agree to anything. His salad was blanketed with a large square of salty white *feta* cheese with fresh tomato and cucumber slices peeking from underneath—and a plate of French fries that dared any fast food restaurant in the world to do them better. Sprinkled with oregano and sea salt, these French fries were perfect as is—no ketchup!

The Greek food was hard to describe. It was normal—meat and fries and salad—but *different*. And delicious. "Greeks take time and great care preparing food," Mom said. "Their special ingredient is love."

Nobody argued her point, and after lunch Elias begged to explore the harbor town. His legs were getting used to walking on land again, and they itched to stretch and run.

Not far from where *Sargos* was docked, an ice cream parlor was busy with couples and families with young children. Elias was too full from lunch to want dessert, but he and Lily checked out the tubs of flavors for near-future reference.

"What's Pista-chi-o?" Lily wondered, as someone ordered a scoop of green ice cream that resembled mint chocolate chip back home.

"Pistachio. It's a green nut, Brainless," said Elias,

as they watched the worker scoop a ball of it onto a sugar cone.

A small shop next door stood empty; its windows were papered over with posters of colorful underwater sea creatures. One poster advertised pictures of marine equipment. Undersea cameras, marine GPS systems—and spear guns!

"Dad!" Elias ran back to the ice cream shop, where his father was putting money on the counter for a pistachio cone for Lily to try. Elias dragged him by the hand to show him the poster. "Can I try spear fishing?"

Hammering noises could be heard coming from inside the empty shop. The paper covering the lower part of the window was ripped off, so Elias squatted low to peer through the glass; a pair of men were in there putting together a display cabinet.

"We'll see about the spear fishing tomorrow. It's time to transform *Sargos* into our mini hotel—it's time for *siesta*."

Elias was concerned. "We're not staying in a hotel? Or with Aunt Kat?"

Dad shook his head. "Apartments on the island are small. There isn't enough space with our relatives and besides, we have *Sargos*! It'll be just like when I was a kid, sleeping under the stars."

Elias and Lily were in no mood to nap like babies (and Greek parents, apparently). There was too much new stuff to look at. Their parents relaxed on the boat while they promised not to wander too far. Petros was no longer around, but they sat on the dock and watched other boats and tourists like it was a reality TV show.

Hours later, after another *taverna* meal, Lily and Elias brushed their teeth in a public washhouse not far from the boat dock and wondered how the four members of the Tantalos family were going to sleep in one small cabin on *Sargos*. They found Mom making up two beds in the little cabin, while Dad was folding down the seat cushions at the stern for a makeshift bed out on the open deck.

"The warm nights of August are perfect for sleeping under the stars," Dad announced. "I remember doing this as a kid!"

Beads of sweat popped from Elias' forehead at the thought of black night creeping into the cramped space of the cabin. "You and Mom take the cabin. I want to sleep outside."

"Don't be silly, honey. You two will be much more comfortable sleeping on the mattress in the cabin."

Nobody knew how Elias felt about small, dark spaces.

"I'm sleeping in the cabin." Lily sat cross-legged in the cabin entry as if her bottom was putting down roots.

"Dad and I will be fine. Go on, now. We've all had a big day and need rest. Fun day on the water tomorrow!"

"Can we go tubing?" asked Lily.

"You feeling okay?" Elias was suspicious. His sister never wanted anything to do with water activities.

"Good idea. I'll inflate the tube now so it's ready for tomorrow morning," said Dad.

"You don't like to get wet, Lil," Elias protested.

"Surprise! Mom and I picked out a new tube— it looks like a shark with gills for handles," Lily explained. "It's so big I won't get wet! I'll wear a life jacket, too."

"Whatever."

In the cabin, Elias crawled to a spot under the porthole. Stars scattered a cold, far-off light; the moon was a sliver with only a weak beam. Lily took up the space next to him and rolled over, asleep before her head hit the pillow.

Elias tossed and turned under the low ceiling, a coffin in the dark. He squeezed his eyes shut and pretended he was outdoors under the higher ceiling of sky. As his eyes adjusted to the darkness, he noticed a soft glow of light coming from the face of his new birthday undersea watch. It comforted his fears and he began to relax—until Lily started snoring like an elephant with a bad cold.

This was going to be one LONG vacation.

7

THE BAD LUCK MAGNET
STICKS AGAIN…

It is official: I am a bad luck magnet on BOTH sides of the Atlantic Ocean. Second day of vacation and I am in my second Time Out. Time Outs are for babies like Lily, so I don't know why they keep happening to me. (Except I know EXACTLY why this time and sure, it was my fault. But it isn't fair.) I have nothing to do, and I am not in the mood to read my birthday book, so I will write down exactly what happened and try to figure out why bad luck keeps sticking to me.

The morning dawned happily enough as Elias and Lily helped Dad push *Sargos* away from the dock for a new day at sea. Then they pulled in the fenders; Lily called them 'boat-balloons', though they knew by now that the plastic fenders were hung over the sides of the boat to protect it from banging into the dock. (*Sargos* was already old and beat-up looking, so Elias was not sure why it mattered.)

Not ten minutes away from Mykonos Harbor, Elias remembered Lily's surprise. "Let's go tubing!"

Dad pointed to the blue-and-white Greek flag hanging limply from a pole at the stern. "Perfect for tubing," said Dad. "No wind today. Flat water this time of year is very unusual. Boaters don't want to get caught up in an Aegean *meltemi*. High winds can last for days. They can send a small boat like *Sargos* clear to Africa before you know what hit you."

"Let's get Sharky in the water!" Lily petted the tube on its gill handle while Mom snapped a life vest over her pink bathing suit and then sprayed sunscreen over every visible part of Lily's body. "Sharky?" asked Mom, while she aimed the spray can at her next victim. "Sunscreen for everyone except Sharky."

The plastic inflated shark tube bared a mouthful of grinning teeth, looking as eager as Elias to get in the water.

"Let's see if Sharkman can float," said Elias, letting Mom spray him.

"It's SHARKY." Lily's hand flew to her hip.

Amazing, Elias thought, *how a second grade girly girl can transform herself into a bossy boss with a single move.*

"Have it your way. Help me get Sharky in the water. On the count of three."

Dad counted in Greek while Elias and Lily heaved Sharky off the stern.

"*Ena, theo, tria!*" Sharky splashed down. "Who's first?"

The tube stayed connected to *Sargos* on a long

line. Elias wore a life vest too, to be on the safe side (Mom insisted) but he dove off the stern to get to the toothy inner tube before Lily had a chance to reply. Mom and Lily were put in charge of watching to see if Elias fell off or made the "cut-throat" signal to stop.

The engine roared and the line snaked out behind *Sargos* while Elias held onto the gill-handles and waited for the tug. As soon as the line was taut, the boat pulled Sharky forward in a rush and Elias gripped the handles. The tube skimmed the surface and water sprayed over the front.

"Wahoo!" Salty seawater soaked Elias, and he gave a thumbs-up signal to communicate with Dad: "*FASTER!*"

Tubing was awesome, until Dad cut my turn short and Lily made my Lucky People list. I swam back to the boat and he pulled on the line to bring the tube in close so she could board Sharky without swimming (even with her life vest on she acted like a baby). Then, she made Dad drive so slowly she didn't get wet. A boring ride and only ten seconds later she made the cut-throat signal to stop. She calls that tubing? What's the point? Seriously. And, Lily got Dad to pull the tube—with her on it—right back to Sargos. Yep, completely dry just like she wanted. I got another turn, but then my luck ran as dry as Lily Tantalos in a bathing suit.

Dad hauled Sharky onto the boat, where it took most of space, and then he steered *Sargos* into the turquoise waters of a quiet inlet. The air was still and quiet; it seemed as if the terns and other creatures of land and sky had abandoned the island. The sun climbed high.

"Wow, we've tubed far this morning." To Elias, all the islands of the Aegean Sea resembled each other, but this one looked especially abandoned with no trees and no houses. A lonely mountain rose from the middle of it. It gave Elias a creepy feeling, but after setting the anchor Dad brought out snorkeling gear—and spear fishing equipment.

"*Yesss!*"

Elias slipped fins onto his feet and walked like a duck.

Spear fishing lucky? Sadly, no. I'll keep writing. You keep reading.

Dad made his son listen to the rules, for EVER it seemed. Elias learned to 'point the spear only at fish, not people' (stuff everybody already knows. Elias wasn't dumb, in spite of all the red-slashed homework papers Mrs. Struggles marked down!). Then Dad let him hold the spear gun and taught him its parts.

"Can we get in the water yet?" His fingers itched to try.

"Go ahead and spit in your snorkel mask, son," said Dad.

"Spit? Are you serious?" Elias tucked the spear gun under his armpit and held the mask at arm's length.

"It'll keep the mask clear so it won't get foggy underwater. Try it!"

His father spit in his own mask, rubbed the spit around and reached over the side of the boat to dip it clean in the sea. Elias spit in his mask and could hardly wait to get his face in the water to see if the spit trick worked. Following Dad's example, he put his lips around the mouthpiece. Breathing through the snorkel made him sound like Darth Vader from his favorite old movies. He gave a thumbs-up.

"That reminds me," said Dad. "Hand signals are important. Thumbs *up* means 'All clear' and it's safe to pull the trigger. Thumbs *down* means—"

Phhwhooooopht!

It was one of those moments when you wish you could jump in a time machine and relive the last second over and do it a thousand different ways other than what just happened. Elias had put on the mask and was holding the spear gun in his hand, waiting to get in the water, when suddenly his eager finger touched the trigger ever so lightly and—*Phhwhooooopht!*—the spear point lodged in Sharky the Tube's nose.

Air whooshed out of the tube at an alarming rate, and Lily blubbered. "SHARKY! Elias, what did you do?"

"—thumbs down means *WAIT*," repeated Dad, retrieving the small pointed spear from the tube, which had deflated into a lump of red-slashed gray plastic. "I'm very disappointed, Elias. We'll deal with Sharky later. The tube can be fixed, Lily. If you can't listen, son, we're done here."

"I'll listen! I didn't pull the trigger on purpose. It was an accident."

"All right, then. I'll give you the spear gun after you get in. It must be loaded in the water, NOT on the boat. You saw what just happened. You're lucky it was the tube that got hit and not a person."

"Careful, *boys*." Mom lifted her ocean-gray eyes over the top of her book, looking worried. "Mike, shouldn't this wait a few years? A spear gun is dangerous. It is not a toy."

Yes, my luck can get worse than popping Sharky. A LOT worse.

"You heard your mother," Dad said sternly. Are you going to take this seriously?"

"Yes Dad," Elias said meekly, anxious not to have the spear fishing adventure cancelled.

A blue world met Elias' gaze through the clear mask when he jumped in, falling on his back as he'd been shown, flippers in the air. *Awesome!* He thought, staring around him. It was like being on another planet!

Dad plunged into the water next, and tapped Elias on the shoulder. Together they swam further out into deeper water, their masks making the water crystal clear for easy viewing of the rocks and fish around them.

It was impossible to stop what happened next. Silver lightning whizzed over Elias' left shoulder; he swizzled round and watched them excitedly—just as Dad said, "Here you go, son," and handed over the spear gun. The azure water burst into a million tiny white bubbles, and only when they faded back to blue did Elias see his father again.

Both coming up for air, in his Darth Vader snorkel voice Elias asked, "Were those fish the sargos? Those fast, small fish our boat is named after? Did you get one?"

Dad waved empty hands. "I already gave the spear gun to you!"

Their faces changed from excitement to panic. The spear gun was no longer in either of their hands.

They held onto their masks, took a deep breath and plunged under the surface. The spear gun was fast disappearing into the depths beneath their flippered feet.

Elias dove deeper and tried grabbing it, but the flippers got in his way. *Missed!* He had to come up for air.

Dad went straight down. Elias held his breath, too, hoping for a miracle. He kept checking his watch. Twenty seconds, thirty. How long could his father hold his breath? He wished he had timed him in their Olympics.

It felt like an eternity, the twenty, thirty, forty seconds that followed. Elias kept his mask face down in the sea, watching for any sign of his father. After what seemed like ages, the snorkel, mask and body of his father appeared.

Dad came up empty-handed.

Silence followed for several seconds while they trod water and stared down at the blue sea. It was an uncomfortable quiet, one that tumbled with anger and disappointment and remained unbroken—until another powerboat came into view.

Dad and Elias waved until the boat motored closer. They shouted across the water to the three young men on board, two of them dressed head to toe in SCUBA gear. "Can you help us?"

"Something is wrong?" The driver, wearing yellow Hawaiian print bathing trunks, spoke with a heavy Greek accent in halting English.

Dad explained in rapid Greek what happened, pointing to the sea. It was easy for Elias to understand Dad was explaining the spear gun was lost down there and he grew hopeful, but one of the men in SCUBA gear shook his head. "Here the sea is too deep. Even with SCUBA gear, it is impossible. I am sorry."

Their boat powered away, and Dad looked puzzled for a moment—they weren't *that* far off shore!

A dark, don't-talk-to-me-now expression shuttered

his face when he turned back to Elias. "I know it was an accident, son, but we are done. Back on the boat."

"Time out. NOW." Mom meant business, too.

Elias crawled into the cabin wishing (for the second time in one day) his new watch had a time-turner feature. Peering through the porthole, he could see the men's boat had swung round and returned, pulling close to theirs. It was similar in size to *Sargos* but shiny, newer. Muffled voices came through the door; his father was talking with the men in Greek. A left-out feeling crept over Elias, and he wished he could speak the language. The name *WunderSea Adventures* was written in gold along the side with a picture of a snorkeler shooting colorful fish with an underwater camera.

Their engine roared to life and the boat turned away. Elias could see the name painted across the stern too: the words *Mykonos Island* and a telephone number. On a whim, he used the back of a home-work paper (one that wasn't too covered in red ink) to record the telephone number. When his family got too annoying, maybe they'd take him along on an adventure.

Not that I have a telephone. Or cell phone. Or whatever.

8

... AND AGAIN

To Elias' surprise, *Sargos* did not follow *Wunder-Sea Adventures*; the boat gently rocked on the sea. Utter calm and quiet pervaded the cabin, and he yawned, suddenly craving the oblivion of sleep.

Hours—or minutes—later (he had no idea which) he woke up, confused, forgetting where he was until he heard the sharp sounds of his father swearing in Greek, and realized *Sargos* still was not moving. A knock on the cabin door made him gear up to protest it could not be his fault.

Mom opened the cabin door and said, "Dad needs your help. The boat isn't starting."

The sun had moved higher overhead and by the empty feeling in his stomach Elias guessed it was past noon.

Dad was standing at the captain's wheel scratching his head. "We might be here a while."

"Do we have anything for lunch?" Lily asked.

"What's in the cooler?"

Mom opened it and Lily helped pull out its meager contents. A few water bottles and a couple of cheese-filled Greek 'pies' from a shop near the dock. "I was sure we'd be back on Mykonos by lunchtime. I only packed these snacks."

The closest island had no visible buildings, sugar-cube style or otherwise. Barren and gray against the omnipresent backdrop of blue, the island in view had a low mountain smack in the middle of it.

"Maybe we can get help—and fast food—somewhere over there," Elias suggested hopefully. As he spoke, an eerie feeling shadowed the words. "Only—I don't see anything except rocks. Piles and piles of rocks."

"Where are we, Daddy?" Lily's voice grew squeaky when she got nervous or shy.

"Not sure. We'll have to find a mechanic to look at the starter, but first we need a way to get the boat over to the island. It isn't far, but we need a tow." Dad kept turning the key in the ignition, but no luck. "Son, did you mess with the electrical system?"

"Of course not, Dad!"

The sun beat down bright as ever but the sea had lost its sparkle. "Wait—I've got an idea," Elias said hopefully. "We could paddle to shore."

"This boat's too big, son. No oars." Dad sighed.

"I've got it!" Elias punched the air and scrambled back into the cabin to find the piece of paper to scribble down the numbers. "Got it!"

"What are you talking about?" Mom asked.

"The telephone number! On the stern of *Wunder-Sea Adventures*. Those guys were helpful; maybe they'll come back and tow us to shore."

"Smart thinking, Elias, thanks!" Dad punched the number into his cell phone.

The Tantalos family did not have to wait long at all. A boat's engine rumbled from a distance, then closer and louder until Elias could easily see the driver, still wearing the Hawaiian print bathing suit shorts. No sign of the two passengers.

After listening to their tale, the young man shook his head. "Can't tow you all the way to Mykonos. Thirty minutes from here. Sorry. Wish I could help more."

Dad nodded toward the barren island not far away. "Could you tow us to a place here we can set anchor?"

The driver tugged his hat down to shade his eyes. "You want to stay on *this* island?" He questioned the choice, but tossed a line to *Sargos*. Elias caught it, and Dad tied it to the bow.

"Sure, just look for a strip of beach where we can set anchor. We'll take it from there," Dad told him.

"You're the boss." The driver pulled *WunderSea Adventures* away slowly, and *Sargos* followed in its wake like Sharky the Tube.

As they neared shore, the small island showed off a messy jumble of rocks scattered around the base of a low central mountain. A small arc of gray pebble beach looked like a promising place to anchor, but the driver offered to take them further. "There's an old pier not far away. Keep your feet dry."

"*Efharisto,*" said Dad. "That's thoughtful. The pier it is!" A minute later, the two boats rounded a bend and the pier came into view. *WunderSea Adventures* eased *Sargos* to its edge, and when Dad tossed him the line the driver pulled it on board and waved, roaring out of sight around the eastern end of the island without waiting for another thank-you.

Elias could see no buildings that weren't a heap of rubble. No people. No trees. Lifeless.

Dad held onto a post with one hand and untied

the line, handing it to Elias. "Jump onto the pier and take the end of this line with you."

Elias hopped off the bow over the watery space between boat and land. A few rusty cleats on the pier offered the only places to tie up. Elias looped the end of the line around the cleat a few times, trying to remember how to make the correct knot.

"Can I tie the cleat knot?" asked Lily, reaching for Dad's hand for help walking the narrow strip of deck between the captain's wheel and the bow. She hopped off *Sargos*, her face shiny and eager. "I've been practicing."

"Show off," Elias teased, but he handed her the line. "I'm too hungry to think straight. Let's look for a fast food place," he laughed.

Dad watched as Lily tied a cleat knot, and was explaining the importance of tying knots correctly. He reminded them: "Strong winds whip up here in the Aegean Sea without notice—a special kind of wind storm in this area is called a *meltemi*. If a boat isn't tied properly it could end up in Africa." Dad chuckled and checked Lily's knot. "Not bad! Now, let's see if I can fix the boat as well as Lily ties a cleat knot!"

Lily threw an 'I can do it better than you' face at Elias while Dad tilted the engine out of the water to see if an object had gotten stuck in the propeller.

"I don't see anything wrong back here. Must be a bad fuse or loose wire." Dad patted the hull of the old powerboat. "I'm sure I can get her going again, but it will take some time to find the source of the problem."

Up close, the mess of rocks began taking shape into a very old city, ruined and smashed into pieces beyond recognition. The high afternoon sun bounced off massive pieces of white marble that dotted the city in such brilliance it was hard to look straight at it. Smooth dirty-white trunks—stone columns—stood straight and tall, reaching to the sky like a pale, leafless forest. Other columns lay toppled, scattered in round chunks on the ground.

"Good news and bad news," said Dad, looking around. "The good news is I know exactly where we are."

Elias and Lily and Mom cheered.

"Don't get too excited. The bad news is that driver left us on an island called Delos. He did what I asked him to, but I wish I'd known where we were being towed before he took off." Dad tapped the redial button on his phone, but after a minute slipped the cell phone into his shorts pocket. "No answer. We're on our own."

"What's wrong with Delos?" asked Elias, scanning the rocky landscape for clues.

"If I remember my history lessons from school in Greece," Dad said, "the last time people called this island "home" was two thousand years ago."

Reality about his joke sank in. "No fast food?" Elias' stomach growled instant concern.

Crumbling stone walls crisscrossed the hillside and seemed to outline where buildings once stood. Now roofless, broken. No *tavernas* on this uninhabited wasteland. Worse, no boat repair shops.

"You mean everybody here is *dead?*" asked Lily. Her blue eyes grew wide and her voice squeaked higher.

"Ooooo." Scaring his sister eased his own fears. "After two thousand years, any boat mechanics left in this city would be nothing but bones!"

Lions of Delos, guarding the dry Sacred Lake

9

RUINED

A bony pair of skeletons popped into Elias' imagination. Wobbling on sun-bleached leg bones, the two figures clattered right onto the deck of *Sargos*. One skeleton scratched his head with skinny, white finger bones analyzing the boat's engine. The other rubbed empty eye sockets with his knuckles, unable to see the source of the problem with the starter. Like a movie, the scene played in his mind, and Elias laughed at imagining how confused ancient beings would be over twenty-first century boat parts.

"What is so funny, Elias? Nothing amusing about this situation." Mom frowned and wiped sweaty bangs from her forehead and applied a thick glob of sunscreen to her arms. "Whew, it's hot here. Not a single shade tree." She passed the tube around the family.

"Can I explore?" After the cramped space aboard *Sargos*, Elias was anxious to stretch his legs.

Mom hesitated. "I'm giving your father a hand with

the boat."

Lily chimed in. "Can't we go our own? We'll stay together." She glared at Elias, daring him to say no.

"I guess it will be okay. Stay together within sight of the pier, and don't wander too far. And put on shoes. And sunscreen."

"We will, Mom," chorused Elias and Lily enthusiastically and in unison, with that fake-companionable sibling knowledge of what makes their mother agreeable.

However, Mom was not finished setting the rules. "Don't climb on the ruins; it could be dangerous. Be extra careful around antiquities."

"What are ant—ant-thingies?" asked Lily.

"Antiquities are objects from the ancient past. The tall columns that you see, or small things like clay pots that once held olive oil, for example," Mom explained while she coated their backs with sunscreen. "Don't stay under the sun too long—and remember the water bottles and *tyropita* from the cooler for a snack. I'm afraid that's all we have."

Elias ducked into the cabin for his backpack and shoved the water bottle and cheese pie next to his new *Myths and Legends* book.

"While you're in there," said Lily, "get my bag, too."

He found Lily's pink *Dazzle It!* bag next to her pillow, and in the sunshine it sparkled like a pink bomb explosion.

She made room in her bag for the water bottle and *pita* next to a notebook and a pen with pink feathers sticking out the ends. "Daddy, how did everything on Delos get wrecked?"

Dad was on hands and knees locating a tool box in a compartment under the back bench. "Delos used to be a trading port. The merchants got rich selling things like olive oil. Built a city right here, where they could meet traders from all over the Mediterranean Sea. People built temples to the Greek deities, and Delos became a religious center with temples built to gods of other lands, too, like Egypt. Grand place, too, it must have been, with the white marble buildings. People can have a selfish streak—true long ago and, unfortunately, true today. The buildings got destroyed and the treasures picked over by invading armies and pirates. Not much left now but broken chunks of marble."

"Pirates were here?" Elias shoved a water bottle and a large cheese *pita* into his full backpack and zipped it shut. "Cool! I wish I could have met a pirate!"

Mom gave them final instructions while Elias and Lily slipped T-shirts over their bathing suits. "Stay in sight. Not more than an hour and a half. Do you have your watch, Elias?"

He flashed his wrist to show her it was there, but he was already off the boat and heading toward the ruined city.

"Let's explore!" Free from the confines of *Sargos*, Elias called back over his shoulder as he ran down the pier with swift strides and turned left onto a wide unpaved path. He'd forgotten how much he loved to run! Like ghosts awakening from the ruins, clouds of dust trailed after him.

He slowed to a jog when he came upon a large rock with letters chiseled into it in both English and Greek languages:

AGORA
MARKETPLACE

The *agora* must be the place where people bought and sold goods. Until the pirates came and wrecked their marble city.

"WAIT FOR ME!" Lily lagged far behind.

Elias slowed down, but not for her. The sun glared against two hunched figures in the distance. What kind of creatures were they? One could be a man, but the other was the size of a deer back home, or maybe a large dog; was the Greek sunshine playing tricks on his eyes, like a mirage in the deserts of Egypt? Elias tensed, poised to move if the creatures threatened to come closer.

Rising from the shimmering heat, the man—trick of the sun or flesh—vanished and left nothing of his presence. In his place was a large animal carved from white stone. Elias stopped short from surprise, and Lily plowed into his back.

"Check this out, Lil!" Beyond the first statue he saw another. And another and another. A row of stone four-legged creatures were poised atop stone pedestals. "These are statues of lions!"

"What are you talking about?" asked Lily, breathless. Distracted, Lily kept looking over her shoulder and her eyes constantly roamed the ground at her feet.

"Scared?" he scoffed. "The lions aren't real."

"I know THAT. I'm not afraid of the statues, but Delos is creepy," said Lily. "So quiet. If people lived here long ago there might be—you know, *dead people*." She whispered the last word, her eyes scanning the dust under their feet. "I'm trying not to step on anybody's old bones."

"Delos isn't creepy. Just deserted," Elias said, but he couldn't help glancing around for half-buried skeletons, too—only he hoped to find one. Among the purple and white wildflowers pushing through the dry earth he hoped to see a finger or toe bone sticking out. Walking into middle school with a souvenir skeleton would *guarantee* him a better year, wouldn't it? Even bullies like Kincaid and Brandon would be impressed with a skeleton, wouldn't they?

Another chiseled stone marked the name of the place:

AVENUE
OF THE LIONS

Not seeing any bones (yet) Elias gave his attention back to the lions. Craftsmen from thousands of years ago must have carved those mouths gaping open in a silent, permanent roar. In fact, the eerie silence was getting to his nerves too, but he'd never admit it to Lily. Tossing back his brown wavy hair, he broke the quiet.

"Rooooar!"

The only living things on the island he could see were half-dead wildflowers and dried-up weeds. There were no signs of people, living or skeletal. The only sound was a soft *whooshing* in the background: the sea washing over pebble beaches.

Elias and Lily's sandaled feet made crunching noises on the path. He squatted to inspect it: count-less small stones, bits of hardened red clay and millions of tiny chips of white marble columns from ages past.

"Let's get out of here," repeated Lily. A huge dark-ened spot on the side of the island's single mountain caught her eye. "What's that black hole up there?"

"Looks like a cave. Let's go!" His stomach growled, but he ignored it in the prospect of real exploration.

"We can have a picnic there," suggested Lily."

"Good idea!"

Elias found a path of granite steps that zigzagged

up the slope to the cave's waiting mouth. The mountain path was steep, and it was slow going. Many of the stone slabs were broken or wobbly.

Part of the way up, they stopped to sip from their water bottles. From this lookout, the sea was full of changing colors. Pale green waves swirled around the shallow edges of Delos, gradually becoming the brilliant cobalt blue they knew to be deeper waters.

Sargos bobbed on its mooring, small as a toy boat. Lily waved.

"Mom and Dad can't see us up here," said Elias, rolling his eyes.

"If they can't see us, we have to go back down. We promised." Lily's eyes darkened.

Elias could sense Lily's bossiness about to surface. "We'll go back in a minute."

With a bird's-eye view from the mountainside, Elias' brain got busy putting the scene back together to how it might have once been before its destruction. Like a jigsaw puzzle, he put the pieces of Delos back together, with its houses and narrow streets bustling with people, tall columns supporting important buildings, and merchants selling honey and lemons.

Only one house among the ruins, on the far eastern end of Delos, had its roof. Today, the city was in fragments and the earth was parched. All white and dry and brown and... *green?*

In the center of a perfectly round patch of green bushes, a single palm tree stood tall. No other place on the entire island was green. During their day's journey on *Sargos* there had not been a single palm tree on any of the islands they'd passed.

"C'mon, Elias. Let's see the cave," said Lily, urging him the rest of the way to the top of the hill.

"I thought you didn't want to get out of sight of the boat."

"We're up this far. I want to see what's in there."
They trudged up and up and up the granite steps,
not stopping again until they reached the top. Elias
guzzled the water bottle while Lily squatted on her
heels, pushed some weeds from another carved signpost and read:

MOUNT KYNTHOS
AND THE GROTTO
OF HERAKLES

"What does 'grotto' mean? And does 'Herakles'
mean Hercules? Wasn't he that strong dude in Dad's
old Greek stories?" asked Lily.

"A grotto is a cave." Elias scratched his head trying
to remember Dad's ancient myths. "Yeah, Hercules
was the strong half-man and half-god from Greek
mythology. Herakles might be an old Greek spelling
for the same guy."

The signpost pointed them a short distance down
a narrow path. The path, unfortunately, wound its
way through a thorny patch of prickly weeds.

Ma-a-aaa! Ma-aa! Ahead of them, a young goat
pranced along the path with easy steps and disappeared up the mountain.

"If that goat can do it, so can we!" Lily maneuvered
optimistically to the cave's entrance with only a few
scratches, and Elias followed.

A few feet in front of the cave was a large block
of hollowed-out marble, rounded like a cup without
handles, better suited for the hand of a giant. Standing on tiptoes, Elias could barely see over its lip. The
other ruins he had seen on Delos were either statues
or columns, but this "cup" was large enough to fit
a person inside. Elias threw a leg over the top, but

something tugged on his backpack straps, holding him back. "What's the big idea, Lil?"

She threw him a severe look that rivaled his mother's, which meant only one thing: Lily was about to say the three words that big brothers everywhere hate worst of all to hear from little sisters: "I'll. Tell. Mom."

"Mom said not to climb on ant-thingies."

"Whatever. And the word is 'antiquities'." Elias sighed and lowered his leg. "You win. Wait—where are you going? "

Thick slabs of rock made a frame for the cave's opening and formed a pointed, arched ceiling inside, like an old church back home. Lily skipped inside, but he kept a hand on the giant's cup. Most caves were dark and damp and smelled funny, and his stomach curled at the thought of it.

"Come on in!" Lily's voice echoed and bounced off the natural stone gothic ceiling. "Check this out!"

For most of her years, Elias had managed to keep his sister away from knowing he was afraid of the dark (and he had no intention of letting her in on that secret now) but he did not want Lily to have adventures and great discoveries without him. His stomach flipped in protest, but he took some deep breaths and stepped into the darkness.

The air inside was dry and cool. The interior was dimly lit; the sun sent shafts of light that pushed through slits in the roof where the slabs of stone were not fitted tightly together.

His eyes adjusted to the light inside the cave very quickly, and he could see weeds poking through the high stone walls. In fact, Elias thought it was not much of a cave at all, and was rather disappointed.

"Lily, what's so special in here?"

His own voice echoed around the cold walls, but the only answer that bounced back to him was silence.

10

HIDE AND SEEK

L ily?"

Drifting from somewhere behind the cave's back wall came a high-pitched voice. "You gotta see this! It opens into a huge room back here with cracks open to the sky. Like skylights. And some of those stalag-thingies!"

"It's 'stalagmites'... never mind." In the empty cave, his sister's voice was ringing... up, down, everywhere. "Lil, I can't see you."

He took a few slow steps. A slash of black on the back wall became an almost-unnoticeable crack in the granite, wide enough for a small person to slip through sideways. Lily's muffled voice had come from there.

Elias dropped his heavy backpack on the ground to make his body thinner, but when he squeezed through, the darkness swallowed him whole. His heart pounded and his brain swam. A damp, musty smell stirred the air, like the salty scent of the sea combined with sweat socks from his locker.

A small creature swooped past Elias' head, its soft wings whizzing next to his ear.

"Something's in the cave!" Elias choked out, unable to breathe and unable to see anything. "I'm getting out of here." He realized a soft glow of light was coming from the face of his watch. It shone dimly on moist rock and made him feel a little better. The last memory of fifth grade assailed him anew.

He was cleaning out his locker after the final bell rang. He'd pinched his nose and aimed an old pair of sweat socks, stiff from dried sweat, at the waste bin—and missed.

"Good thing you're not on the basketball team."

Why did he never hear them coming?

Kincaid and Brandon hovered over him with a dare. "Bet you fit inside."

"In... the locker?" Elias stuffed bleeding homework papers into his backpack, but Kincaid and Brandon smiled.

"Truce?" Kincaid slid into the locker. "See? I'll go first." He asked Brandon to close the door, and Kincaid's muffled voice slipped through narrow vents at the top of the door. "Easy."

Brandon pulled up on the handle and the door sprung open. Kincaid emerged and winked at Elias. "Your turn."

Elias weighed the factors. Could his (former) best friends be sorry? Was this a test of renewed friendship? Elias would show them he wasn't afraid. Not of them. Not of anything.

Smiling, Elias stepped in. The metal door whacked his elbow as it closed. The darkness and lack of air surprised him. His heart rate quickened, and his throat felt strangled but he choked out a laugh. "OK, guys... let me out now."

The handle jiggled; the door didn't budge. Elias forced down panic. "Throw your weight into it," he suggested. Brandon could bust anything.

"Looks like the Wrong-Way kid screwed up again— no surprise. The door's jammed, Tanta-loser." Brandon taunted.

"Maybe the kid who gets assigned this locker in September will let you out," said Kincaid, reasonably.

"If you're still alive!" Brandon whooped and banged on the metal door.

Through ringing ears, Elias heard their footfalls retreat. He tried kicking at the door but his shoelace was stuck. Full panic set in—if he didn't get home from school his family would miss their flight to Greece! A terrible thought struck. What if they left him behind? Lily had a spectacular talent of being able to talk their parents into anything.

All concept of time vanished. Minutes passed—or hours? His cramped body ached, and a headache pounded. Elias cheered up when he remembered having an atomic fireball in his pocket, but he couldn't move his arms to reach it.

A girl's voice in the hallway sounded like music. "It's me. Kennedy. You're really in there?"

"How did you know? Never mind—just get me OUT!"

She jiggled the locker handle furiously, but the door remained stubborn. "I see the problem... your shoelace is jammed in the door. I heard Kincaid and Brandon taking bets if you'd shut yourself in the locker. Thought I'd better check out what those idiots were talking about." Kennedy told Elias to sit still (as if he had a choice) while she ran for a janitor.

The beautiful sound of a crowbar scraped against the door and popped it open. When daylight flooded in, he felt blinded.

"Are you all right?" Kennedy was peering in at him anxiously.

Now, in the cave, Elias smelled the musty air like his old sweat socks and remembered Kennedy's eyes. Light green, speckled with yellow. Eyes that made him think of a freshly mown soccer field on a sunny morning after it rained.

Too bad they were no longer friends. After she had helped him out of the locker, Elias opened his mouth to thank her for saving his life, but a bitter liquid crept in. He dashed to the trash bin, where his stomach heaved out the half-digested remains of his lunch. Without a backward glance, he'd run down the hallway and out the door and had not stopped until he was home.

Lily emerged from the Grotto of Herakles looking pale as a ghost—but a smiling one. "Scared of a bat? There's more to the cave back here. Don't you want to see?"

Elias ducked as another winged creature sped past his head, looped around and disappeared into the depths of the cave. Squishing his body back through the narrow crack, he dashed back outside. Two tall, strong-looking rocks supported the cave entrance; Elias leaned against one and closed his eyes to focus on breathing while the heavy fog of bad memories rolled over him with a crushing weight.

Opening his eyes again, he took in the scene of Delos and the surrounding sea until his breathing slowed and relaxed; the blue sea and barren gray landscape reminded him how far away he was from school. Restless, Elias swung his backpack over his shoulder and was picking his way through the thorny path when he heard Lily hollering after him:

"You're leaving behind a sister, you know!"

He glanced over his shoulder, but Lily wasn't following. She'd set up her picnic snack on a flat rock in front of Herakles' cup, so he went back through the prickly weeds to join her. Medusa—uh, Marina—the doll was propped up next to Lily's *spanakopita*, and Lily alternated between eating, talking to her doll and writing in her glitter-covered notebook with her pink feather pen.

His stomach felt sick, and not so hungry anymore. "I thought you were the one who said we had to go back to where Mom and Dad can see us, remember?"

"Mom waved to me just now—you can see the pier from up here. They can see us, too, so you were wrong. Why did you leave the cave so fast? I wanted to show you the big room in the back. Not scared of bats, are you?"

He said nothing; Kincaid and Brandon would have a field day if Lily let it slip that he was afraid of dark, closed-in places. He ignored her and pulled out the *Myths and Legends* book from his backpack to see if Pindar had confronted the lions yet. Long ago, did Pindar's ship of raiders attack this very island? Were his lions real—or stone?

"Hello Delos!"

I shout into the sunset, gathering courage. At last— my first raid! Excitement flows hot in my veins, eager to prove I am as brave as my father. The sun coming up from behind the mountain in the east is giving me strength. It flares red on white beasts lined up near a small lake, poised as if to strike.

Motionless, standing in a neat row, are the lions. Carved from stone! I laugh at my earlier fear.

Two, four, six... I mentally count the lions as I run past, struggling to remember the raider's island map finger-drawn in the dust. Where am I to run next?

The cold metal of my sword knocked against my leg. Ten, twelve, thirteen... I pass more. My young sister will like to hear about these magnificent white lions.

The memory of my family's teary farewell threatens to make my purpose falter. Mother had said, "Pindar, you are too young to see blood on your sword!" (at which point I remember Philippa had begun to cry, and could not stop until Mother promised to let her make an offering at the city altar in front of the temple to pray for my safety).

Father retired from the King's army, and he understood: at nearly fourteen, I am ready to prove myself a man. He gave me this, his own sword. I will prove him worthy of the gift—before the sun sets this day!

Stone lions! He had to go back to the Avenue of the Lions and count them. Maybe a few were hidden in the brush? Did other Greek islands have stone lions, or was Delos the only one?

In the view spread out below, the green palm fronds of a tall tree—the only tree—waved a cheerful welcome to him from the center of the green bushy circle he had noticed earlier, not far from the Avenue of the Lions.

"Are you done eating yet?" Elias shoved the rest of the cold cheese *pita* in his mouth. He put the sandwich wrapper into his backpack and took a swig from the water bottle. "Let's head down to that palm tree next. It's near the lions." He checked his watch. They had almost an hour before expected back on *Sargos*.

Going down the mountain was much faster than up. A reviving spirit of exploration surged through his veins. He waded once more through the prickly path to the stone staircase, and the rest was easy.

At the bottom of the long trail of broken steps they had not gone very far along the narrow streets of the ancient city, when something very much alive scooted across their path.

"WHAT WAS THAT?" Lily jumped on a block of marble, still as a statue.

"Aren't you glad? Delos isn't deserted after all. People don't live here, just lizards!" As if scheduled to prove his point, two tiny olive green lizards emerged from the base of a sun-warmed terracotta jar and chased each other in a game of lizard Hide and Seek.

"You thought *I* was the scaredy-pants." Elias caught sight of a thick, dark brown tail just as it slithered over the doorstep of a roofless shop. He took a few steps in its direction, but the large creature slipped out of sight. "Follow that lizard!"

A LIZARD SUNNING HIMSELF ON DELOS ISLAND

11

FINDERS, KEEPERS

"What I saw was BIG!" Lily did not move off her plinth. Two creatures, no bigger than a finger-length each, ignored Lily and played a game of chase around the wide lip of the jar. "I'm not talking about you, cute little lizzies."

"I think the big one's gone." Elias was disappointed.

"The lizards must be more afraid of us than we are of them," Lily decided and hopped down.

Now that they paid attention, the reptilian residents of Delos were everywhere, spending the hot summer afternoon running about their playground of city ruins. None of the lizards were as big as the first.

"Where did he go?" Elias ran about searching. "If you count his tail, he was three feet long—he's got to be here somewhere!"

Elias and Lily joined the lizard's game of Hide and Seek, with the elusive creature as 'It'. Searching through open doorways and glassless windows, Lily found the lizard first and whispered. "There he is—

sunning himself."

Elias followed her gaze to the *agora*, where they found the biggest lizard either of them had ever seen outside a cage, sitting on top of a grand high-backed marble bench.

The lizard was soaking up the sun and minding nobody's business but his own, motionless. Elias and Lily froze too, so as not to startle him. Time stood still and, while the three of them were at an impasse, Elias noticed details. Thick yellow lines ran down the middle of the lizard's back, in dashes, from his head to the tip of its tail.

"His back looks like the middle of a street back home," said Lily.

"More like a highway," said Elias, "because he's so *fast*."

"That's a good name for him." Lily tiptoed closer. "Do you like your new name, Highway?"

At her approach the lizard scooted away, speedy as a race car. Elias chased the large creature around the ancient marketplace until it all came full circle, to where he helplessly watched Highway's long tail slip into a dark gap under the grand white bench.

Lily flopped, panting, onto the seat and rubbed the smooth, cool marble. "This is a good place to sit," Lily announced. "Even if it is a zillion years old."

"Dad said two thousand, not a zillion."

"Here." She patted an empty space on the broad seat next to her. "Try it!"

But Elias had other ideas. He squatted on his heels and peered into the crevice after the lizard. Sprawling flat on the ground, the sharp marble and pottery rubble poking sharply into his stomach, Elias could not see a thing.

When he put a hand inside the crevice, Lily stopped him. "What if Highway bites you?"

"I can feel something in here." He reached inside as far as his arm would go.

"OUCH!" Elias pulled out a bleeding finger and sucked on it. "There's something in there!"

"Highway bit you. I knew it," said Lily, who took Elias' finger in her hand to analyze his wound like the kindly no-nonsense school nurse back at Evamere School. "Mom will take care of it. Let's go back to *Sargos*."

"Not yet. There is something else in here. Not the lizard." Elias pulled his finger out of his sister's grasp and reached his arm back inside until his fingertip curled around the object. It was cold and hard. "Got it! It's heavy," he said, surprised.

Lily's brown eyes grew rounder as Elias tugged the mysterious object into daylight, and when he got a good look at the thing he almost dropped it.

In his hand was a perfectly formed circlet of golden leaves.

Dozens of gold leaves, long and pointed and gleaming rich yellow in the sunlight. Amazingly, the object looked new. Out of place on this island, covered with dust and broken pieces of rock as old as time.

"This must be what scratched me." Elias gently ran his finger along the edge of a pointed leaf. A delicate thing, despite its weight.

"Wow," said Lily in a faint voice, mesmerized. She reached for it.

"Don't touch!" Elias jerked his hand back. "Lil, have you ever seen anything so fantastic?" He traced the veins of a gold leaf with his finger. "What could it be?"

"It's a crown." Lily spoke with confidence.

If anybody knew about things like crowns, it was Lily. Her closet at home was filled with dress-up costumes and princess gear.

Elias held it high and put it on. The leafy wreath of gold sat heavily on his head.

In a small voice, awed, Lily whispered. "You should see yourself, Elias. A Greek god from Dad's stories come to life. Can I try?"

Winners of the ancient Olympics always got crowns of leaves, Dad had said. Green leaf crowns. This crown of gold leaves made him feel like a champion—no, more than that. Royalty. Like a king. Or a god. Magnificent!

He shook his head. "Not yet."

Famous. Standing alone in a bright white spotlight, his family, classmates—the entire town, probably—everyone would want to be friends with the hero in a golden crown.

"I am so LUCKY!" he shouted into the too-quiet deserted Delos air.

With ten fumbling thumbs, Elias took the splendid thing off his head and nearly dropped it a second time, but he caught the wreath of gold before it hit the ground.

"Luck sure is slippery," said Lily, laughing.

"Lil, can you get the old Superman beach towel out of my backpack?"

"We don't have time for you to run around with a crown and cape pretending you're a superhero. Put it back under the marble bench and let's get back to Mom and Dad."

"Put it ba—No way! I don't want to pretend—I want to—here, you can hold it. Just for a minute. AND BE CAREFUL." He put the crown onto Lily's lap and she held it gingerly. Finding the towel himself, Elias spread it out and took back the crown, centering it on Superman's "S" shield. He wrapped it around the crown so the sharp stem wouldn't poke him.

"How did a crown like that get lost under a bench?"

Lily asked.

"Who cares? That's not the point, Lil—I'll be rich! Famous!" Elias shoved the wadded towel to the bottom of the backpack. With the bag of fireballs on top, nobody would know a piece of ancient gold treasure was in there. "There." He zipped the backpack shut and put the straps on his shoulders.

"You can't take it," said Lily. "It's not yours."

"Aw, nobody saw."

"It's an ant . . . ant-thingy-whatever. The crown belongs right here."

"The word is *antiquity*. Get it right someday, would you? And drop it about putting it back." Elias walked away at a brisk pace and yelled over his shoulder. "Whoever it belonged to must have died a couple thousand years ago, so what's the big deal? It's mine now. Finders, keepers."

HEADLESS STATUES ON DELOS

12

WRONG-WAY

E lias ran to get away from his sister and her
nagging. He stopped to catch his breath near
a pair of statues. Dressed in long robes, at
first they appeared to be two women, but he was not
sure. Faces and hairstyles didn't help identify them.
The pair didn't have faces. Or hair. Or heads.

Disconcertingly, their bodies began at the neck,
from which stone robes flowed down to toes, which
the craftsman who made them had graced with
sandals. Being headless was something of a fashion
for statues on Delos.

When Lily caught up, she unfortunately had plenty
of breath left to pester him. "Put the crown back," she
insisted, her hands on her hips. "What if somebody
saw you take it?"

"Who could be watching us? These two?" Elias
said. The stiff figures stood tall, life-sized. "They don't
have eyes, Lil. These dudes don't even have *heads!*"
Elias made a ghostly sound. "Ooooooo!"

"You can't scare me!" Lily took a step closer to one of the marble figures and touched its robe with the tip of her finger. It looked soft but was made of rock, not fabric. "They're not dudes—they're a couple. A man and a woman."

One statue had a figure like Mom and the other one held the front of his robe with an air of authority, like Napoleon. He touched it, and the white marble under his finger felt hard and cool on the hot day. The woman held up her long skirt with bent knee, ready to take a step. The sun overhead was beating on his brain and, as the heat shimmered in around the statues, it was easy to visualize the couple stirring to life.

In his imagination, they sprouted heads, and their marble skin turned to flesh and blood. Hopping off their bases—a big step—the statue-people stumbled, but helped each other straighten up, allowing their long, elegant robes to trail on the dusty ground. The man noticed Elias first and held out a hand to shake; Elias was astounded to see his own hand reaching back from brown robes, similar in style to the man but of much poorer quality. Lily, too, was dressed in a simple robe. The woman greeted them with open arms. "Welcome to Delos, children!" She linked elbows with Elias on one side and Lily on her other. "Come, stroll with us," they said. "Let us show you the fair white city."

"They must have been rich to dress so pretty." Standing on her tiptoes, Lily traced the hollow of the woman statue's headless neck with her finger.

Interrupted by Lily, the daydream popped to reality, the statues stiff upon their bases.

"If I sculpted them, I would have carved a necklace for her," said Lily. "And given her a pretty face. Where did their heads go?"

Elias shrugged, deciding his sister would think he was crazy if he described the living faces of the statues that weren't headless in his daydream. Instead, he touched the hand of the man who had shaken his and marveled at the craftsmanship of the person who made them over two thousand years ago.

Each figure was shaped out of one huge hunk of marble, including their robes, which the craftsman had managed to make look soft as draped fabric. Elias knew that sculpting marble could not be easy; in art class he'd made pottery once. His clay ended up as a lumpy mess formed into a jar that his mother said was perfect to store wooden spoons in the kitchen—but he knew the truth.

Elias, checking his watch. Twenty-seven minutes left. "Back to the lions? I want to count them."

"Okay," Lily agreed, but she headed down a path in the opposite direction, away from the Avenue of the Lions.

"The statues might be headless, but you're brainless," Elias teased. Lily ignored him and kept stomping off in the wrong direction.

"You're going the WRONG WAY! The lions are this way," he shouted.

Lily faced him and put her hands on her hips again and shouted with a voice that cracked with her crying. "Look who's talking, WRONG-WAY TANTALOS. You're not my boss. I'm not brainless, and I'll go where I want." She began to run.

That was a low blow. *Wrong-Way.* Memories stung him for the second time that hour. Why did Lily have to dredge up the worst moment of his life?

Red and orange leaves swirled in the cool air that blew through the fifth grade playing fields behind Evamere School. The championship game. On the last play. Score tied, and Kincaid passed the ball to him, the Evamere Wing's fastest runner. Elias' moment of glory.

"Could have happened to anybody," Coach David had insisted afterward, bravely attempting to pretend it didn't matter.

Kincaid had kicked high, so Elias spun around to get in a better position to head the soccer ball. The smack gave him an instant headache, and he dizzily ran in a fog of confusion wondering why the opposite team's goalie had split into three people who all strangely resembled Kennedy.

Nobody came close to catching up to him. He kicked the ball as hard as he could into the net—and sailed it past her, scoring the game-winning point past Kennedy for the other team. Time ran out. Elias had run the wrong way. A simple mistake. Everybody said so. But nobody else had done such a stupid thing.

He knew it. Kincaid knew it. Brandon knew it. Kennedy knew it. For the rest of fifth grade, Kincaid and Brandon led the masses of classmates up and down the hallways of Evamere School, calling him "Wrong-Way Tantalos."

Now that he thought about it, Lily never teased him about it. Not once.

Until now. Let *her* go the wrong way.

Suddenly, with a horrible wrench in his gut, Elias noticed his sister was heading straight for a large black hole in the ground. It was a rectangular pit, very neat in shape, the size of a car. No ropes or wall prevented anyone from tumbling in, and Lily was acting angry, not paying attention to where she was going.

Elias froze, watching his sister barrel for the pit's edge with a kind of horrible fascination, until a memory jarred his mind, like being struck by one of Zeus' lightning bolts: in spite of his whopping mistake that day on the soccer field, Elias knew his were the fastest running feet in the entire student body of Evamere School. Kicking those feet into high gear, he tore after his sister.

Sending up clouds of sand, clay bits and marble dust with every step, Elias caught up just as she gained awareness of the danger; her toes rocked on the edge, trying in vain to stop at what was indeed a pit several feet deep.

Up close, it was worse. Dark, unmoving water filled the pit, like a swimming pool that hadn't been cleaned in a thousand years. Puffs of green algae made thick balls of floating scum on top of the black water. Deep, certainly over the head of a girl afraid to swim.

Elias grabbed Lily's arm and yanked her to safety.

"You could get hurt falling into that muck. Be careful next time, will you?" Elias did not mean to sound so snappy, but it came out that way.

"Ouch," she said, wrenching her arm away from his grasp. With a sleeve of her T-shirt she wiped hot tears away.

"See if I bother saving your life next time," said Elias. In a heartbeat, his mood flip-flopped from angry to worried, and now annoyed. "I'll tell Mom you called me names."

"I'll tell Mom you started it."

He was tired of his sister acting like a baby, and he was tired out from his energetic burst of speed. Resting on a large rock next to the pit, Elias noticed the chiseled words:

FOUNTAIN
OF THE MINOANS

The signpost stood at the head of a wide staircase across one end of the pit; at least twenty steps led down into the black water. The steps gave the hole a man-made look. Elias did not see how this square cavity could have been a water fountain, which he thought of as clean water spouting up in the air.

If the water was clean in ancient times, maybe the ladies of Delos had walked down these very steps to get their drinking water?

Elias picked up a rock and tossed it into the pit to check the water's depth; he could not hear any clunk of the rock hitting bottom. Shimmers of the midday heat lifted from the pit and his imagination kicked into action again.

Ancient Greek women gathered on the steps, long robes flowing like the carved fabric on the headless statues. Dainty bare toes in leather-sandaled feet stepped down to the water level and the ladies helped each other drape their long skirts over their arms to keep the edges from getting wet.

They lowered the narrow lips of their water jars, or 'hydria', into the well. The air filled with their chatter, until soon the clay jars were heavily filled with fresh, sparkling drinking water. The tall clay pitchers were painted red and black, and some of the women balanced them atop their heads, held up carefully with graceful hands so as not to spill a drop. Another lady held her hydria with one hand on her slim, bare shoulder. Another set hers on a hip and waited for the others.

"Thanks for saving my life," said Lily, her squeaky voice interrupting this daydream. "Can we get out of here now?"

The algae-filled pit of the twenty-first century stood before them as before. Elias had liked it much better in his daydream when it was sparkling in sunlight with fresh water.

"Whatever. I'm not your babysitter." Elias checked his watch. "We have a few minutes left. I'm going to count the lions."

Sweat pouring from his brow, Elias ran toward the Avenue of the Lions without looking back to see whether Lily was coming or not. It wasn't far. It was getting to be very late in the afternoon and the sun was blasting hot. As he drained the last drop of water in his bottle, he wished the Fountain of the Minoans contained fresh water.

He counted nine lions standing in the weeds at the edge of the wide path. Hunks of misshapen stones stood where other lions might have been, giving hints they might have once been their bases. He noticed that every lion faced the exact same direction.

Lily caught up and brushed past Elias without speaking to him, but waded through the weeds to kneel beside a lion. She got down on all fours, arched her back and roared.

"What are you doing?"

"Pretending I'm a lion. They're staring at that palm tree," stated Lily, her confidence returned. She got up and brushed dust from her knees.

"Why would the lions be doing a stupid thing like that?"

"I don't know. It's the only tree on the whole island, maybe that's why."

"That's dumb."

"Fine, don't believe me." Lily pouted and stomped off down a path that disappeared into the thick area of bushes that surrounded the palm tree like a wide green circle.

He looked from the lions to the palm tree, and back again. Feeling ridiculous, Elias got down on his knees near the lion. He glanced left and right to make sure nobody else was around, and tried Lily's idea. Indeed, the lions made a proud row, their muzzles facing the direction of the wide green bushy area.

The fronds of the palm tree stuck out over the bushes and barely moved in the hot, still air. A sign-post marked the path:

SACRED LAKE

Why was this marked as a lake? Tall green bushes, weeds and wildflowers made the circular patch, not water. No source of fresh water was available on Delos, since the black sludge at the bottom of the Fountain of the Minoans didn't count. No lakes, no creeks. There was the Aegean Sea all around Delos, of course, but that was salty sea water. Could a lake have existed here two thousand years ago? What happened to it? Could it be the very same lake Pindar ran past all those centuries ago? It must be!

Goosebumps tingled up Elias' arms, making the hair stand up. *Pindar the Raider Boy* might be a legend, but could it be true?

PART TWO

Like what tender tales tell of the Pelican...

St. Thomas Aquinas, hymn

13

PALM OF THE TWINS

Lush green vegetation and a thick pad of dead grasses muffled sounds in the waterless Sacred Lake. It was too quiet. Where was Lily? If he got separated from his little sister and she went back to *Sargos* without him, Mom would make him clean the Port-o-Potty for the rest of their vacation.

Elias squeezed through the scratchy bushes and, like a swimmer, waded down the narrow path. The path led through a mass of evergreen bushes, and Elias followed the Christmas-tree scented trail. Underfoot was a thick cushion of long grasses, matted down as if they had been trampled by many feet. But whose? Lizard feet couldn't have pressed those grasses.

The piney bushes were too thick to see over, around or through. No sign of his sister.

After rounding a curve in the path, Elias found himself in an open, circular space. At the very center of it, one tree—the tall palm—towered above the clearing. Other paths drew to it like spokes of a wheel, with the palm tree at its hub. Which path did Lily take? Must he waste *all* his time chasing after his sister?

He checked his watch. Fifteen minutes to report back to the pier. Big trouble was in store for him if he showed up minus a sister! The bushes blocked Elias' view. If only he were taller and could see over them.

The palm tree! From the top, he could see the entire island.

Afraid the heavy load in his backpack would throw him off balance, Elias left it at the base of the palm. The brown earthy trunk swelled out like a pineapple, and its ridges proved perfect for climbing. His sturdy sandals with rubber soles gripped the stubby layers of trunk. Hand over hand, Elias pulled himself up as easily as climbing a ladder.

A slight breeze stirred the sweltering heat, and under the green palm fronds that feathered down through the vivid blue sky Elias' spirits revived. In the cooling shade of the tree, he worked his refreshed muscles harder to climb as high as he could. When he got near the top, he held on tightly with one hand and leaned out to peer between the fronds. He shaded his eyes with the other hand, and was so busy searching the ground for his sister that he did not have a chance to hide before it happened.

The carpet of matted grasses gave him no warning. Only a single swish of grass, too late, hinted that someone approached. The heat glimmered like a mirage across the green Sacred Lake, and directly down one of the paths Elias saw a lion stretch tall on its base, open mouthed and roaring with silent fierceness. Poised for action.

For several heart-pounding seconds, Elias imagined the lions springing off their bases to defend what was once theirs, nine angry beasts, one charging down each path, gathering around the palm tree in the clearing to pounce on his backpack. The gold crown of leaves would be scratched from its hiding place, his homework papers blown straight into the hands of Mom and Dad, his secrets exposed. He'd be trapped at the peak of the palm, with no place to run or hide, with the lions of Delos nipping at his ankles.

Elias shook off the sillies and repeated the facts. The lions were made of stone. Not moving. The heat of the Greek sun must be messing with his head.

Coming to his senses, he called to his sister. "Lil! It's time to go!"

Swish. No answer. If it were Lily, why didn't she answer?

Swish. Swish.

Something was coming! Elias froze, and with one hand pulled a palm frond over himself as cover, wishing he were invisible—or at least able to merge into the tree trunk and disappear.

A knobby walking stick was the thing Elias noticed first, sending a sinking feeling to the pit of his stomach. This was largely due to the fact the cane was being pointed straight at his face. Or (he hoped) that the cane was pointing angrily at the palm tree, while he had miraculously achieved invisibility.

Fat chance!

A ring of white hair showed under the brim of a floppy sun hat, which hid the face of a man who shuffled into view, swishing slowly around a bush. The man lifted his head and revealed a pair of ice-blue eyes under the brim, staring without blinking straight at him.

In the second it took Elias to realize it was an old man and *not* a pack of wild stone lions, he had no time at all to wonder where the stranger came from or why he was angry at a palm tree. This crinkly-faced old man, whoever he was, was angry with *him,* and had no issue with the palm tree.

Elias' knees shook, and his palms began to sweat. He lost his grip and slipped a short way down the trunk. Wiping a hand on his shorts he hugged the tree tighter.

The old man turned his face up and shouted at him—if one could call it shouting—in a thin, wheezy sort of voice:

"Child, you must get out of Apollo's tree! NOW!"

Indignant, Elias did not like being called a child—but neither did he like the cold, squinty eyes or the thin, wrinkled face. The old man had eyes like chips of ice. Weird to think of ice on a day of such heat...

Glancing down at the frowning old man, Elias could not get his muscles to cooperate. His legs felt stiff and refused to move.

"GET OFF THE SACRED TREE THIS MINUTE!"

No other boats were at the pier, and the only living things they had encountered for hours were lizards and weeds. Where had this man come from? Half of Elias' brain tried to move his legs as ordered, but the other half was puzzled, filled with questions. What did a palm tree have to do with the Greek god Apollo? Why *sacred*? *Sacred* meant something special and holy, like church, didn't it? What was church-like about a palm tree? And the dried-up lake— it, too, was 'sacred'?

The cane shook harder in his direction, as if it were a sword. Elias' gulped, seeing that the man was taking determined steps on the soft grasses, and making a beeline for Elias' backpack.

The crown!

At the bottom, wadded up inside his old Superman towel, was his ticket to fame on the soccer field, and popularity at the middle school back home. The man took another step closer. What if he stepped on the delicate golden leaves by accident? Could he know about the secret treasure within?

Elias wished the backpack was safely on his back, where it belonged. Whispering promises to himself, he muttered, "If I get out of this mess with the crown intact, I will never let it out of my sight again!" Desperation woke up Elias' muscles at last; he had to reach his backpack before the old man got to it!

He was inching down the ridges of the trunk when he heard Lily singing to herself down one of the other paths. There was no way to warn her of the danger.

"Here you are, Elias. What are you doing up there?"

Lily took a step backwards when she realized they had company. The old man put down his walking stick and leaned on it. His blue ice-chip eyes sparked like fire.

"Children," he said in a stern tone with a strange accent, "you must not harm the sacred palm of Apollo. It was on this spot, according to the old legends of Greek mythology, that the twins of King Zeus were born. Apollo and his sister, the goddess Artemis, were born at this place, which is the sacred heart of Delos. Tree-climber—" he glared at Elias, "—you are climbing on the birthplace of gods!"

The man's scratchy, wheezing sort of voice sounded different. He spoke with an accent different from other Greeks, but Elias could not place it.

"Of course, this is not the same tree; a palm is kept planted on this spot to remind us of Apollo and the good things he represented. Light, music, wisdom, and, most of all, beauty. His twin, Artemis, was a strong goddess of young women. And the hunt." The old man glared again at Elias. "The myth says Artemis helped her mother bring Apollo into the world after she herself was born. The stone lions continue to guard the palm in the Sacred Lake."

"Are *you* Apollo?" Lily asked, while Elias continued to climb down the tall tree.

The old man leaned on his knobby walking stick and laughed. "Apollo? Am I the Greek god of life's beautiful things? Sunlight and poetry and music and learning? Am I the god who was so handsome many statues were carved to capture my likeness? Would you want to own a statue of this crinkled old face?"

Lily acted shy around the laughing old man, not sure if it would be rude to laugh along.

"You might say I am an old friend of Apollo's." The stranger laughed harder, his sunken, wrinkled cheeks stretched into an awkward smile as if his face wasn't used to doing it much. Likewise, his wheezy voice did not sound as if it was accustomed to talking to people often.

Close enough, Elias jumped the last four feet off the tree, grabbed his backpack and slung the straps over both shoulders. With the happy weight back where it belonged, he breathed a sigh of relief and released some tension by laughing.

The old man turned a stern face to Elias. "My name is Alexander le Meilleur. I am an archaeologist responsible for uncovering Apollo's ancient city. You see, men built an amazing city around Apollo's famous palm tree. They ordered craftsmen from other islands and around the known world to make statues and mosaic floors and art for the walls. They built grand columned temples to hold gifts to the gods. Three grand temples to Apollo, especially, but many more countries put temples to their gods right here on Delos."

Alexander's blue eyes had been twinkling at Lily; maybe it was a trick of the light, but it seemed his ice-chip eyes could bore a hole right through Elias—

sear through his backpack like an X-ray. Once again, Elias had the uncomfortable feeling that old Alexander le Meilleur was hiding something. Elias' feet itched to run far away as fast as he could, and he wished for a fireball to suck on, but he didn't dare open his backpack for one.

"Your boat is the one at the pier?" asked Alexander. "Do your parents know where you are?"

Elias nodded and was pulling the straps of his backpack tight to hold it close against his body when Lily twisted his arm to see the watch face. "Elias—we have to be back at *Sargos* in one minute!"

The brother and sister stumbled over each other in their haste to leave, but Alexander called a warning after them.

"Stay away, children. You must not disturb the ruins on Apollo's sacred island!"

If they are already ruined, why should he care? Elias wondered as he darted down the bushy path to reach the wider Avenue of the Lions. Once on the Avenue, it would take only a few seconds to get to the pier and their home-sweet-boat. Through the corner of his eye he caught a last glimpse of Alexander the old archaeologist pushing aside a bush with his cane. He disappeared as swiftly as Highway the lizard, but Elias was not fooled. The old creeper would be back.

"Run, Lily, run!"

STONE SIGNPOST AMIDST THE RUINS ON DELOS

14

WHAT PINDAR FOUND

W hat's an arch-o-gist?" Lily asked, panting beside him in a sprint past the row of white lions. "Alexander said he was one."

"*Arch-ae-ol-o-gist.* Loves old stuff from the past. Digs in the dirt to find it." It was hard for him to talk and run at the same time, so he waved a hand around the ruins of the ancient city to show his sister what he meant by 'old stuff'.

"Alexander sure likes Apollo," said Lily. "Are you sure he isn't Apollo?"

"Can't be. You know Greek mythology is made-up stories from a long time ago, don't you?" Elias shuddered. "Besides, this Alexander guy was creepy with a capital C."

"He wasn't creepy. Just ancient. That's why he's Apollo."

"Lily, why are you sticking to your Alexander-is-Apollo theory? That's just brainl—I mean, the Greek gods and goddesses are not real." Elias stopped himself from teasing; he needed to get to the boat on time and couldn't risk Lily running off mad, and needing her life saved again. He couldn't turn up at *Sargos* empty-handed without a sister, or Mom would be angry.

"Did you see how he snuck up on me and then—poof!—he disappeared?"

"I'll bet he saw you take the crown from under that bench, Elias. That would explain why he followed you into the Sacred Lake and trapped you up the palm tree like that. Did you hear what Alexander said about priceless ruins?"

"If he wants it for himself, he can't have it," said Elias. He gripped the straps of his backpack tighter and picked up his pace to the pier. "*I* found the crown. It's *mine*. And about the crown, Lil. Better not tell anyone yet, okay? Not Mom and Dad, either. Keep it a secret between us until I figure out what to do with it. You have to promise."

They jogged close together and linked pinkies in an unbreakable pinky-swear, and Elias felt happy he had saved her from a bad fall in the nasty Fountain of the Minoans.

Standing on the bow of *Sargos*, Mom had her hand across her eyes like a visor, watching for them. She smiled at their red, sweaty faces.

"Good for you, being on time. And good news! Dad fixed the problems—he replaced a fuse. The engine works fine. Let's get going. We aren't far from Mykonos, and it'll be time for dinner when we get there."

Now that Mom mentioned dinner, Elias remembered his skimpy snack at the cave and rubbed his stomach. "Let's hurry!"

Later that night, after a delicious Greek dinner of pork *souvlaki* and crisp French fries sprinkled with oregano, he needed to be alone to think, so went down to the cabin. Inside, he slid open a compartment to find his flashlight. He had to get the heavy crown out of his backpack and find a place to store it, but where? Too risky to carry it around with him.

Keeping it wrapped in the Superman towel, Elias tucked the valuable wad into a compartment Mom had said could be used for his stuff. Next, he balled up his T-shirt and stuck it on top in what he hoped was a casual-looking pile.

After Lily came in and they settled in to sleep, *Sargos* rocked them gently on the water like a cradle. Elias stared at the low ceiling and listened to the ruffled sounds of Lily's breathing while inches away sat the gold crown, hidden. The treasure, and the possibilities its wealth created, filled the crevices of his mind even more than his dinner crowded the corners of his stomach.

Elias did not know how much the gold leaves were worth, but he was sure of one thing: he wanted to get back to Delos as soon as possible. Finding the crown was so *easy*—maybe there were *more* treasures on Delos, just waiting to be picked off the ground!

Unable to sleep, Elias reached for his flashlight and the *Myths and Legends* book.

My heart races as if begging to escape my chest. It pounds with the pace of my feet down the Avenue of the Lions. And what a grand Avenue it is! I grow dizzy looking left and right at the white-columned buildings everywhere. I am forced to slow down coming upon a horde of shoppers in the agora. I recognize it at once, though I have never been to this island before. Agoras look the same in every part of the known world!

What a mass of people!

Men, women and children crowd the sellers' stalls, most of them dressed in the simple robes of slaves, just like at home. I hear snatches of conversation as I make my determined way through the agora, too crowded at this place to run. I pass a group of boys placing bets; one brags he will win the athletic games in the upcoming festival. A group of men I pass analyzes the skill of actors on stage in the local amphitheater the previous night.

"Honey for sale!"

"Spices here!"

Slaves, sent by their masters, respond to sellers' shouts and stop at stalls for things their owners require for the evening meal. It is the same all over the Mediterranean world. Smells of grilled meats reach my nose and I feel hungry, even though the old raider gave me a small supper.

My feet trip over a young girl about my sister Philippa's age, not more than nine, so small I do not see her as she bends over a heavy-looking jug of olive oil nearly half her size. An older slave catches up with the child (are they sisters, I wonder?) and helps her, before the pitcher drops its precious load on the marble floor. I hear the older girl scolding the younger, who takes it bravely and does not cry. In my city, a slave would have been severely punished for spilling a drop of olive oil.

A twinge of guilt strikes my soul for the first time since embarking on this journey across the sea to join the raid for the great King of Pontus, Mithridates. These slave girls have no idea a battle is about to rage around them, changing their world forever—will they survive the onslaught of my fellow raiding warriors?

I shake off the feeling that I must warn the two girls, and push myself out of the throng. Back on the marble street where it is more open, I set my feet to a quick running pace. I must find Apollo's treasure!

Elias wished the book had a map. What route had the raiders taken? He had never heard of a country called Pontus, and he had no idea where the Aegean Sea was in relation to the Mediterranean and the Atlantic. Were they connected?

Which way to Apollo's temples? I have no clue. I slow to ask a slave at the edge of the agora and find there are three temples to the god. Skirting a few more slaves on errands for their masters, I find them: a forest of gleaming columns, leafless and smooth stone trunks of white marble. These are the temples! The treasure-filled temples of Apollo that the soldiers talked about endlessly on the journey!

I am overwhelmed that I am first off the ship to see them. Painted carvings of the gods richly decorate the building, but I can't make out the colors with which they are painted. The sunrise coming over the low mountain streaks everything in shades of red.

So many temples in one city! In my wildest dreams I had never thought such a place existed. The men on the ship did not exaggerate the riches of this place. I turn my running feet toward the largest, grandest temple, and do not stop until I reach the foot of its broad marble staircase. Their 'secret weapon', the old raider had called me! He had promised to block the way of those who would try to stop me. Nobody would guess, they said, that the smallest raider would be the one to take away their brightest crown. The Temple of Apollo will give up its richest treasure—the Crown of Victory sanctioned by the sun god himself—for the glory of Mithridates—to me!

Elias yawned and fell sound asleep to the rocking of the boat, and in his dreams he wandered the stalls of the *agora* on Delos. The marketplace was no longer crumbling in ruins, but was part of a shining white marble city. He ran from one shop to another, interrupting the sellers hawking their goods, asking if they had seen a boy about his age wearing a sword too big for him.

In the dream, Elias was anxious to find Pindar and ask if he found anything half as magnificent as his very own crown of golden leaves.

15

BOAT NEIGHBOURS

At the first moment of dawn, sunshine streamed through the porthole far too early for Elias to be awake on vacation. The spine of *Myths and Legends* heaved up and down on his chest. Forgetting where he was, Elias sat up too fast and cracked his head on the cabin's low ceiling. The book spilled off his chest and landed on Lily.

"*Ouch!*"

He had forgotten his sister was sleeping a mere two inches away!

A knock on the cabin door was followed by a burst of Greek sunlight. Amazingly, Lily rolled over, snoring.

"Awake in here?" Dad peered in through the cabin's low door. "Come on out, Elias. I need a hand."

First, Mom needed Dad's help to transform their bed into the boat's back bench; his mother must have been off the boat to find breakfast, because she had already put a basket of bread and honey on a tablecloth spread over the cooler. The deck dipped under his feet as Elias stepped off the bow onto the firmer footing of the dock.

"*Kalimera!*" Two white-blonde-headed kids, a boy and a girl, repeated good-morning to him in Greek, then English, but they didn't appear to be either Greek or American. They were eating breakfast on the deck of a boat docked side by side next to *Sargos*. Boat-neighbors!

"*Kalimera.* Where are you from?" Elias replied 'good morning' in Greek but switched to English, too.

"Hi! I'm Annika," said the girl, who looked about Lily's height. "From Sweden." She switched languages to English, too, but her version of the language sounded more like music.

"He doesn't care, Annika," said her older brother, who, when he stood up to say hello, seemed about the same age as Elias but taller. Everyone was taller. Elias sighed. The boy rolled his eyes at his sister and smiled shyly.

"That's okay; I've got a sister, too." Elias rolled his eyes just the same, and both boys laughed. "My name is Elias. From America."

"The United States or Canada?" asked the tall, blonde boy.

"Oh." Elias sometimes forgot that North America included other countries like Canada. Mexico, too. "We live in the States. Between New York City and Boston. My Dad grew up in an apartment in Athens, so I'm Greek-American."

He was relieved these boat-neighbors could speak English. Dad had filled some of the long hours on the plane trip by giving Elias and Lily a language lesson, but he did not know many Greek words beyond 'good morning' and 'thank you'.

"I'm Jon. You're lucky to be part Greek—it's warm and sunny here! Do you travel to Greece a lot? Have you been to Mykonos before? We arrived last night." For English not being his first language, the new boy asked good questions.

"This is my first trip since I was a baby."

"Come, join us." Jon's formal English made Elias smile, but he was pleased to be invited onto Jon's boat. While he answered more of Jon's questions, he had a chance to admire Jon and Annika's boat, which was a beautiful sailboat with two cabins and a living room space inside.

Unfortunately, the gathering was interrupted before too long.

"Sorry to break up the party, son," interrupted Dad. "I'd like your help with errands this morning."

Reluctantly, Elias followed his father down the dock and turned once to wave goodbye. Bright sunshine played on his new friend Jon's hair, making it almost white. Jon waved back.

Lily was awake and up, and meeting the boat neighbors, too. She and Annika were hugging like long lost cousins.

Other boaters were drinking coffee or putting their boat-beds away and making ready for the new day. Elias hoped to see Christos again, but the fisherman's *cacique* was not at the end of the dock, and Petros the pelican was nowhere in sight.

Souvenir shop owners were busy, too, pulling racks of T-shirts and dozens of neon-colored blow-up beach toys onto the sidewalk. Next to the ice cream shop, a store window was plastered with photos of colorful fish, and divers wearing bright yellow tanks on their backs.

Two men dragged out a large sign on boards and stood it up in front of their shop:

NEW TO MYKONOS!

WunderSea Adventures

Explore the Wonders
Under the Sea

Lessons and hourly rates
Snorkel trips/Night diving available

Elias made to go in, but one of the men said they were not yet open for business, so he and Dad walked around the harbor, stopping in shops for two cups of coffee, orange juice, and bottles of water.

Father and son wandered down a narrow alley until they came to a place so steaming hot it made the air around the harbor feel cool and breezy by comparison. A hand-painted sign above the open door read *fournos*. Far too hot outside already to go into such a fiery overheated shop. Elias was ready to dash past it when the most delicious aroma drifted into the alley. A *fournos* was a bakery—but not the kind of bakery Elias knew back home. All he knew of bakeries was the kind tucked into the corner of the grocery store that sold pink-frosted cupcakes that tasted like cardboard.

The *fournos* smelled heavenly, and boasted round loaves of bread with thick crusts. Cinnamon-scented cookies filled bins. He didn't think any of Dad's old

Greek stories included bakeries, but Elias was sure if the Greek gods had a bakery on Mount Olympus it would most definitely be a *fournos*.

"*Yassas*," shouted men in smudged white aprons, who smiled a welcome but looked uncomfortable, sweating heavily next to hot brick ovens. Using long-handled wooden paddles, they brought out hot *pita* that Dad bought for lunch. *Spanakopita* for Elias and Lily, but Mom preferred plain cheese pies to the spinach-filled ones. Dad's favorite had the flaky *pita* dough wrapped around a sausage.

Even though the smell in the *fournos* was divine, Elias was soon sweating like the bakers and was glad to leave their human-sized oven. Politely, he said, "*Yassas*," as they left. Similar to *aloha* in Hawaiian, it worked just as well for 'good-bye' as 'hello'. Easy to remember.

Dad walked past the dock and row of shops and *tavernas* that lined the waterfront. At the last building on the strip, he turned up another narrow alley. Red geraniums bloomed out of old olive oil cans being used as vases by doorways and on steps, and bright pink bougainvillea hung in full bloom over tiny balconies overhead.

"Here." A small sign hung by the door advertised *Marine Repairs*. Dad led the way in, and Elias rubbed his stomach. Had he bad-lucked the boat's starter?

One of the mechanics reached out with a darkly tanned arm and shook Dad's hand, then shook Elias' hand too.

"*Yassas. Kalimera*. My name is Nick."

Nick wore oil-spotted jeans, a friendly smile and a T-shirt that said *May I help you?* written in five different languages on the front, including English.

"*Kalimera*," said Dad. "I'd like a mechanic to check out the wiring on our boat before we take her out today. She's a pretty old tub—we ran into some trouble yesterday."

Elias squirmed and shifted his weight from one leg to the other and his stomach hurt; *Sargos* was fine—she *had* to be!

"I can help with electrical work this morning, sir," said Nick. "I've got time now. Why don't you show me the way to your boat?"

After an hour of tinkering, Nick set down his tools and gave them the verdict. "Your electrical system is old, but not too bad. I tightened some of the connections and everything checks out okay now."

Nick was paid, and thanked for his time. The Tantalos family put away the food for lunch and packed ice around the water bottles in the cooler.

"Aren't we ready to go have fun yet?" Lily was back from Annika and Jon's boat, dressed in another bathing suit destined to stay dry.

"Not yet. Who wants a job?"

Elias jumped to attention. Work on a boat was *way* more fun than any chores back home.

"Untie the cleat knot, then wait for the signal to push out. After I start the engine. Got it?"

"Aye, aye, Captain!" Elias untied a line from one of the cleats and held onto it. While he waited for Dad's signal, he practiced tying the cleat knot, ready to untie it again.

Lily was slipping her arms into a life jacket, but it didn't stop her from getting bossy and reaching for his line. "That's not how to tie a cleat knot."

"That's a good cleat knot," said Elias, pulling the line away from her grasp. He held it in his hands, frowning at the cleat.

"No, it isn't," she insisted, snapping closed her life jacket's buckles and stepping onto the narrow ledge that surrounded Sargos' deck.

"Yes, it is. Move out of the way. I've got to see when Dad gives the signal."

"*Sargos* is too small a boat to hold these arguments." Mom displayed her talent for knowing exactly what was going on. "Be helpful, Lily, and bring in the fenders."

"You tied that knot wrong." Lily acted as if she had not heard Mom. "Let me show you." She placed one foot on the dock and both hands on her hips.

While they argued back and forth, nobody noticed how *Sargos* was slowly and silently moving away from the dock—until it was too late.

"HELP!"

Lily's legs were dividing into a great wide split over the water, one foot planted on the dock while the other one remained on the floating *Sargos*. She was helpless to move one way or the other.

16

CHRISTMAS IN JULY

Lily's legs split further and further apart. Her toes gripped the edge of the drifting *Sargos*, but it was no use.

"HELP!"

Kerplunk! Lily fell into the sea in the narrow watery place between the boat and the dock. Her curling hair rose and stretched out weirdly at the water's surface, like some sort of hairy blonde octopus.

Thanks to the life jacket she had snapped on moments earlier, Lily's head bobbed to the top. She coughed and spat out a mouthful of salty sea water. "What did you do that for?" she spluttered angrily at Elias. Her arms flailed in the water, splashing but not going anywhere.

"*My* fault?"

In a heartbeat, Dad leaped onto the dock and grabbed the slack line from Elias' hands. Mom calmed Lily and talked her into doggy-paddling around to the stern. As soon as she reached the back, Dad pulled the line hand over hand to tug the boat closer to the dock, where he re-tied *Sargos* firmly to the cleat.

Trying to be helpful, Elias climbed over the back bench to lower the ladder into the water. He reached a hand to help a sopping wet Lily climb into the boat, but she slapped it away and pushed past him. Her teeth chattered from the unexpected dunking, even though the morning was already hot.

After Mom wrapped a towel around Lily's shoulders, she rounded on Elias. "Lily is still learning how to swim—what if her life jacket was not on yet? She's not the fish of the family, like you are. If the boat was running her legs could've gotten cut to ribbons on the propeller blades!"

Elias thought he was finished being scolded, but Mom was just warming up. "If you and your sister cannot learn to work together this might well be our last boating vacation. Understood?" Mom's eyes flashed and her gray-blue eyes looked stormy.

Elias had rarely seen his mother this angry. "But *she* was the one who—"

Mom interrupted. "Maybe it will help you remember not to be such a stinker to your sister if you spend time cleaning out the boat's Port-o-Potty."

Lily was towel-drying her hair and lifted the towel to speak in a low voice that mom wouldn't hear. "HAH—you're the Pooper Scooper!"

"It's not fair to get a stinky job just because *you* didn't pay attention," he grouched at Lily, who grinned at him before letting the towel hide her face, but she wasn't fast enough for Mom.

"I saw that. You can help him, Lily. We don't pick on others. Especially family."

The day had not begun well for Elias, but nobody could stay in a grumpy mood once *Sargos* putted out from Mykonos Harbor and sped into the bright blue that was the Aegean Sea. The sky and sea had a calming effect on the Tantalos family. Before long, the mood of all aboard was as sunny as the day.

The day went from hot to hotter, and they decided to stop for a swimming break at one of the pretty pebble beaches. Mom wanted to swim, too, and Lily was talked into putting on a life jacket to wade in shallow waters where she could collect smooth stones.

As *Sargos* motored past a small island neighboring Mykonos, Mom used binoculars to choose a nice shallow cove with clear, greenish water. It took some time to set the anchor, maneuvering the boat forward and backward until the anchor gripped the sea bottom.

"Jellyfish!" Floating in the sea only an arm's length away from Elias were two clear jellyfish the size of his fist.

Elias scooped the jellyfish into a bucket with plenty of sea water to keep them alive. Everybody bent over the bucket of water to get a good look at the sea creatures. In the clear water the transparent jellyfish were almost invisible.

"The tentacles might sting," warned Dad.

With one finger, Elias touched the top of the jellyfish. "Slimy!"

Lily took a plastic drinking straw and gently tickled the tentacles of one of the jelly-like creatures. The sunlight played on the wet gooey strands until they sparkled like—

"Christmas lights!" she shrieked with glee.

"Christmas? It's July. Make sense, will you?"

When Elias looked in the bucket of sea water he saw tiny white lights blinking up and down one jellyfish's body, in tidy rows. "Let me try." Elias took the straw and tickled the other jellyfish, until both were decked out with miniature lights and twinkled like a holiday display. "Lil, it *does* look like Christmas lights!"

"We should have Christmas in July every year!" Lily danced with her doll around the boat.

Elias poured the jellyfish back into the sea.

Lily's first turn tubing on Sharky had been short, so she wanted to try again. The injury from the spear gun had been repaired, and they happily got the tube ready.

"Dad, remember to keep the boat going straight. When you turn in circles I feel like Sharky will throw me into the water, and I've been dunked enough for one day."

After several minutes tubing, she made the cut-throat signal—she was ready to stop, and *Sargos* slowed on the western fringe of a small, rocky island with a low mountain. At its base, the fronds of one tall palm tree stuck out in the middle of a bushy green circle.

"Tubing is fun, but my hands got tired of holding on." Lily unhooked her life vest. "Do you want a turn, Elias?"

"Not this time."

"You always want a turn!"

"Lily." He spoke low and soft, but with an undercurrent of excitement running through his voice. "Do you see where we are? Hello, Delos!"

The piles of ancient ruins surrounding Mount Kynthos suddenly seemed to Elias debris brimming with treasures waiting to be discovered—*by him!*

Inside his chest, his heart fluttered with excitement like the wings of a bird trying to escape its cage. "I'm getting hungry," he said, forcing his voice to remain calm. "Can we have lunch and stay for a while?" A big idea had come to him, and he could barely breathe. He had never dreamed he'd return to the treasure island so soon.

"Sure—this spot is as good as any," answered Mom. "We can swim first and then eat lunch on the boat. We'll take a *siesta* before heading back to Mykonos."

"Son, could you help get the anchor ready?"

Elias jumped up to help his Dad with the job. He pulled the anchor's long, heavy chain out of its compartment and Mom helped Dad maneuver the boat back and forth to set the anchor. Then everyone went swimming for the second time that day. Mom and Dad trod water, and even Lily was hot enough to take a dip with her life jacket securely fastened.

Elias needed his sister's help to treasure hunt, so he swam close enough to discuss his new plan in a whisper.

"I don't want to hear it," she said. Her dark eyes flashed a warning. "You should take that *you-know-what* right back where it belongs. Don't look for more old stuff. If you take anything else, I'll tell."

For a kid of eight, Lily could put on a fierce act when she set her mind to it. Elias had to get on her good side about this treasure-hunting business, but his sister doggy-paddled back to the boat and refused to hear another word about it.

For lunch, the family stayed on board to eat under the shady canopy. The spinach and cheese pies tasted delicious, warmed by the sun. He and Lily shoved huge bites in their mouths and licked their lips. A more peaceful, contented moment between them may never come. It was time to insist Lily join his plan.

"Lil—we can cover more ground together," whispered Elias. He took another big bite of *spanakopita*.

"A hunk of spinach is stuck in your teeth." Lily pointed to her front tooth to show him where it was lodged.

"Whatever. When we find more treasure we'll sell it," he said, picking his teeth. "I'll split the money with you. You can have a TV for your bedroom. And a computer!"

Lily refused.

"And more bracelets?"

But his sister would not agree to their top-secret treasure-hunting expedition until he added a new wardrobe of matching outfits for herself and Medusa (uh, for Marina—because he also had to promise to stop calling the thing 'Medusa').

Lily's help was proving to be expensive, but with more treasure lying around Delos for easy picking, Elias did not worry too much about the cost.

"Time for a *siesta*," Mom announced after she cleaned up lunch. "If you're going to stay out on the deck for your rest, kids, put on more sunscreen. We'll snooze in the cabin."

"Sure, go ahead! Have a good nap!" Elias could not believe his luck. "I'll read. Lily, do you want your book, too?" He tucked *Myths and Legends* under his armpit and passed the loaded *Dazzle It!* bag to Lily.

Mom raised her eyebrows over her sunglasses at this unnatural display of thoughtfulness. Lily pulled out her notebook and pink feather pen.

This *siesta* custom was finally coming in handy!

Elias had to be patient until he was sure Mom and Dad were asleep. His parents talked in low voices, but it soon grew quiet on *Sargos*.

He read a few sentences of the book, intending to stop the moment he was sure they were asleep, but reading Pindar's story made him forget where he was, transporting him back two thousand years ago to the time when Delos was still a grand city worshipping the god of the sun.

The temple buildings are quiet. After the busy agora, I enjoy the peacefulness, and with light footfalls ascend the stone steps. I keep my eyes on the door; I invent a story to tell in the event that a priest comes to ask my business.

Nobody does. Not seeing a priest (and failing to concoct a good explanation for my presence if I come across one), I boldly draw out my sword at the top step. Its sturdy weight gives me courage.

An olive green lizard darts between my leather-sandaled toes and the door. I had not seen it hiding in the shadows of the columns. Normally I like lizards, have caught them at home for Philippa's entertainment when we finished the day's work, but now— my nerves high—I jump, startled, and lose the grip on my sword.

The second that it takes for my hand to lose my grasp on the hilt is long enough for it to fall. The metal blade screeches against the stone floor. It is loud enough to warn the entire population of the impending battle. I spin in alarm, not knowing which way to turn.

Lily's elbow jabbed Elias in the ribs and jerked him back to reality.

"*Hey!*" He whisper-screamed and rubbed his side. "That hurt."

"Sorry. My pen ran out of ink and I was shaking it. Didn't mean to bump you," Lily whispered back. "Dad's snoring."

"You would know."

After what seemed like an eternity, the glorious sound of sleeping parents came from behind the closed cabin door. Elias set his book on the cooler and checked his watch.

"Lily, we've got a good two hours while Mom and Dad take their siesta. This is our chance to pick up more treasure!"

DOLPHIN MOSAIC FLOOR IN THE HOUSE OF THE DOLPHINS, DELOS ISLAND

17

PICTURE PUZZLES

Mom and Dad won't like it. We'll end up with more than one day of Pooper Scooper duty."

"Shh... I'm hoping they forget about that. Plus, they didn't specifically say *not* to leave the boat. We'll be back on *Sargos* before they know we're gone."

"Are you *sure*?"

"We're wasting time." The boat rocked gently as he stepped over the back bench and climbed down the ladder, and they panicked at the small snapping sound when Lily fastened her life jacket, but the cabin stayed quiet. Luck was on their side!

Elias took a few steps down the ladder at the stern and slipped into the sea without a splash, then held the ladder steady for Lily to follow. He swam with one arm while holding both pairs of their sandals overhead to keep them dry. Lily doggy-paddled after him, but stopped halfway to the beach.

"Wait! I don't have my bag."

"We don't have time to go back for that thing."

"But—"

"You don't need Medu—Marina. We don't have time."

Elias swam ahead of her and sloshed up the beach, waiting in silent agony for her to paddle faster. Who knew how many more gold treasures were just beyond his reach, sitting in dark nooks for the past two thousand years?

When his sister finally waded onto the beach she took forever unbuckling her life jacket and finding a place to leave it on the pebbles. "It'll be too hot to walk around Delos with this on. I'll leave it here and pick it up when we come back," said Lily. "I'm not sure about this. Why do we need more treasure?"

"You've got to be kidding." Elias did not understand her reluctance. Like holding a winning lottery ticket, treasure fixed so many problems in his life! The gold crown was the best treasure he'd seen. "There's LOADS of stuff we can do with more treasure. Dream big, Lil! We can buy our parents their own boat so we don't have to borrow this old tub from Uncle Costas next time."

"You mean *Theo* Costas. And I LOVE *Sargos*. Don't talk bad about her."

"Whatever. It's time for ACTION!"

Elias scanned the arid landscape and led the way up what appeared to be a main street—a path about four feet wide covered with sand and stones and some bits of the typical broken marble and pottery that littered the place. The main street trailed away from them and led upwards toward the mountain.

Elias spied a large lizard skittering on the path ahead. "Is that Highway?"

"No. This one is almost as big, but it has a bright yellow head, see?"

Elias hurried to agree to keep Lily happy. "Let's see

where it's going. Maybe it will lead us to treasure, like Highway did."

It worked. Lily cheered up and ran ahead down the street after the lizard. "Let's call her 'Sunny'. Maybe she's friends with Highway."

The main 'street' was intersected with narrower alleys, barely three feet wide, lined with crumbling stone walls and covered with more of the white crunchy marble and red pottery bits. Sunny darted into another ruined building with another one of the now familiar, chiseled stone signposts:

HOUSE
OF THE DOLPHINS

"This must be an ancient neighborhood." Roughly cut gray and reddish-colored stones formed walls that gave shape to roofless houses. Lily ran inside the Dolphin House, but Elias slowed down, looking for a place that could hide treasure. Another marble bench? One of the huge terracotta vases? Or a big crack in the stone walls?

Elias could tell at once that House of the Dolphins was special. Tall columns stood at the corners of a courtyard surrounding a colorful picture laid out in a square in the middle of the floor. The floor-picture was big, about the size of his bedroom at home. At knee-height a rope had been slung all the way around, fastened to a post at each corner.

Sunny proved to be just as good at Hide and Seek as Highway; this new lizard had simply vanished.

"This floor looks like an ant-thingy!" Lily stared at the floor with a crease in her forehead.

"Antiquity," Elias reminded her automatically.

The picture looked painted on, only Elias could

see it was not made with a paintbrush. It had been created like a puzzle with colored bits of broken-looking tile. Unlike the other ruins on Delos, this tile seemed broken on purpose—cut, in fact. Circles of blue-tiled sea waves rolled around the edge of the picture. In each corner, pairs of dolphins leaped playfully over blue-tiled waves. A black tile gave each dolphin its eye.

"The people who lived here put creatures of the sea on the floor to make their houses pretty," said Lily knowingly. "It looks like a fancy rug."

"I think you're exactly right, Lil! Greek summers are too hot for carpets and rugs on the floor like we have at home."

Lily stayed behind the rope but knelt on her hands and knees. "Look at this one—a cute little man is riding on the dolphins! How many tiny pieces of tile make up all these dolphins and waves?"

"Don't know... hundreds... thousands." Elias checked his watch and rolled a pebble between his thumb and forefinger, then chucked it through a glassless window in frustration. Mom and Dad would wake up soon, and there wasn't any treasure in the House of the Dolphins, at least not any that he could fit into a backpack. "We don't have time to count tiles, Lil. Let's go see if there's another house. *Treasure*, remember?"

Lily dashed out of the doorway but came back with a handful of the red and white bits from the path; she sat cross-legged on the floor and sorted the stones into piles by color, then began piecing together her own floor-picture.

"You go treasure-hunting, Elias. I want to make a picture."

Sunny chose that moment to come out of hiding. The lizard scooted under the rope and settled onto one of the dolphins in a ray of sunshine, remaining frustratingly out of reach.

Elias put a foot over the rope, but Sunny skittered away and disappeared over the doorstep and around the rough stone wall.

"DO NOT STEP ON THE ANCIENT MOSAIC!"

Elias spun around, startled.

A man's head poked over the glassless windowsill. His wrinkled face was scrunched up and turning a funny shade of red that Elias was pretty sure was not from sunburn. It was *him*—the same old archaeologist who'd yelled at him for climbing Apollo's palm tree!

"The rope is there for a reason, young man." Alexander's voice calmed, but Elias could see his hand shaking on the knobby walking stick.

"Sorry." Elias took a giant step back over the rope. In spite of getting yelled at, he could barely keep his eyes away from the beautiful mosaic tiles.

"Young man, you have a talent for disturbing antiquities sacred to Apollo's holy island."

Elias could tell this was NOT a compliment. He had forgotten how much the man's squinty eyes resembled chips of blue ice. Even though the day was hot, Elias shuddered in the company of this odd archaeologist.

Lily had been absorbed in making her floor picture but looked up when she heard the archaeologist's voice. "Hi! *Yassas*, Mr... Mr. le Meilleur!"

The wrinkles on his thin face crinkled and stretched into a smile when he saw Lily.

"*Yassou*, child. You may call me Alexander; it's much easier for you to say, I think. That is a very nice *mosaic* you're making," he said to her, but Elias noticed the man's icy eyes kept straying back to him, watching.

"Young man, you must step back from the rope."

Elias took a step away from the rope.

"One more giant step."

Elias thought he'd better do as he was told. It would be a tragedy if old Alexander insisted on waking his parents to scold him.

"That's much better. *Efharisto. Merci.* Make sure you do not step on the priceless mosaics in these ancient houses. Antiquities on Delos could never be replaced." Alexander took off his cap. A halo of white hair surrounded his glistening, sweaty scalp.

Lily knelt outside the rope and pointed to one of the dolphins. "Look, Elias! This dolphin has a wreath of leaves in its mouth, kind of like the one—"

Uhk-khmm! Uhk-khmm! Elias threw a fake coughing fit to draw Alexander's attention from his sister's next words. He glared at her but attempted to speak in a normal tone of voice to the old archaeologist. "Yeah, Lily, just like the seaweed crown Dad wrapped around my head when I won our family Olympics the first day of vacation. Um... Alexander, do I see a dolphin carrying a ring in its mouth? What's that about?"

Alexander replaced his cap on his head and nodded approvingly. When he spoke, he talked about the old designs as if they were friends. "That dolphin is the victor in a game. You see, Apollo loved the leaves of the laurel tree very much, but that is a long story. The god made sure its leaves would never decay but would stay ever green. The laurel wreaths of Apollo were important to the ancient Greeks. A crown of golden laurel leaves was always given as a sign of victory to kings who won battles—"

"—and to the winning athletes in the Olympic Games!" shouted Elias, forgetting to be nervous; he understood why his father had given him a 'crown' of seaweed in their watery version of the Games.

"That's right." Alexander finally gave Elias a rare, weird crinkly smile of approval. "Crowns of golden leaves were made for kings and other wealthy men to offer to the storehouses of the gods in exchange for favors. Increased trade, fair weather for their generals' ships, and the like. There was a special one, one golden crown in particular was known in legends as the Crown of Victory. Anyone in possession of it— well, let us just say that their lives would be free of troublesome things like poverty or being on the losing side of battle or business. I doubt such a crown actually existed. Apollo having a special laurel crown was merely a story, like the gods and goddesses themselves, designed to give hope and answers. The wealthiest residents of Delos liked to commemorate stories of the gods and goddesses in art like this mosaic."

"Why did Apollo love trees so much, Alexander?" asked Lily. "First a palm tree was where he was born, and now a laurel tree? Was he a envi-ro-ment-list?"

Alexander wheezed when he laughed, but his face lit up and his smile stretched wider as he began to settle into a story. "No, this love was more a matter of the heart, not born of the earth. As the story goes, Apollo loved a beautiful nymph named Daphne, but she did not return his love. In fact, Daphne ran away from the god's attentions. When he had nearly caught up with her, the nymph turned herself into a laurel tree! For ever after, the sun god loved the laurel tree, even though it meant the loss of his love. Statues of Apollo often show him wearing a laurel leaf crown. It is his symbol, a message of hope and victory."

The glow faded from the old man's face now that he had reached the end of his story. The man's wrinkled forehead creased severely down the middle, and the corners of his lips turned down in a frown. "Now. Where are your parents?" he asked, all serious and almost angry once more.

"Um..." began Elias, who had absolutely no idea what to say.

"I did not see your boat at the pier today."

"Oh... our parents... um... our boat, *Sargos,* is anchored off the pebble beach... around the bend from the pier."

"Time to go! *Yassas!*" Just as at their first encounter with Alexander, Lily took action. She grabbed her brother's arm and pulled, not waiting for the archaeologist to say another word.

Not knowing or caring whether Alexander was following them, Elias and Lily stumbled through the maze of stone alleys back to the pebble beach as fast as they could. Their hearts pounded in their chests, and their leg muscles burnt like they were on fire. But it was not fast enough.

"LILY! ELIAS! WHERE ARE YOU?"

18

UNDER A STARRY SKY

When Elias saw his mother's puffy, tear-streaked face getting sterner and redder and madder by the second, he was not sure if he would rather face Alexander's icy blue eyes or Mom's stormy gray ones. Both made Elias shiver in the hundred degree heat that permeated the Greek islands in summer.

Both parents were pacing the beach when Elias and Lily ran pell-mell onto the pebbles; Dad was gripping an orange life jacket with white knuckles. "ON THE BOAT—NOW!" The tone of his voice left no room for argument. Dad put the life jacket around Lily's shoulders without comment and snapped the buckles shut.

Mom, however, had plenty of comments, but she was so angry she had trouble speaking in complete sentences. "How *could* you—? What were you—? We woke up—the boat—*EMPTY!*" For the entire thirty minute boat ride to Mykonos, Mom continued ranting in single syllables. "How. Could. You. Do. That?"

When the windmill spokes of Mykonos came into view, Dad spoke up. "Thank God Lily left her life jacket on the beach. At least we could be pretty sure she hadn't drowned." Sarcasm dripped from Dad's voice, at which Mom burst into tears in another unrelenting chorus of "How could you?"

Unfortunately for Elias, by the time they reached Mykonos Harbor and docked Sargos for the night, Mom had found a few more words. "You've already got one day on the Port-o-Potty job tomorrow. Add the rest of this week. And the next."

"What about Lily?"

"Your sister can help you clean it out tomorrow. She is younger. Lily looks up to you and follows your example. You should have known better. Your father and I are very disappointed. Get ready for dinner and think about what you did. Two weeks, young man."

Elias' cheeks burned hot, and his fists clenched. "I will think about how UNFAIR you and Dad are! Punishing me for two weeks—and Lily barely a minute! I'll be the Pooper Scooper on my birthday!"

He slammed the cabin's small door behind him as he crawled inside, but it made a wimpy *click*, making him angrier. "NO FAIR!" he yelled again, making clear to the entire world exactly how he felt.

After laying flat on his back in the cabin to remove his damp swim shorts, Elias overheard his father talking to someone whose voice he did not recognize. He flipped onto his stomach to peek out the porthole and gulped.

Out on the dock, dressed in navy blue pants with gold pins shining from the collar of a stiff short-sleeved blue shirt adorned with a sleeve patch that read *Municipality of Mykonos* was an attractive woman with fair skin and bountiful red hair tied up

126

in a messy bun that stuck out from a sun visor.

A police officer.

Freckles dotted the officer's cheeks, but Elias could see the seriousness in her eyes and he felt the air in the cabin evaporate. Did she know about the crown?

A group of boat-neighbors joined their conversation, including his sister, Annika and Jon. The officer's next sentence made Elias break out in a cold sweat and duck out of sight from the porthole.

"No need to be alarmed, folks." She switched easily from Greek to English. Tourists came from so many different countries that English was a common language understood by many. "We'd appreciate help, especially from you boaters. Please be on the lookout for any suspicious activity you might see during your rides around these islands."

"For what we should look, Officer... what is your name?" Jon's face shone with eagerness, and Elias knew why. What boy wouldn't want to catch a bad guy? He rubbed his stomach, which had started to ache, but he put on an innocent face and joined them on the dock.

"Calm down, kids. I am Officer Maria. Stolen antiquities, selling ancient statues, vases, that kind of thing. Someone could be transporting bulky packages by boat."

Elias asked, "What should we do if we see something suspicious?"

"We don't want any boaters—especially you kids—taking on these antiquity pirates single-handed. That could be dangerous. If you see anything unusual, simply leave a description at *astinomiya*—the police station. A few blocks behind the harbor, that way." Officer Maria pointed toward one of the ubiquitous flower-laden narrow alleys. "People who understand the value of ancient objects are not your typical bankrobber, hold-em-up-with-a-gun-in-their-pocket kind of crook. But don't let that fool you; modern pirates can be dangerous, especially when a lot of money is at stake." The police officer straightened up. "The Aegean Sea covers a vast area; we can use the extra eyes. Safe boating out there, everybody. *Kalispera.*"

The gold pins on her uniform collar flashed in the warm evening sunshine as she strode briskly down the dock, stopping at the end to repeat the story to a group of fishermen. The dark-capped men were bent over their fishing nets after another day's work, untangling the snarls and stitching holes that had gotten too big.

"I need to change clothes for dinner," said Dad. "You and your sister may walk around the Harbor area for a few minutes." His forehead creased in the middle and his voice got serious. "Do *not* wander away from the immediate dock area. Do I make myself clear?"

Elias promised, and he meant it. His stomach ached and he was in no mood for more trouble.

"Have you met the famous Mykonos pelican yet?" Lily was asking Annika, who shook her head. "I'll show you. Let's go find Petros." With arms linked at the elbows, Lily and Annika skipped down the dock past the other boats.

Elias had a sudden inspiration. "Wait right here, Jon—I'll be right back." Elias used his hands to motion 'wait' in case Jon didn't understand the English. He leaped onto *Sargos* and in a moment was back with a treat to share. "Would you like an atomic fireball?"

"Never had one, but I will try." Jon popped the red candy out of its plastic wrapper and began sucking on it as the boys walked after their sisters.

"Lily never makes it past thirteen seconds," Elias explained, slipping one in his own mouth and keeping his eyes on Jon's reaction. The blonde boy's eyes grew bigger as the candy heated up. After a minute and a half, his blue eyes watered and dripped.

"The trick is—and please don't tell my sister—if it gets too hot, put the fireball next to your cheek. It'll take the heat off your tongue and let you keep going. Breathe in through your mouth to let the air cool your mouth."

"Your secret is safe with me, thank you!"

The boys kept keen eyes out for Petros, but there was no sign of the oversized white and pink pelican anywhere. Sitting in a pile of nets in the *caicque*, however, was the bird's best friend, Christos the fisherman. Yellow nets draped over his knees, and his hands worked to repair holes.

A tourist wearing a Mykonos T-shirt and a video camera strapped around his neck came up to chat with Christos at the same time.

"Excuse me, Christos, have you seen the pelican?" Elias' stomach gnawed; he did not feel well.

"Ho yes, Petros is never too far away. If you are looking for the pelican, my friends, don't worry. He will find you. You can be sure of that!"

Annika and Jon' parents called them for their dinner. Jon pulled a wry face. "Thank you for the—what did you call it?"

"A fireball. Here, take some!" Elias dug in his pocket and pulled out a few extra candies to share with his new friend. "See you later!"

"Any news from the police?" the tourist asked the fisherman.

The men standing around had steered the conversation away from birds and back to thieves. Elias strained his ears to hear every word. It seemed that rare, ancient objects were coming up for sale on many islands of the Aegean Sea. Tourists, especially, were spending a lot of money on the antiquities without knowing they were being sold illegally.

"A few people have been arrested at the airport trying to take antiquities out of the country. Illegal, you know." Christos looked round at their foreign faces when he said this.

"Why would people get arrested for buying something if they paid a lot of money for it?" His stomach was twisting tighter than one of Lily's knots. "That isn't fair."

"Ho now, by law any antiquities found must be turned in to the Greek authorities. Expert archae- ologists examined the items and discovered they are truly ancient. The buyers were released when they returned the treasures. The strange thing," rumbled Christos, playing with the end of his moustache, "is that nobody knows where the crooks are finding the antiquities. Museums have not been broken into, and as far as the police can tell other archaeological sites—like the one nearby at Delos—have not been vandalized. Yet objects keep turning up in the wrong hands."

Elias felt a nudge in his ribs. Lily. He ignored her. "Do the police have any clues?"

"No, ho! I suspect I have more fish in my nets than the police have got clues, or I'm not Christos the fish- erman!"

Lily tugged on Elias' T-shirt and nudged his ribs with her elbow a second time.

"OW, Lil—hang on, you don't think—" He stepped away from the men and ducked under the doorway of a tiny white chapel built close to the dock. The chapel was crowned with a blue dome that matched the color of the Aegean Sea, just steps away.

"Come in here—" Elias pushed on the door and they went inside.

The chapel was empty and dark, but sunshine filled

the space with streams of light that fell on slim yellow candles stuck in a deep layer of sand in a brass tray. The candles were lit and had a heavy, waxy scent, although the chapel had no other patrons; warm yellow light flickered against saints painted in rich colors, reds and blues and greens, their halos and clothes adorned in gold leaf paint covering every inch of the walls. His eyes followed the beautiful art to the high domed ceiling where hundreds of gold stars had been painted against a nighttime-blue. The ceiling stars twinkled, reflecting candlelight.

"Nobody knows about *you-know-what*," he said to his sister. "No how, no way."

Lily's stared up at him and didn't say a word.

"How could anyone know? It is our secret. We pinky-swore on it." Elias rubbed his stomach.

"I *told* you. You should have put—*it*—right back under that marble bench!" Lily's hands flew to her hips.

"This is *different*, Lil. I found—*it*. Those men were talking about stuff being *stolen*. I didn't steal anything. It was simply there."

"Kids? Here you are!" said Mom brightly. She entered the chapel with Dad, both of them dressed nicely for dinner. Mom wore gold earrings that swung over her suntanned shoulders, and her hair was pulled back in a low ponytail. "The fisherman said you had come this way. Having fun exploring?"

"Sure, fine," Elias and Lily said hastily.

"I want to light a candle to thank God you were found safe and sound this afternoon," Mom said. Her face glowed in the candlelight as she smiled in Lily's direction; Elias could see Mom's eyes were teary again. "Then we can eat dinner."

Dad dropped some coins into a box. "Let's all light some candles." Dad handed them each a taper. "As for me, I am thankful that the old girl *Sargos* has stayed in one piece for this trip!"

Grateful that his father's change in subject would make Mom laugh instead of cry, Elias pressed the wick of his candle to another that was already burning. The wick flared tall and bright, then settled into a slow-burning flame. Elias shoved it deep into the sand so it would not tip over. "I am going to thank God it is almost time to eat dinner!"

"Your stomach is a bottomless pit," said Lily. She pushed her own candle into the sand. "I'm thankful Elias hasn't dropped Marina overboard."

Laughing, the Tantalos family headed outside.

"I want to see the windmills up close." Lily pointed to the huge bicycle-spokes that showed on a hill above the flat rooftops of the sugar-cube white houses and shops.

"We haven't seen much of Mykonos Town yet. If you're not too hungry, let's look around for a few minutes and make our way to the windmills to watch the sunset over the water before dinner," Mom suggested.

Elias agreed to the detour when Dad promised he could choose the *taverna* for dinner. The famous Mykonos windmills proved a tricky destination; the streets became a winding maze lined with tiny tourist boutiques and coffee shops. Alleys going off the main lanes dead-ended at small hotels with blue painted doorways framed in colorful red and pink flowers.

A gray-haired islander was leading a slow-footed donkey through the alley, and Dad asked the most direct way to the windmills. Elias doubted there was a fast, direct way to anything on that island, but they followed the donkey. Baskets tied to the animal's back were stuffed with leafy greens, fruit and vegetables in a rainbow of colors, and the food looked so fresh and good Elias was tempted to pick a tomato right off the cart and bite into it.

Vroom! A young man zipped down the street on a bright red motorbike, driving it within an inch of Elias' flip-flopped feet. Strapped to the back of the 'bike was an old wooden box decorated with the picture of a smiling pizza on it. A delivery boy! They didn't deliver pizza like this in Connecticut, he thought, and (in spite of nearly losing a few toes) smiled, glad to be reminded he was far from home.

"Let's try the side streets. Might not be so busy," suggested Mom, leading them down one of the shopping streets for pedestrians only. There were no pizza delivery bikers or donkeys on this alley, but Elias had never seen such a skinny street. If he reached out one hand to touch the shops selling sunscreen on his left, he could at the very same moment touch the jewelry shops on the right.

Every store window had a display more enticing and beautiful than the one before. Even the shops selling flip-flops and beach towels had a dressed-up appearance. And the gold! Twisted into earrings and thin chains, the smallest pieces of gold put on display in shop windows were priced at hundreds of *euros*. If Elias put all that gold jewelry together in one lump, it would not come close to the amount of gold wrapped in his old Superman beach towel. Elias did not need proof that his crown was pure gold. He had never been more convinced of anything in his life. Even if he didn't find more treasure on Delos, this one would be enough to buy him anything he could want!

"Look!" said Lily, who was bouncing up and down in front of a rack of postcards that stood tall on the street corner. "It's Petros!"

Looking down to pelican-eye-level, Elias could not see Petros or any other overgrown bird. "What are you talking about, Lil?"

"Look up." On the postcard rack next to glossy pictures of the Mykonos windmills, several cards displayed photos of the island's favorite show-off: Petros the Pelican, Mascot of Mykonos.

Tourist maps and guide books filled the next rack. *Cycladic Islands of the Aegean Sea* and *Cooking with Olive Oil* were some of the titles. One book cover showed a big yacht cruising in front of a small, dry island similar to Delos. *Boating World: The Greek Islands* was the title.

"Hey, Dad—can I have a few *euros?*" It turned out to be a good time to ask for money; Dad handed him the coins and didn't question the purchase, because Mom was attempting to lure him to one of the jewelry store windows. Elias made the transaction, remembered to say "*Efharisto*" to the sales clerk, and tucked *Boating World* into his backpack next to *Myths and Legends.*

Lemons hung from the branches of trees that grew wedged in between shops, and flowers grew out of big old tin cans that advertised olive oil. Shops along the flowered alley sold old-fashioned white statuettes, and vases in black or red terracotta with pictures from Greek mythology painted on them in gold. Elias picked up an ancient-looking vase with handles. Dolphins, painted in black, splashed around the sides of the red clay vase.

He had a really funny feeling about those dolphins, and could not get them off his mind. A few more knots turned in his stomach—and he was sure they were not from hunger.

"Dad, can you come here?"

Mike Tantalos was clearly happy to have a reason to be pulled away from the jewelry store. Mom soon got distracted by an artsy-looking store next door, and Dad turned across the narrow street to see what Elias wanted. "Thanks for giving me an escape route, son. That jewelry was expensive!"

"Why would people want old stuff like this?" He showed Dad the vase decorated with dolphins and it hit him. The mosaic floor in the ancient house on Delos had dolphins exactly like these.

Dad took the clay vase from Elias. "This one is not old. It's a replica—a copy of things archaeologists have discovered in ancient Greece. The original objects are housed in museums, and are special because they teach us about life thousands of years ago."

"You mean ant—antiquities?" Lily said, jumping into the conversation and getting the name right for a change.

"Why would people make fake copies if they can buy real ones?" asked Elias.

Dad smiled. "Real objects from long ago are too rare to be handled. And breakable. Take a clay vase two thousand years old. Copies are made that people can touch and appreciate. If the real deal is used and broken, it is impossible to replace."

"Can't people have a real antiquity if they pay for it?" Elias remembered what Officer Maria said about thieves selling antiquities. If somebody was selling, that meant someone was buying.

"Son, antiquities are part of our cultural heritage as Greeks. Priceless treasures belong to *all* the people. Museum curators know how to take care of ancient artifacts so everyone can see them and enjoy them."

Mom must have given up on the jewelry, because she came along carrying a shopping bag. Elias guessed correctly that she'd bought something with the sun on it. A sun clock. Mom collected suns, ever since Elias was five and made her a Mother's Day present in kindergarten—a sun made from modeling clay with his initials scratched in the back. Elias remembered painting a smiley face on the sun so his mother would always be happy. Now, their kitchen walls were covered in suns, some handmade gifts from him or Lily, some as Christmas gifts from friends and relatives, too. The kitchen suns were a daily reminder, Mom liked to say, that they should always be optimistic and look at the sunny side of life.

"Are we done shopping yet?" Elias and Dad hoped.

"Boys!" Lily frowned, and Mom laughed. "Let's go see the windmills."

Elias followed his family through the winding streets, thinking. By the time they reached the imposing windmills, the sky was changing into bands of pink and orange and purple.

The replica with the dolphins was a fake but not inexpensive. His crown had to be worth a lot more than a hunk of clay shaped into a vase, right? And if the tiny bits of gold jewelry Mom liked were expensive, how much could the gold crown be worth? He could not get it off his mind.

Priceless.

The sunset painted the whitewashed windmills and houses a rosy glow. On the horizon, the Aegean Sea gleamed, a deep blue watery blanket sprinkled with dust of gold. The darkening waves gently rocked a sleek, white yacht similar to the one pictured on the cover of his new book. The yacht was anchored out in the deeper waters, near a tall, expensive-looking four-masted sailing vessel. The sun, now a red ball of fire, dipped close to touch the horizon.

Lily was disappointed that they were not allowed to go inside the windmills, but Dad announced it was time for dinner, and Elias could not take his eyes off the shiny yacht. He liked *Sargos*, but he admitted to himself that he would trade it in a second for that one.

Another beautiful boat came close to shore, much smaller than the sleek white yacht and the four-masted sailing ship—and vaguely familiar. About the same size as *Sargos*, it looked twice as fast with twin engines at the stern. Three men standing on board wore shiny black wetsuits, and as the powerboat went by Elias knew why it was familiar: *WunderSea Adventures* was painted along the side in gold letters, with a picture of the SCUBA-diving photographer chasing colorful fish. Real SCUBA gear, oxygen tanks and fins, was loaded in the cockpit behind the captain's wheel.

The sky glowed blood red, and *WunderSea Adventures* motored past the white yacht, and out past the sailing ship, whose tall masts were now silhouetted against the lingering sunset. The powerboat picked up speed near a large cruise ship anchored further out in deep waters. Points of light from the cruise ship's countless portholes reflected on the dark water and looked to Elias like thousands of stars in an upside-down sky.

"Dad, did you see *WunderSea Adventures?* The new SCUBA place must be open for business now! Can we check it out tomorrow morning?"

Dad did not answer. When Elias turned around, his family was gone.

Windmills on Mykonos Island

19

IN COMMON WITH PIRATES

A heavy scent of lemons, flowers and grilled meats teased his nose as Elias breathed hard, instantly worried. Mom's rule for getting lost was to stay put, but his family was no longer in sight at the windmills. He saw no choice but to plunge into the crowd at the base of the slope near the restaurants to look for them.

His heart pounding in his throat, Elias quickly became shuffled along like a fish in a school of sardines.

Lively *bouzouki* music filled the air and pushed his footsteps faster, but there was no space to run. Lantern-lit tables were squeezed onto narrow sidewalks at the edge of the sea, and Elias used his soccer footwork skills to wind his way around tables while trying not to fall off the sidewalk's edge into the water.

People spilled thickly from alleys and shops. Couples, families and groups had settled in for long dinners, positioning themselves close to the water's edge for a prime-time spot; sunset-viewing here was like a spectator sport, or TV. Feeling like a fish swimming upstream, he jumped up and down, trying to see anyone familiar, but no luck. He dodged doorsteps lined with old metal cans-turned-planters, their peeling *feta* cheese labels obscured by mounds of red geraniums. Garlands of pink bougainvillea hanging overhead made it feel like a party, but Elias had nothing to celebrate.

Elias squeezed between couples holding hands and groups of laughing teenagers.

Mom's other rule—for desperate times only—was to ask a family with a baby stroller for help (since people with babies are used to taking care of others pretty much around the clock and might be willing to help one extra kid). Elias tried that approach, but his bad luck magnet was in full force because the family couldn't speak English. Sweat beaded on his forehead and his palms felt clammy.

Incandescent light spilled from boutique windows next door to shops selling T-shirts and coffee. Elegant tables with white tablecloths glowed under candlelit lanterns; those expensive-looking outdoor restaurants butted cozily next to cheerful *taverna* tables dressed in traditional blue-and-white checked paper. Everyone smiled, laughed, sang and ate, skin glowing from another day under the Greek sun. Elias walked and searched faces, feeling invisible.

The music hit a lively tune and a group rose from their tables to dance, men and women grabbing each other's shoulders in a circle. Children ran to join in, grabbing adults and each other around the waist, hopping from one foot to the next trying to keep up. Most tables were filled with people, and everyone acted relaxed and happy.

Elias had never felt so foreign and alone.

The delicious aromas coming at him from all sides made his mouth water. He found a fireball in his pocket and the familiar fire of the candy on his tongue made him feel a bit better—but it didn't take his mind off his troubles.

Where was his family?

The buzz of conversation at *taverna* tables reminded him of the school cafeteria back home. A young woman sitting at one of the lantern-lit tables by the sea was eating a bowl of white yogurt as a dessert. She held a spoonful of golden honey several inches over the yogurt and watched it drip onto the creamy white mound. It reminded him of the day Kennedy Anderson had smiled at him from the lunch line on French Toast Styx Friday. Everyone's favorite lunch, the rectangular pieces of bread swam in maple syrup that looked to Elias like honey.

In the cafeteria that day, everyone was excited because it had begun snowing outside and they hoped school would be cancelled early. Kennedy Anderson was in the lunch line ahead of him and smiled—and he tripped over his feet, knocking her down, and with airborne trays of French Toast Styx, they sprawled on the linoleum cafeteria floor. Like a baseball player sliding into home base, he belly-smacked across the floor and didn't come to a stop until he was halfway under Kincaid and Brandon's table. Ever-lucky Kennedy avoided the mess, but the trays landed sticky side down and syrup oozed into his ears and dripped from his hair.

Elias could still smell that sweet maple syrup—and hear Kincaid and Brandon's applause echo around the cafeteria. The motherly cafeteria lady, Mrs. Rhodes, came to his rescue and took him to the cafeteria sink where she rinsed his head under the cold water sprayer.

Elias shook away the bad luck memory and continued searching the endless stream of people for a familiar face, but felt lost in a maze. Every direction ended with the same view: dark sky overhead, well-lit alleys with white buildings, and blue-painted doorways smothered in red flowers.

If he could find the harbor, he could find *Sargos*—and, eventually, his family. He set off down one street, and then another.

His feet ached to run, to keep pace with his pounding heart, but Elias could not make any headway through the crowd. In the narrow streets it was not easy to look over the throng. How long would it take his family to notice he was missing in a crowd like this?

His heart sank when he remembered the trouble he had caused on this vacation in such a short time—the boat's ailments, and getting scolded for disobeying and sneaking away...

A scary thought grabbed him in the gut and did not let go: What if they were *glad* he was missing? They'd be *happy* to be rid of a bad luck magnet like him. Lily probably convinced them they were better off not bothering to look for him. He could drop dead in the middle of the street from starvation and nobody would care.

A chapel across a square gave him hope that he had found the harbor dock. Elias made a beeline for it, knowing *Sargos* was just beyond, but on closer inspection, he realized his mistake. This chapel's dome was painted red, not blue, and it was not at the harbor but in the middle of a small square lined with bustling, great-smelling *tavernas*.

Elias slunk onto a low wall next to the chapel without any idea what to do.

The Greek *bouzouki* music changed tune, growing louder and faster, until lively young couples got up to dance. Others joined in, old adults, children... everyone wrapped their arms around each other and danced in a circle, laughing.

An odd sensation that he was no longer alone came over him, and Elias realized someone familiar was moving closer, as if he had nothing better to do than wait for a lost Elias to realize he was there.

The pelican!

"Hi Petros, am I glad to see you! Have you seen Lily?" Elias sat on his heels and stroked the bird's creamy feathers. The softness calmed him, and his pounding heart rate slowed to a normal pace.

Stay put. That's what Mom always said to do if they got lost.

After a short while someone's French fries dropped under a *taverna* table, and Petros waddled away to investigate. Elias was not sure what to do next, but spending time with the pelican had made him feel less lonely and afraid.

"*Yassou!* Do you need help?" A woman strode toward him carrying a red bag and matching sandals—and she spoke to him in English!

Elias nodded and blinked to ward off tears.

"Where are your parents? Are you a visitor to Mykonos?"

Embarrassing. Elias stared at his feet and knew he should not talk to strangers, but he did not know else what to do. "I was looking at the windmills with my family and I... I don't know. We got separated," he said, looking down at the white lines painted around the flat stones paving the square.

The woman nodded. "Very easy to do here in these

crowds. Maybe I can help you find your family. Do you know the name of your hotel? Where are you staying?"

"We're staying at the harbor. On our boat. We had been talking about getting dinner, but I can't find them, and I don't know the way back to the boat. Probably left without me."

"Don't worry. Mykonos is a small island. Let's go find them." A questioning look crossed the woman's face. "Do I know you? What is your name?"

Elias picked up his chin and wiped his face with his T-shirt sleeve. "It's Elias. Elias Tantalos."

The woman beside him stared.

"My dear, you look just like your father! I've seen you in photographs since you were a baby. Just on my way to meet Costas at the ferry from Athens. We have plans to meet your family for dinner tomorrow."

Elias stood rooted to the spot. She talked to his parents? How did this stranger know him?

The woman knelt down to look in his eyes and spoke kindly with a Greek accent. "The last time I saw you, Elias, you were a baby covered in olive oil at your baptism. I am your *Thea* Katerina. If you like, you may call me Aunt Kat. Easier, *neh?* I would know you anywhere from photographs, but I'm sure you don't know me, do you, *koukla?*"

Come to think of it, she *did* look familiar; he'd seen her face with Uncle Costas in pictures at home, too.

Aunt Kat's soft tone made his worries gush out; he couldn't stop tears flowing down his cheeks. "I didn't mean to get lost, it just happened, and I'll probably get in trouble again but—"

"The towns on these Cycladic Greek islands were designed to be winding and confusing on purpose," his aunt said kindly. "You are not the first to get lost. Can you guess why?"

Elias shook his head.

"The streets were designed to confuse invading pirates."

"There were pirates around here? Tell me more!"

But Aunt Kat didn't hear him; she had pulled a cell phone from her red bag. "Let's call your parents and find out where they are."

Why didn't I think of that? He did not have a phone, but he knew his parents' phone numbers. Any of the shopkeepers could've telephoned his parents, if he had thought to ask. That would have been better than talking to a stranger (even if she *had* turned out not to be a stranger).

"Don't worry, I'll get him to Little Venice safely," Aunt Kat hung up and slipped her phone back into her bag.

"Little Venice? What's that?"

"It's a part of town where buildings sit on the edge of the water almost as if they're floating on the sea. Just like in the famous city in Italy. I hear it looks something like that in Venice. I haven't been myself— have you?"

She didn't wait for his answer but gently ushered him down a less crowded lane. Aunt Kat chattered on about the history of Mykonos, and Elias fell silent. What if Mom and Dad did not *want* to find him? That afternoon on the pebble beach his mother had cried with relief to find Lily's life jacket, but did Mom say anything about being happy *he* had not drowned? No, she did not.

The alley opened at the sea with *taverna* tables lining the sidewalk, glowing warmly with lanterns and buzzing with the voices of so many tourists eating dinner that it did not register at first that many of the voices were shouting for *him.*

His family ran to him, waving their arms in the air.

"Elias! We thought you were right behind us," said Mom, hugging him in plain view. He'd worried that she would pile on more Pooper Scooper duty, but she squeezed him so tightly he could barely breathe.

"Thank goodness you are all right." Mom held tighter.

"You gave us a scare, son." Dad joined Mom in an increasingly embarrassing public group hug. The entire population of Mykonos was watching.

"What would I do without a big brother?" Lily had her hands on her hips, her eyes blazing mad. "Don't get lost ever again!"

When he tried backing out his family only pulled him closer, laughing and crying and talking at the same time. He felt his neck get hot again. "You—you are *glad* you found me?"

"Why, honey—" Mom smiled, holding him out and looking at him from head to toes. She laughed and shook her head, making her earrings and ponytail swish around. "Don't you know?"

Elias shook his head.

"You and Lily are our treasures," said Mom. "Nothing you do or say will change that in a hundred million years. We love you."

Dad nodded and grinned and rubbed the top of Elias' head.

"We're together at last!" Aunt Kat said from the outskirts of the family huddle.

"How can we ever thank you?" Mom hugged Aunt Kat and then hugged Elias again. His mother did not let go of him but turned to Aunt Kat and asked, "Let's sit down and catch up. We have a table right over here. You'll join us?"

"I'm on my way to Mykonos Harbor to wait for Costas at the ferry. Good thing I was early."

The *taverna* overlooked the darkened sea, and

soon their paper tablecloth was weighed down with chicken and pork skewered on long sticks and sprinkled with lemon and oregano. Olive oil was drizzled on top of salads loaded with tomatoes and cucumbers and *feta* cheese.

Now that he was no longer lost, Elias was famished. He licked olive oil from a chunk of tomato and slid a piece of pork off a skewer with his teeth while Aunt Kat explained to Elias and Lily how she was a schoolteacher during the year in Athens, but had started Sunny Days Camp to bring kids together in summer. It didn't matter where they were from or what language they spoke, everyone had a good time exploring the islands together.

"You are welcome to join the *pedia*," she invited Elias and Lily. "We go on outings—beaches to swim, and caves and sometimes explore ancient ruins," Aunt Kat said, her eyes sparkling. "Ancient Greek art has such stories to tell! I'll show you my collection during your visit."

Aunt Kat found a small business card in her purse and stood up. "It may be easiest to reach me here, at the number for Sunny Days Camp. If you'll excuse me. We will meet for dinner tomorrow, *neh?*" Aunt Kat looked at Elias. "We have a birthday to celebrate soon! Have you enjoyed your new *Legends* book?" Her eyes twinkled and he nodded, smiling back at her.

When the family was together it was somehow easy work meandering through the narrow flowered alleys back to Mykonos Harbor and *Sargos*. Catering to people on vacation, the shops in Mykonos Town stayed open late. When they neared the dock, Elias noticed the new SCUBA shop had opened for business. "Let's look at spear guns, Dad. I want to get one for you."

"You can't afford it, son—and neither can I."

"It can't hurt to look, can it? Let's see which one you'd pick if money was no object. If you had your choice of anything in the store."

The owner, who was still dressed in SCUBA gear, introduced himself as Yannis. The shop was new, Yannis explained, because the Greek government had only recently allowed diving in the waters around Mykonos.

"The sea floor is littered with ancient objects that people tossed overboard or lost in storms and ship-wrecks centuries ago." The owner chatted animat-edly. "SCUBA diving takes you where the sea life is incredible—and you wouldn't believe how long antiq-uities can survive intact underwater. Thousands of years. Isn't that right, Thanos?"

The owner's partner came through a back door of the shop and joined the conversation. Elias recog-nized Thanos. Both were young men with black hair, but Thanos' was shaved short and Yannis' hair curled down his neck. "Of course, the Greek government doesn't have the time or money to dive for antiquities. But they protect the ancient objects by setting many laws against tourists diving for them. Many places are off-limits for diving, like Delos, because there are many ruins left underwater. You don't want to dive without an organized tour like ours. Too easy for marine police to catch you where you don't belong. Tourists can see a lot of interesting sea life right here, around Mykonos."

"I want to try it! Dad, can we?" Elias did not care how much it cost. The bottom of the sea was waiting to be explored!

"You're too young for SCUBA. Come back when you're older, OK, kid?" Yannis smiled at Elias and his teeth flashed in the sunshine. Trying not to stare, Elias noticed that a tooth near the front was capped in silver. "Night diving trips are especially beautiful," he said. "The colors of fish stand out with undersea flashlights."

A broad-chested man dressed in a blue and white T-shirt brushed against Elias' backpack on his way to the counter. In English, his shirt had the phrase *It's all Greek to Me!* on its back.

"Hey—watch it," muttered Elias. Dad gave him a look that said (without saying) he was being rude.

"I'm looking for an underwater camera," the man said in English. "Lost mine in the sea. Whaddya got?"

Thanos put both hands on the shoulders of the tourist. "*Yassas*, welcome back, sir. What can we do for you?"

When Elias put his head on the pillow, soon after leaving the shop, he promised himself he would buy his very own cell phone as soon as he sold the gold crown. He never wanted to feel lost again.

20

PINDAR'S NEW PLAN

Elias woke from a restless sleep in the middle of the night. The low ceiling kept him feeling trapped, coffin-like, and the black of night dusted with only a few stars through the porthole did not help. He tossed and turned, his mind drifting back and forth between the raider's loot and what his father said about objects from ancient Greece. *Priceless!* Worth so much it can't be counted! Elias remembered something else Dad said, too, the part about museums, but who cared about dusty stuff in dumb old museums? Not him. He pushed that memory into the furthest, darkest back corner of his brain.

Front and center: Priceless was enough to buy whatever he wanted. A lifetime supply of atomic fireballs. New soccer uniforms and cleats for the entire Evamere Wings team. Like one of Zeus' lightning bolts, the reality of his new wealth jolted into his head. Springing up, he cracked his skull on the low ceiling.

Rubbing his head, he was too excited to feel the pain. When he sold the gold crown back home, he'd have money to buy Dad a new spear gun. A new boat, too, with money left over. Everyone would be very happy with Lucky Elias Tantalos!

His brain spun like a top, and he couldn't sleep. Reading sometimes helped, so he decided to see what was happening on Pindar's raid.

My whole body is shaking, like the clattering of my sword down the hard, marble steps of Apollo's Temple. It shivers through my bones like an earthquake, a warning loud enough to rouse the island's citizenry. Will my first raid end this quickly in failure? Sweat pours from my forehead, and I determine to carry out the old raider's plan even if it means finding Apollo's Crown of Victory and running to the ship with the whole of Delos at my heels.

I scramble to pick up my sword, and sigh with relief when its hilt is once again clutched in my grip. Nobody emerges from the temple to question the noise! Not one soul alarmed! I boldly hold my sword, raised in front of me.

The door opens easily to my light touch, and I step inside. I congratulate myself on getting so far so fast without further incident, but the sight that meets my eyes takes my breath away. A towering row of columns lines the sanctuary like a forest of marble and frames, a glittering sight of treasure on the altar table that even my wildest dreams could not have imagined. I had not known the world contained such a trove of finely crafted objects—and so much gold! As blinding in its beauty as the white marble city, the gold is staggering in its mighty triumph. If I had known I would see such things I would have begged my father to let me join the raids as soon as I was old enough to hold a sword.

I wish for a bigger bag.

At the far end of the room stands a bigger-than-life statue of Apollo. For it must be him, the god Apollo, god of harmony and light. Anyone could tell from the crown of laurel leaves carved right onto the god's marble head, painted with gold.

I am confused. If that crown is part of the statue, real as it looks, what is it I am meant to take?

I walk as in a trance to stand in front of Apollo. When I get close to the altar table—so loaded with offerings that I am surprised it does not groan under the weight—I set down my sword.

Clay figures, toys, lie atop silver and gold; I push aside these weak offerings from children and the poor and grab at everything and anything that shines with value. Pulling the sack from behind my vest, the one meant to carry Apollo's Crown of Victory back to my comrades, I begin shoving in the riches.

Next to Elias, Lily's elephant-with-a-cold snores ripped through the small cabin. If he sold the crown, he knew exactly what he would do with the money. He'd buy a bigger boat, one with an extra cabin he didn't need to share with his sister. And wouldn't his teammates be happy to have him back when he showed up at school with new equipment and uniforms for everyone?

The stars winked at him through the porthole, and he winked back. With the money he'd make from selling the gold crown, Elias would get back on the Wings' good side. And, he supposed, he'd give Lily the stuff he promised.

His wishes expanded until they outnumbered the stars. It was halfway to morning before Elias drifted off to a most comfortable sleep.

21

STINKS

M om knocked on the cabin door for a second time to wake Elias, but he slept on and his gold-tinted dreams merely changed form. A clomping herd of elephants wore gold crowns and kicked soccer balls towards a flock of pelicans that scooped them into their beaks and flung them into the air, where they turned into balls made of gold. When Mom knocked a third time, the elephants turned and dropped golden plops of poop that turned magnetic and stuck to a metal shield Elias held in front of his chest.

"The Port-o-Potty will not clean itself!"

Finally, Elias woke up and groaned. He shook Lily out of her snores. "Lil, Mom didn't forget Pooper Scooper time. Let's get it over with."

While *Sargos* was docked in Mykonos Harbor, the Tantalos family used a nearby public toilet, but there were many hours at sea when each family member had, at one time or another, no choice but resort to the Port-o-Potty. Every morning, before they could set out for a new day on the water, the system had to be cleaned out.

Elias took a few deep breaths of fresh morning sea air and tried his best not to moan through the chore. If he complained, Mom might tack on more days. But it wasn't easy. He swallowed a groan when Mom insisted they each put on rubber gloves that went up to his elbows. But did they have to be neon pink? His sister liked them, but seriously? He was almost eleven!

"Your ears are turning just as pink!" Lily, laughing, grabbed one handle on the Port-o-Potty and helped him carry the sloshing waste container down the dock to the marina's emptying station.

Still laughing when they reached their destination, Lily attracted attention by waving her free neon pink hand at fishermen and tourists. Elias was glad nobody could see what was inside the thick plastic container they carried. That would be more embarrassing than the gloves!

He twisted the cap to open the container's tube, but it wouldn't budge. He turned it to the left as hard as he could. Nothing.

"Maybe it goes the other way, Elias," Lily suggested.

He almost dropped the container on his toes. "Oh— so I'm turning it the *wrong way*. Just say it. I'm the Wrong-Way Kid. You know you want to."

"Hey, I'm sorry. I didn't mean it that way," she said. "Honest. I'm not like those boys on the team who used to be your friends. They are meanies."

Lily's brown eyes held onto his with an expression that he could describe only as *soft*. Elias had a flicker of memory, someone else's eyes searching his in the same way. Who was it?—oh yes, Kennedy. Green eyes. Soft eyes. Eyes that looked at him as if he wasn't worse than the slop in the Port-o-Potty container.

He took a deep breath and let out a long sigh.

"Okay, Lily, but stop rubbing it in, won't you? Those boys..." his voice trailed off as he turned the cap to the right as hard as he could. Nothing moved. It was hopeless. "I'm sorry. I didn't mean to jump on you like that. Those boys said—and don't tell anybody—but they said... um, they want to use my head for the soccer ball next season." Remembering, Elias gave an angry tug on the plug and it came loose. "Yes! Got it! Lil—you know what they did?" He spoke in a low tone so nobody could overhear, even though they were quite alone. "Kincaid had a ruler and everything. To measure my head to see if it was regulation size."

"They were joking, right?" Lily's eyes grew wide.

"I guess, but... just don't tell, all right?"

Lily nodded solemnly.

For reasons he could not explain, Elias felt better after sharing his feelings, more light-hearted, than he had in months—even though the job still stank like a barn. Lily took a step toward him, acting as if she were about to hug him, but the poop container he held between them luckily stopped her from getting too close.

Secretly, Elias had been worried about himself. His brain kept making wrong turns. In fifth grade, he'd frequently say or do something stupid that got him in trouble with teachers. He had been a pretty good student in fourth grade, but in fifth his grades fell off a cliff. Would he always be a bad luck Wrong-Way mess-up?

Elias finished the stinky job and added fresh water to the emptied waste container, and Lily helped him carry it back to *Sargos* as quickly as humanly possible. Mom was waiting to add the chemicals into it, and Elias hoped nobody would need to resort to using the Port-o-Potty again today—but almost always, one or more members of the Tantalos family did.

Every morning for a week, Lily helped him with the Pooper Scooper job, even though she didn't have to. She simply called it her early eleventh birthday present to him. In spite of the disgusting job in the mornings, the days grew into a pattern that came as close to paradise as Elias could imagine. The weather stayed calm, perfect for boating, swimming and tubing.

During one especially hot afternoon siesta, Elias opened his new book, *Boating World: Greek Islands*, and smiled, humming to himself with the confidence born of the surefire plan to make everything right with his newfound riches. He dug in Lily's *Dazzle It!* bag for a pink highlighter and circled the picture of the best boat that he would consider buying with some of his treasure. Then he studied a map of the islands until he located Mykonos and Delos. He circled those, too.

Flipping open *Myths and Legends*, he found Pindar loading his sack with treasure from the Temple of Apollo. The raider boy worried that the gods did not approve of his trespassing in their sanctuary:

Do the gods see and hear? Do they care? Will Apollo, the god of light, beauty and harmony, be angry at the dark acts that my fellow raiders will inflict upon the beautiful white city this night? It is, indeed, the most beautiful place my eyes have ever seen, but even as my hands defile the treasure store my heart gives thanks that it is witnessing this holy place.

I pause, listening for any signs of danger, still seeking

the piece of treasure that the raiders have sent my speeding feet ahead to find—the Crown of Victory.

Where is it? I study each object on the altar for the one thing of beauty necessary for our raid's success.

Apollo's crown. Legend says it is a magnificent mass of delicate gold leaves, laurel of course, for laurel leaves are Apollo's special symbol of victory. There are other gold leaf crowns here, crowns that must have been offered by kings and athletes, but this one—this one is different. If I manage to find Apollo's own Crown of Victory, our raid will cut Delos to its knees!

Curses upon it! Where is this thing?

I admit it is difficult to concentrate with so many splendid treasures here for the taking. My hand rests on a gold snake bracelet coiled to fit on a slender arm. Like my mother's. I slip it into my pocket rather than into the sack, still listening for an answer from the gods. I keep my eyes locked on the statue of Apollo and my ears wide open for any sound. Afraid to breathe, I wait for almighty Zeus, father of Apollo, to send one of his lightning bolts to strike me down for my actions.

Or Zeus may choose to tattle to one of his priests, sending his feet to the Temple and my feet running for the door.

No answer comes, heavenly or human.

I stand open-mouthed and draw out my sack, forcing my hand not to tremble as I load it with treasures. I pick up a clay horse and matching chariot that look as if made by a skilled craftsman. Perhaps a child my sister's age had offered this to the god.

Philippa will like this. Removing my helmet, I toss the toy into its bowl.

Philippa would say 'yes'. Not to the toy, but 'yes, the gods hear and care'. She is too young to understand how much wealth these raids bring to our country and, indirectly, to our family. Why should one small city keep so many riches for itself when others have so little and need much?

I see a glint of yellow light from above, and it is like an answer to my prayer. My eyes stray upward to meet Apollo's, and I no longer feel fear. So taken was I by the multitude of treasures at the god's feet that I had not gazed long enough upon its head! In plain sight, the crown is sitting atop the statue. Not carved as one with the statue's head, as I had thought earlier, but in the fading light of day I see that it is, in fact, a separate piece. Removable.

A crown worthy of the god of champions. Gold laurel leaves. A victory crown. This is what the raiders counted on! It is within my reach!

I leap for it, scrambling on the altar and then the god itself to reach the head. I was correct—the crown could be taken! Without hesitation, I removed it, but where to put the sacred object? I do not attempt to cram the golden leaves of Apollo into my too-bulging sack. Instead, I force it onto my own head.

MINE!

Mom's cheerful, freshly-rested voice interrupted the silence and jerked Elias two thousand years forward into the present. His parents never took naps at home in Connecticut, but afternoon siesta was one Greek custom they seemed to like a lot. Elias had never read so many pages of a book in his life, but what else was he going to do when his parents insisted on acting like three year olds and take naps every afternoon?

"*Siesta* time is over," she said, but he was only half listening. A new wave of excitement was busily flooding his brain.

"Elias? Are you listening? Time for one more swim before dinner."

"Sure, Mom. Thanks!"

Pindar's story had given him a lot to think about, and swimming would give him time.

In lazy circles, *Sargos* had toured the coastline of the island closest to Mykonos that day and was approaching Delos. Elias recognized the barren island at once, with its jumbled mix of rocks and ruins.

"Absolutely, positively NO going on shore," Dad said, as if he needed to remind the kids of their prior disaster. "Don't even *think* about it." Off the starboard side Dad's eyes took in the pebble beach of the gray island an easy swim away.

"Did we have to end up at this barren pile of hot rocks again?" Mom grumbled, preferring sandy beaches with an abundance of olive trees for shade. "The ruins are interesting, of course, but in this heat—"

"Sure, no problem. No going on land," Elias answered with the most agreeable attitude he could muster, even though he was disappointed. Grabbing his snorkel gear, he dove off the port side away from Delos.

Lily finished rubbing the sleep out of her eyes and snapped her life jacket on. She jumped off *Sargos* with a splash and doggy paddled closer to him while he treaded water. Both of them stayed a dutiful distance away from shore.

Elias mulled over Pindar's discovery. It all fit. Did it matter if two thousand years had gone by? The lions pointed to the Sacred Lake with Apollo's palm tree at its heart—and it was clear as a Greek summer day that Pindar's island was the same as Delos. The crown had to be one and the same!

Fact: the new owner of the legendary Crown of Victory—the ancient golden laurel that guaranteed victory in battle—was none other than Elias Tantalos. He possessed the world's best good luck charm! Everyone would want to be near him for his good luck to rub off on them!

A few boulders jutted into the sea, and Lily doggy-paddled around them.

"Elias—*quick!*" She waved her arm. "Down in the water! There's something yellow!"

A few strong swimming strokes took Elias close to his sister. "What is it?"

Lily's face beamed; her wide eyes and big smile could mean only one thing:

Treasure!

22

THE SUN GOD'S REQUEST

I can't reach it," Lily said. The life jacket kept her bobbing on the surface, so she tried grabbing the bright yellow object with her toes.

Elias was so excited he could barely breathe—until he put his face in the water and looked through the mask. Like a bubble, his enthusiasm grew, burst and evaporated in an instant. The colorful object was not gold but plastic—a big fat clue that it was not made thousands of years ago. A twenty-first century toy, perhaps dropped overboard by a toddler on a ferry.

Fresh disappointment washed over him. Ancient Delos hid its treasures well; gold was not found on its ruined shores as easily as pebbles on a beach.

"Can you help me get it?" Lily begged. "I'm not a good swimmer like you. Please?"

Elias drew a long breath and entered the blue world beneath the surface. Deeper than it appeared, the yellow toy was at least ten feet down, but not hundreds, like the dark blue water now home to

Dad's spear gun. He swam toward the bottom for several feet until his fingertips scraped the edge of the smooth plastic. He could not get a good grip. Flipping over, Elias grabbed the thing with his toes and pushed off the sea bottom.

"You did it!" Lily squealed.

Elias handed the plastic junk to his sister. It was not much bigger than his hand, like a computer gaming toy. He treaded water and Lily bobbed in her life jacket, as the pair checked out the discovery. Bright yellow plastic encased a screen like a mini computer. A stylus dangled from a cord attached to its side.

"Is it some kind of underwater video game?" said Lily. "Do you think I can keep it?"

Only one fishing boat was in sight, and it was far out at sea. "I don't see anybody hunting for it," Elias reasoned. "Somebody must have dropped it off a boat. A tourist would be long gone by now. We can figure out what the thing is later. I'll put it in my backpack to keep for you. Your bag is too full of dolls and bracelets and notebooks and pink feathery pens and stuff."

Lily made a face at him but laughed and handed it to him, and they swam back to *Sargos*.

For several days the heat wave raged like a *fournos*, and Mom kept sending Elias to buy more sunscreen. At *siesta*, Elias rested in the shade and occupied himself by debating whether or not he should confide in his sister the amazing news of his Crown of Victory. If he had to keep the wonderful secret inside himself for a second longer he might rip a lung. He studied a map of the Aegean Sea in his new book, *Boating World: Greek Islands* and realized he had a way to tell her right there in his hands.

"Lily, check his out," he said, his finger twirling over the map. "These islands are called 'Cycladic' because they form a sort of circle. What do you see here, roughly in the center?"

"Mykonos!"

"Yes, but look closer. What is this tiny one in the heart of the circle?" Lily leaned over the book and read aloud. "Delos."

"Yes! Do you remember what that old archeologist Alexander said? Delos is the 'sacred heart' of the islands. This is what he meant—Delos is in the middle, or the 'heart' of the Cycladic islands."

Elias showed her a photo in *Boating World*. A white stone lion against a blue sky told him the page was about Delos. It had a brief paragraph about its glorious history.

"Listen to this, Lil. This book says the ruins weren't just old houses. They were temples. To Apollo and Artemis. Other gods and goddesses from Greek mythology, too. Even gods from other countries had temples on Delos. People used to visit Delos from all over because it was a holy place!"

Elias put his head close to Lily's and whispered: "There's more. In ancient times, people visited temples to offer prayers and sacrifice objects to the gods. People made offerings to please the gods or gain protection from them. Children made offerings, too! Kids gave clay toys, like dolls, to the temple altars, and wealthy adults gave objects of great value." Elias closed *Boating World*. "Objects of great value, Lily! What if the gold leaf crown was on Delos for a special purpose? What if it was meant for the temple of someone who loved laurel leaves so much they were made into gold?"

Lily's eyes grew wide. "You think the crown was an offering to Apollo?"

In a rush, barely breathing, he confided his theory about Pindar, the raider boy he was reading about—a boy who was sent to raid Apollo's temple and steal the Crown of Victory, an offering so special it meant eternal wins for whoever possessed it.

"Lily, I don't know how Pindar lost the crown—I haven't gotten there yet in his story—but Lil, swear you won't tell?"

Lily did not look very happy, but when Elias held out his little finger, she extended hers and they solemnly shook on it.

"Lil, I didn't find just any gold offering to Apollo. It all makes sense. I found Pindar's lost crown of Apollo. The Crown of Victory is mine!"

Grapes hung from an arbor over the heads of Elias' favorite *taverna*, where the Tantalos family met *Theo* Costas and Aunt Kat to celebrate his eleventh birthday. The moon, rounder each night since their arrival, added its nearly-full glow to the table lanterns. The *taverna* was crowded with tourists, and Elias happily stuffed a pork *gyro* into his mouth. Life couldn't get much better than this, being eleven with his problems ironed out and refreshing cucumber *tzatziki* sauce oozing down his chin.

A conversation at the next table got heated, and Uncle Costas casually leaned over to ask what was happening.

"No stopping the thieves. The tourist business will crash and then where will we be?"

Elias recognized the dark blue cap over a salt-and-pepper gray bushy line of eyebrow, complete with matching moustache. Christos the fisherman must have finished another hard day's work fixing thick piles of fishing nets, and was having dinner with a fellow fisherman.

"Any news?" asked *Theo* Costas.

"Not about the thieves, they're slippery," said the friend.

"Hard to hold in one place," agreed Christos. "Treasures from other islands were rounded up recently at their airports by customs agents. Santorini and Crete. The thieves are keeping well out of sight, yessir!"

"Those islands are too close to Mykonos for my comfort." Elias' uncle pushed back from the table and rubbed his full stomach. "Not good for island tourist business with robbers running around in the height of summer. Not good for my wife's day camp business."

Aunt Kat joined in. "You can't keep me away from giving kids a good summer. I trust island police to keep Sunny Days Camp safe from those crooks."

L ater that night, the waxing moon rose over Mykonos Harbor and brought comforting light through the porthole, but Elias' eyes wouldn't stay closed. He had already opened his birthday gifts, so he hadn't been given any more, but he didn't care. He had the best gift of all. A gift meant for a god. A gift that *made* winners.

Nobody believed in mythology anymore. If the crown was lost for two thousand years, was anyone left to care? If anybody was in need of something that promised victory to its owner, it was one bad luck magnet—Elias Tantalos! That was a fact, too. Finders, keepers.

A new dilemma cropped up and began to weigh heavier on his mind than when the gold crown sat atop his head. It guaranteed winning as long as it remained in his possession. If he kept the crown, he would never be a bad luck magnet again. He'd win the State Cup next time and his (former) friends would like him again. It wouldn't make him famous, because it would have to be kept a secret, and if he was on TV wearing the crown the Greek police would come for him.

On the other hand, he could sell it online as a good replica. With the money, he could replace his father's spear gun. And buy a new boat so they didn't have to borrow the old one with the faulty electrical system. He could buy the stuff he'd promised Lily, and a bigger boat so Lily could snore in her own cabin.

Reading the next part of *Myths and Legends* that night did nothing to help him feel less confused:

Earlier this morning, as our ship had drawn nearer to the island, our captain gave us final instructions: on the King's direct orders the people of Delos will not see another sunrise—or be enslaved.

The older boys and men taught me tricks with the sword, and at mealtimes in the galley they terrified me with stories of past raids, mocking the faces of men trying in vain to defend their lands and wealth.

The raiders laugh in the face of fear, and say the islanders have no defense. No army of theirs could be as strong as ours.

Before this day ends, the time will come to put my skills with the sword to the test.

I am afraid.

A heavy, trapped feeling spread from the top of Elias' head and on down, until it felt like a clamp had caught his body in rings of gold. A tornado of thieves, golden leaves, dolphins and knobby walking sticks pointed to museums and spun out of control. Elias drifted into such an uneasy dream that it made him scramble for a scrap of homework paper to write on as soon as he awoke:

Bouzouki music played, bright notes rushing over themselves, blaring on loudspeakers, but I was standing in a crowd at a small-town carnival back home. I held a prize by its hair: a perfect white head of stone, yet weirdly topped with brown, wavy hair like mine. A crown of golden leaves circled the hairy head of stone with living eyes staring at me from its stiff, chiseled face. In the dream I did not find this unusual. I turned the face away, holding the head by the hair, so it wouldn't keep looking at me.

Colors whirled around me, reds and yellows in crazy patterns of light from the rides and games and ice cream stands. The Greek music shifted to carnival sounds, fast-paced tunes and shrieks of children braving the scarier rides. A short distance away, the rest of the head's statue was on its knees, alive with its hands searching the stump of neck. I waved the head about in a slow-motion dance. "Mine, mine, all mine," I shouted, unafraid.

An arrow struck the ground near my feet. Startled, I saw a super-sized woman, standing on top of the Ferris wheel. Fearlessly standing, she rode it down, her robes flying out around her shoulders. This woman did not look like a statue but was very real. She jumped off and held a firm stance a few paces from me.

"I am Artemis, twin of Apollo. I can spear you as easily as meat on a stick." Artemis reached for another arrow from the quiver slung on her back. The arrow had a shining gold point. "On your signal, brother." She nodded at her brother-statue. The head in my hands nodded back.

Paralyzed, I watched the hunter Artemis set the arrow in her bow and point it straight at my heart. As I focused on the arrow's gold point, it changed into a bright red ball. An atomic fireball that exploded into flames and aimed for me.

The huge headless man-statue stood up and wandered with his arms out in front, trying to find his twin. The crowned head spun around to me and spoke.

"I am Apollo, god of many good things. Light. Harmony. Reason and Learning. And Beauty. By stealing my crown, which of these qualities have you displayed?"

"N-none... but—I didn't steal it, I found it... um... Highway found it—Highway, yeah, that's a fast lizard, not a highway... um, never mind."

I dropped the crowned head and it rolled on the ground, but as the face rolled away it said,

"Restore my crown to its rightful place. I am depending on you, Elias Tantalos."

Sweat dripped down his face, and his undershirt stuck to his chest. Elias felt out of breath, as if he had been running a race. Lily was breathing noisily next to him, and he exhaled slowly. *Thank goodness.* A bad dream.

He shivered at the memory of Artemis' shining black arrow exploding into flames, and Apollo's talking stone head.

Reading sometimes helped change bad images in his head, so he thumbed through *Myths and Legends* to find his place. Elias' chest felt tight with the dangerous dream, and felt he couldn't breathe until he found out if Pindar had survived the battle.

"Kids? Are you awake?" Mom swung open the cabin doors.

Elias rubbed his head. Half his brain was stuck in the awful dream, and the other half was stuck two thousand years ago with Pindar. He had never been so happy to hear his mother's cheerful voice in his entire life, but he needed a few more minutes to read. *What had happened in the raid?*

"Today, we're not going out on the boat. I need you to run some errands with Dad in town. Please dress, so we can have breakfast and get started."

"I just need five minutes to wake up, Mom," he pleaded, and luckily she went away.

Myths and Legends. Without warning, the legend

of Pindar ended abruptly. The writing on this page was different, more like a school textbook with facts instead of the story:

Inscribed on a fragile fragment of papyrus, the ancient legend of Pindar the Raider and his Crown of Victory did not withstand the test of time. The ancient piece of papyrus on which this story was discovered was severed at this point. The full story has never been recovered. A report of fact, or a fancy of imagination? The truth may never be known.

Apollo's Crown of Victory, if it existed—which most archaeological experts doubt—was lost to time. King Mithridates of Pontus and his men successfully raided the sacred island, killing thousands of Delians. Some escaped, and some women and children were sold into slavery. It has been suggested that one group of Delos residents hid well and survived the attack, but were never able to completely rebuild their once-great city. The island remained vulnerable to future pirate attacks and looters who helped themselves to marble for building materials.

The Greek island of Delos was never the same again and to this day, the great white marble city lies in ruin. An archaeological museum has been planned but has yet to open to the public.

"What!?! Where's Pindar?" Elias frantically flipped through the book but found nothing more, and he chucked it across the cabin. *Myths and Legends* landed with a smack on Lily's feet. She rolled over, but did not wake up.

A few minutes later, Mom knocked more insistently on the door. "Lily, I'd like your help with housekeeping today. *Boat*-keeping, I should say." Mom closed the cabin door after agreeing to five more minutes.

Yawning, Lily sat up and stretched, bumping her hands against the low cabin ceiling. "Ouch!"

"Lil—I've got to talk to you before you go see what Mom wants," Elias whispered, panting. "I had a nightmare... about *it*."

His little sister grew wide-eyed as he recounted the unreal, but terrifying, encounter with the god and goddess (but he made it less scary for her sake and left off the part about Apollo's talking stone head being removed from its body).

"Apollo asked for his crown back? We have to take it back to him!"

"As much as I want to keep it, I think you're right, Lil. We have to get this crown back to Delos. More than that—we have to find out where the crown belongs and... I don't know, put it in its proper place, wherever that is... maybe in one of Apollo's temples? That's what Apollo wanted. This sounds crazy but in my dream he was asking me to do it. Counting on me."

Deep inside his own head, however, a different voice spoke up—his father's words: *Real antiquities belong in museums, for everyone to enjoy.*

The words spun around in his head like the carnival rides in his dream. The ancient crown might have the power to make him a winner, or rich and famous, but deep inside he had not wanted to admit the truth to himself: *If I keep it, I'm just like the raiders and pirates. A thief.*

For what seemed like hours, Elias trudged around Mykonos Town with his father doing errands. They lugged bags of groceries and cleaning supplies past the Marine Repairs shop, where Nick stood outside and greeted them. "*Yassas!* Any more problems with

Sargos?"

Elias replied, "*Yassas,*" but he remembered their first day on the boat when he had noticed electrical trouble and pretended it was fine. Not telling the truth caused them to be stranded the next day at Delos.

"No, we've been lucky," said Dad.

"Enjoy the rest of your vacation," said Nick. "Let me know if you run into any more trouble."

"Sure thing, Nick, but we would rather not need your services. *Efharisto.*"

Back on the dock, Elias kicked off his sandals and stepped onto the bow, feeling like a thief *and* liar. He passed the bags one at a time to Mom.

"Lily and I found Mykonos Laundromat this morning," said Mom. "You're just in time to help put away the clean clothes."

In the cabin, waiting to be stowed away in their compartments, he found four piles of neatly-folded clothes. One pile for each family member.

On top of Elias' pile sat the Superman towel.

Could ancient gold be washed and tumbled dry?

In a panic, like a dog digging for a bone, Elias scattered the clean laundry around the cabin. No sign of the gold leaves. He dragged their things from the compartments and came up empty-handed.

His heart lurched, and sank like a rock to the pit of his stomach—only it felt like a boulder. What if he, Elias Tantalos, bad luck magnet, was responsible for the Crown of Victory being lost for another two thousand years!

23

MISSING

Only one explanation crossed his mind: Lily must have taken matters into her own hands and turn him into Officer Maria. He dug through her pink laundry pile. "MOM! WHERE'S LILY?"

Three feet away, Mom was fitting the many food purchases into their small cooler, like puzzle pieces. "The boat isn't that big, you don't need to shout. Every fisherman and boat neighbor in the harbor heard you. What's the urgency?"

"Um... nothing. Where is she?"

"Ah, isn't that sweet. You miss your sister. See, I knew this boating vacation would be good for some *philadelphia*—that's Greek for brotherly love, like the city's nickname, you know," said Mom, her eyes crinkling at the corners happily behind her sunglasses. "In this case, brother and *sisterly* love."

He loved his mother, but sometimes that woman completely missed the point. Did Lily take the crown? Did it get lost at the Laundromat? Would she turn him in to the police? Did she want the riches for herself? *Where was Lily?*

Awful thoughts whirled in his mind like the images from his nightmare. "Just tell me where she is." A note of desperation tinged his voice. "Please."

Mom raised an eyebrow but didn't question. "Your sister finished her chores early, so she joined Aunt Kat's Sunny Days Camp trip. Annika and Jon went, too. We looked for you, but you and Dad weren't back yet. Day Camp is spending the day on another island to explore caves. I'm sorry you missed it."

Elias smiled. Dark, claustrophobic caves. He would rather do a hundred errands with Dad than spend five minutes in another cave. "When do they come back?"

"The ferry returns at 3:30," said Mom.

"I'll go meet the ferry," he offered.

"Why, that's thoughtful of you," said Mom, raising her eyebrow again.

"It's no big deal," said Elias, trying to make it sound as if it was not *the* most important big deal of his life.

"When you're finished putting away the clean laundry I have a few more jobs for you to do." Mom went back to her boat-house-keeping and did not notice the mess he'd made in the cabin. Thankfully, cleaning the Port-o-Potty was not one of his jobs anymore. He had scooped enough poop to last a lifetime.

Where was the Crown of Apollo?

Working hard to stay busy and not watch the time, his watch finally ticked closer to three o'clock. At ten minutes before the hour, he was ready to go. Mom gave him some *euros* to buy more sunscreen from a shop near the dock.

A crowd of parents and siblings waited for the ferry. Lily bounded down the ramp, excited about

Sunny Days Camp.

"*Yassou*, Lily!" Their boat neighbors, Annika and Jon, came off the ferry behind Lily.

"*Yassou, Annika!* See you later—and you, too, Jon!" Lily waved good-bye. Jon and Annika greeted him, too, before being collected by their parents.

Elias waved to their new friends but was glad they couldn't spend time together. He needed the right private moment to question his sister and couldn't blurt it out in public.

Lily bounced along the alley chatting about the stalactites and stalagmites and underground rivers she had seen. Bats, too!

"Stop talking for a minute." Elias turned and put his hands on both of her shoulders to make her stop bouncing and listen. He whispered in a panic. "Lily—Mom washed my Superman beach towel. *IT'S GONE!*"

"Your towel is gone?"

"The CROWN OF APOLLO IS LOST, Lil!"

"Oh, that. I forgot." She pulled on his elbow, leading them behind a Greek vase big enough to hide them both. Red geraniums spilled over the lip of the large vase, hiding their conversation.

As if nothing more important were missing than one of her dolls' shoes, Lily dug through the contents of her bottomless *Dazzle It!* bag. Out came the collection of chunky plastic beaded bracelets in every color and every shade of pink that shouldn't be allowed, pink ponytail ties and Marina the doll. Lily shoved the lot in Elias' hands. "Take it," she said, digging deeper. "The crown I mean. *My* stuff I want back. That crown is too heavy. I don't want it."

His fingers itched to hold his treasure, make sure it was safe. "Where is it?"

"I hid it. As soon as Mom said to get the dirty clothes out of the cabin compartments for laundry. I didn't want you to get in trouble again, so I put it in my bag."

"You did that... for me?" Elias felt bad. His wild guesses about Lily's reasons for hiding the crown were all wrong.

Lily got to the bottom of her enormous pink *Dazzle It!* tote bag but double-checked the coast was clear of tourists before handing the circle of gold leaves back to Elias.

Relief washed over him. The weight of gold was once more in his hands, and the invisible burden of its loss lifted from his chest—but he rubbed the ache of guilt that started twisting once more in his stomach and could not see a way out of the dilemma. He could hide the crown and be a winning thief. He could sell the crown and be a rich and generous one. If he somehow managed to return the crown to Apollo on Delos, he would no longer be a thief. But Evamere Middle School and sixth grade would be every bit as horrible as Evamere Elementary and fifth. Those were the facts.

"Thanks, Lil." Genuinely grateful, he put the crown into his backpack and did not want to be separated from it again. "I owe you one."

He watched his little sister skip down the sidewalk in a game of hopscotch on the gray paving stones outlined with crisp white paint. She pranced past a rack of sunscreen for sale, and he remembered to buy some for Mom. When he came out with his purchase, he found Lily squatting near Petros the Mykonos Pelican, in front of the ice cream shop.

It gave him an idea. Elias excused himself and came out of the shop a few minutes later with a two-ball ice cream cone for Lily.

"Better keep it away from Petros," he said, handing over the treat.

"Wow, for me? Thanks!" Lily's face lit with a happy smile as she caught drips around the cone with her tongue.

While she licked the cone, he wandered next door to admire the pictures of SCUBA divers and colorful fish in the *WunderSea Adventures* SCUBA shop. Elias stared. Most of the posters of undersea life had been removed and a glass cabinet behind the window took their place, with new products on display. Nestled between the waterproof watches and flashlights was a bright yellow plastic case with a screen, exactly like the one Lily found in the water off the coast of Delos with words printed clearly: *Aqua Scribe.*

Elias ran. He couldn't wait to share the news with his sister.

W hy do you want to go back to Delos?" Mom questioned him the next morning over her now-standard cool and refreshing breakfast of yogurt-dripped-with-honey, as he suggested the day's boating destination. "The ancient ruins are interesting, but this heat wave could be dangerous. We're better off swimming on beaches with olive trees for shade."

Elias shrugged easily and dropped the subject. If he seemed too eager, his parents would find out about the gold crown. They would take it straight to the police and he'd be in much worse trouble than Pooper Scooper. He couldn't let that happen!

Vacation days were slipping by as fast as water through a sieve. It was silly... Apollo was a myth, a story. Not real. But... the nightmarish quest to return the crown to its original owner clung to his brain. There must be *some* way he could get it back to Delos, back to Apollo and his twin, Artemis.

He planned to tell his parents about the crown

after returning it. When they were far, *far,* FAR away from Delos.

Later that morning, the Tantalos family stopped *Sargos* in the shallow, warm water near the north end of Syros, a good hour's distance away from Mykonos. No other boats were around, and it was quiet and peaceful.

Swimming, Elias found a jellyfish the size of a melon. He trapped it in the bucket and Mom hauled it over the side. When turned on its back, this jellyfish resembled an enormous raw egg; he managed to flip it over and saw purple tentacles waving in the water, but it didn't do much to lift his low spirits. Dad took him tubing and snorkeling, but his heart wasn't into the water fun.

During every afternoon's *siesta,* Elias researched his book. He'd found a sketch of Delos as it might have looked before its destruction. The ruins were so vast—even if he convinced his parents to go back to Delos, how could he find the exact spot where the crown belonged?

Only one place on the map seemed promising: The Temple of Apollo. He did not remember seeing a signpost for it, but it must be there. There was only one way to find out. He had to convince his parents to go back there. Tomorrow, *for sure!*

A few silver-bellied fish zipped along the starboard side, in perfect timing with his happier mood.

"Sargos fish, Dad! I wish we had the spear gun."

"Let's snorkel to see them better."

The fish were heading straight for the rocky shore, so Dad turned on the engine and allowed Elias to drive the boat while he got out the snorkeling gear.

"We'll see more sea life closer to shore," said Dad, taking over the captain's wheel.

"We don't know this coastline very well," said Mom.

Black spiky sea urchins were visible in the water, and Dad remembered they liked living in rocky areas.

Unwittingly, they had maneuvered *Sargos* into a minefield of underwater rocks. "There's a big one." Elias spread himself flat on his stomach to see over the bow.

The women were doing the "conning'—reconnoitering; keeping a lookout. Lily faced starboard, Mom port; each was needed to help their father spy more unexpected rocks.

"Sargos fish, Daddy. Starboard!"

In the split second that Lily drew attention to the fish, Elias noticed a large rock underwater. He cried out the warning, and Dad turned the wheel, but it was too late. *Thub, thub, thub.*

The awful scraping sound and a rough jolt made the family grab the railings. Mom threw her free arm across Lily to prevent her from flying off the boat.

Thub, thub, thub.

"That doesn't sound good at all," said Dad, cutting the engine. He pushed the button to raise it out of the water.

"Oh, dear," said Mom, pointing to the propeller. It was bent. "Looks like another job for our friend, Nick the mechanic."

"We'll have to limp back to Mykonos as best we can," said Dad.

Having a bent propeller meant *Sargos* kept weaving side to side and the boat was no longer like its fast namesake in the sea. It took a long time to get back to Mykonos harbor, where Dad and Elias went directly to look for Nick at the marine repair shop.

The marine mechanic joined them at once to check on the boat's propeller. Nick rubbed his hands on an oily cloth. "The good news is we can fix it. The bad news is that it's an old engine and we don't have the right size propeller blade in stock. Our shop on Syros—that's the closest island—doesn't have the part, either. It will have to come by ferry from Athens," said Nick.

"Will that take long?" asked Dad. "Tomorrow is our last day of vacation."

"WHAT?" Elias interrupted Dad. "Tomorrow is the *last* day? It can't be! And we're stuck? *Here?*" Mom gave him a stern look, and Elias bit on his tongue to stop himself from saying the complaints lined up to come out.

"If we order the part now," Nick explained, "the blade can be on the early morning ferry and be here by tomorrow afternoon. The repair will take the rest of the day."

"The rest of the day?" Elias was frantic.

Mom sighed. "I agree it is a disappointment, Elias. But we'll never get the boat back to Athens without that part. I'm sorry, kids. We're stuck on land for our last day."

That night for dinner Mom and Dad tried to cheer them up by treating them out to their favorite *taverna*. They sat at a table next to the beach with the best view of a fancy, long yacht that looked gorgeous under the moonlight. Tomorrow night would be a full moon.

Everyone ordered their favorite dishes. Dad ordered seafood, and his mussels came on top of spaghetti in a spicy tomato sauce. Mom's Greek salad came loaded with fresh tomatoes and crunchy cucumbers, with a thick slab of *feta* cheese sprinkled with oregano on top—just how she liked it.

"I don't feel like eating anything," said Lily, who got a mound of plain spaghetti with butter.

"You're missing the best part," Dad insisted, and he kept trying to put one of the black mussel shells on her plate. Lily refused to touch it.

Elias' new favorite food was the small mountain of tiny fish called *atherina*. These salty, crunchy fish were the same size as French fries, and he'd learned to gobble them up head first. Elias liked them even better than French fries. But not tonight. He picked at his plate.

"What *has* gotten into you two?" Mom was staring at Elias, who had never missed a meal before, especially not his favorite food.

Dad looked up from his plate. "We're disappointed we can't go out in the boat tomorrow, but it isn't the end of the world."

Yes, it is.

Elias waited for a better idea to come along, but he had nothing.

"Why didn't I think of it before?" Mom jumped in her seat, knocking over her water glass. She mopped up the mess with napkins. "You two can go to Sunny Days Camp tomorrow. You'll have a great day with other kids, and you won't be stuck here while Dad and I wait for the boat to be fixed. Your Aunt Kat has been begging to spend another day with you." Mom dialed the number.

"Hello, Katerina? It's me, Jackie." Mom related the whole story of the propeller accident. "... and so the boat is out of commission for the day and the kids are stranded on our last full day of vacation. Could they join your group tomorrow? Oh, I see..." Mom's face lost its happy glow. "I suppose that will be fine. Thank you, Kat. They'll meet the ferry in the morning."

Mom put her phone away and reached for the bread basket.

"Well?" Elias and Lily asked in unison.

"Sunny Days Camp is on for tomorrow. I'm so sorry, but it will be another hot day with no shade... and you won't get to do any swimming there," said

Mom in a disappointed voice.

Elias wondered what terrible news Mom was about to tell them. This was the voice she used when she told him he was due at the doctor's office, or dentist.

"Aunt Kat is taking the day campers to see the ruins. On Delos. Otherwise, you'll be stuck here with us tomorrow waiting for the boat to be fixed. It's the best I can do, kids. Sorry. It will be beastly hot there, but we can pack extra sunscreen and water bottles."

Elias tried not to shout for joy. He and Lily gripped both hands under the table instead, until he lost the feeling in all ten of his fingers.

24

SUNNY DAYS DISASTER

Next morning, Lily emerged from the cabin doorway with her beaded bracelets stacked up to her elbows, like she did every night for dinner on Mykonos.

Elias stared.

"Why not?" she asked. "The ancient statue ladies on Delos are dressed up fancy."

Mom packed extra water bottles and lunch to take along, as they would picnic with Sunny Days Camp. In the privacy of the cabin, Elias made sure the crown was safely tucked into his backpack. Finally, he and Lily clambered up the ramp to board the ferry and were happy to see Annika and Jon, who had become regular day-campers.

About thirty children leaned over the ferry's railing on the upper deck to wave good-bye to their parents.

"See you here at three-thirty," everyone called out.

Aunt Kat clapped her hands. "Anyone going into fourth grade or higher can buddy up. Those children going into first, second, or third grade will be in my group." She read off names from a pile of registration papers and checked each one to record attendance.

Lily was going into third grade—she would be stuck with Aunt Kat's group all day.

Aunt Kat clapped her hands for attention. "Visiting Delos comes with rules. No climbing on the ruins. No swimming from the beaches. Do not take *anything*. Everything stays on Delos as you find it. Questions?"

Lily's eyes pooled. "Please," she begged Elias, "I want to help you find Apollo's Temple."

Elias raised his hand. "Can Lily stay with me?" He pressed himself into Lily's side as if daring Aunt Kat to unglue them. With luck, she would think he had leftover anxiety from being lost that night she found him, and would keep them together.

Aunt Kat smiled, and nodded.

The ferry chugged to Delos and he grew impatient to finish the crown business before he changed his mind.

You can take a teacher out of a classroom, Elias thought, *but you can't take teaching out of a teacher.* Aunt Kat gave a history lesson about Delos during the thirty minute trip, beginning with its origin in mythology as a floating island. He already knew the history from his own books, so he watched white terns swoop and play across the blue sky, and enjoyed a cool morning breeze breaking up the relentless heat.

"Boys and Girls, you are about to explore the ruins of a very great ancient city. A few hundred years B.C., about 2500 years ago, Delos was considered one of the most important cities in the ancient world. People came from all over the Mediterranean world to trade their goods in the *agora* and bring offerings to their gods at the many temples. It became a rich city with grand buildings, including houses, a large *amphi-*

theater that seated thousands of people for cultural plays, and even a stadium for athletic games and festivals."

At the word 'offerings', Lily nudged Elias. He had carefully wrapped the crown in a clean, soft T-shirt, and now he patted the slight bulge it made in his backpack.

"Unfortunately for ancient Delians, the island's wealth attracted many unwelcome visitors. In 88 B.C., King Mithridates of Pontus attacked Delos. Many of the residents were killed; women and children were sold into slavery. Merchants' ships were burned, so there was no escaping the invaders. Grand buildings were destroyed. Many of the beautiful marble statues were toppled or slashed to pieces in deliberate vandalism. You will see many of them broken at their thinnest spots, the neck and arms," said Aunt Kat.

While Aunt Kat continued with the history lesson, Elias decided Pindar's raid must have been successful, because Delos was never rebuilt afterward. The Crown of Apollo was the key. Whoever had that crown in their possession became a winner. Leafy crowns are *still* a symbol of winners in the Olympic Games. Whoever has the real deal—like him—can't lose!

Elias trembled and clutched the lump in his backpack. *Could he give it up?*

"Decades later, pirates invaded," Aunt Kat was saying. "More of Delos was torn apart. Over the centuries, people used Delos as a place to pick up marble for their own building projects. Eventually, the whole place was forgotten and buried in dirt. Then archaeologists from France began to uncover the buried city that was once the pride of the Aegean Sea. They are still at work here, developing a small museum to share island treasures with the world."

But what happened to Pindar? If he was a real kid—and the crown was obviously very real—what happened to the real raider? Did Pindar return home a hero and give the horse and chariot toy to his sister? Did his mom like the snake bracelet? Two thousand years ago, that legendary stuff *happened.*

Stuck in the present day, Elias ached to realize he would never know the exact truth.

The ferry's loud horn sounded as it neared the small island. As soon as the boat docked at the pier, he jumped to his feet. Aunt Kat held up her hand.

"Boys and girls, we will meet back here on the ferry absolutely no later than three o'clock. There are picnic tables where you may eat your lunch; all trash must be brought back with you. Leave nothing and take nothing!"

Aunt Kat finished her speech at last. She corralled the younger kids to her side and let the older kids off the ferry first.

"Where do we begin?" Elias stared at the maze of stone walls and ruined buildings. Some of the day campers talked excitedly about hiking up to the top of Mount Kynthos, but he did not have time for side trips. Where did Apollo's wreath belong?

Annika and Jon wanted to see the Avenue of the Lions, but Elias wanted to move away from the group. "We'll try to meet up with you for lunch," he promised Annika and Jon before they split up.

Elias unzipped his backpack and moved aside the yellow Aqua Scribe to pull out *Boating World: Greek Islands.* The detailed map of Delos had a plastic overlay that covered the ruins with an image of what the city might have looked like twenty-one centuries ago. Private homes were marked according to the mosaic floors found there, like 'House of the Dolphins'.

The city was once filled with grand buildings, white columns, statues of marble and bronze, paved streets, shopping stalls, and even a stadium in which the Evamere Wings would have loved to compete. All in ruins.

"There are lots of temples, Lil." He stabbed a finger on the map to show his sister. "Part way up the hill."

Not far up, however, Lily stopped at one of those ropes meant to prevent tourists from walking on the mosaic floors. She read out loud a stone signpost. This one made him shudder to remember the hardened goddess of his dream.

TEMPLE
OF ARTEMIS

"Let's see your book." Lily opened the Glossary in the back. "Artemis. Twin of Apollo. Goddess of the Moon and the Hunt. Children left toys as offerings to the goddess. For girls, it signaled they were ready to be married, sometimes as young as twelve—EW!" Lily handed back the book as if it had cooties. She held tighter to her *Dazzle It!* bag, as if the goddess would sweep out of the temple to snatch her favorite doll. Or make her marry a boy by middle school. *Double EW!*

"Kids back then probably *did* give their stuff to Artemis," said Elias. Artemis' bow and arrow pointed at his heart is not something he would forget soon. "They wouldn't want to mess around with *that* goddess."

"OK, good start! We've found a place important to Artemis. Where would be important to her twin brother?" Lily skipped ahead along a weedy path lined with the ubiquitous stone walls.

Buildings on Mykonos created their own shade

within the narrow streets, but these stone walls were not high enough to block out the blazing sun. Elias wished he had brought extra sunscreen.

The narrow paths twisted and turned like a maze, similar to the modern streets on Mykonos. Were they built this way to confuse pirates on Delos too, like Aunt Kat had told him about Mykonos? *Didn't work too well here*, Elias thought, making his way through the pirate-ruined rubble of the city that was once splendid Delos, one of the world's great intersections of trade, politics, art and religion.

The ancient *amphitheater* was an outdoor semi-circle stadium holding thousands of seats, built into the sloping hillside under Mount Kynthos. "We can sit for a few minutes and have a snack," said Elias. "The best seats are here in front—look! Marble back rests!" He made himself comfortable, just like any respectable ancient Delian.

Elias emptied most of the contents of his backpack onto an empty seat next to him and pulled out the bright yellow plastic Aqua Scribe and *Ancient Lands of Greece* to look at while he ate. Drinking thirstily from his water bottle, he then peeled a few figs.

With an entire outdoor stage all to herself, Lily didn't eat. She danced, and sang her favorite songs as loudly as if a full audience watched.

In fact, Lily's performance *did* have an audience. Running past the front row of marble seats was a large lizard with a thick tail.

"Follow that lizard!" Elias scooped up his book, the Aqua Scribe and the remains of his snack and shoved everything into his backpack. "Is it Highway? Maybe he's here to show us where Apollo's crown belongs!"

"Don't get so excited," said Lily. "This lizard has a yellow head. I think she is Sunny."

"How do you know it's a girl? Whatever—let's

follow Sunny, then." This lizard, whether or not it was agreeable to its new name, proved to be as quick as Highway. Sunny scooted away, across stones arching in a bridge over a dried-up river.

The long chase ended when Sunny disappeared behind one of the stone lions.

"Look where we are. This is getting us nowhere." A glance at his watch proved they had wasted too much time. "It's already two o'clock. Down to our last hour." He slumped on the shady side of a lion's base and kicked at the earth, but quickly choked on the cloud of hot dust he'd disturbed.

Lily's elbow dug in his side.

"Look. Up. *Now!*" Her squeaky voice was, for her, unusually serious and urgent.

The fronds of the mythological twins' palm tree waved in a welcoming breeze over the bushy Sacred Lake.

"Apollo's birthplace! That's it," said Elias, who hopped up with a second wind and sprinted toward the tree, leaving his sister to catch up. When she arrived he already had his arms wrapped around the trunk and had shimmied up a few feet. "It will stay safe from the antiquity thieves up here."

"This is a cinch. You be the lookout, Lil. Make sure to warn me if you see anyone coming down the paths." Elias scaled another foot, and looked out. "Nice view from up here. You should join me – get a better sight of anyone coming!"

A green palm frond slapped him across the face. In the space of a few moments, the cooling breeze changed to gusts that threatened to blow his grip off the trunk.

"Not now!" Elias shouted in frustration at the wind. Only a *meltemi* blowing in from the north could whip up so violently.

"He's coming this way—get down NOW!"

"Who? What? Wait—almost—at—top. Just—a little—higher," Elias grunted out the words and kept climbing. He would *not* be a thief for one more minute! He had to keep going. A couple more feet to the top.

"It's Apollo! Get down!" Down below, Lily's voice mingled with the wind.

"What? Yes, I'm almost at the top—the crown is almost back to Apollo's—"

"I don't mean *Apollo*, I mean the ARCH-O-GIST—*he's coming and you've got to come down!*"

"NO!" he shouted again—not at Lily's command. Not at the strong wind. The sight that took his breath away was of the pier, where a certain familiar ferry boat was being loaded with a long line of day campers.

It seemed too early for the three o'clock scheduled meeting time, but another gust made it impossible for Elias to risk taking his hand off the tree trunk to check his watch. "Lil, the ferry! They're loading the ferry!"

"GET OFF THAT SACRED TREE—*NOW!*" The wheezing voice was fierce. "GET DOWN IMMEDIATELY AND DO NOT MOVE."

Elias slid down the ridges of the palm's trunk and landed with a hard bump on his bottom. He grabbed his backpack and his sister's hand.

"Lil—RUN!" Like young goats they leaped down the thick grassy paths until they were free of the bushy Sacred Lake, and safe—except for one thing: the Crown of Apollo was dangling from his elbow like one of Lily's oversized bracelets.

At the end of the Avenue of the Lions they could see the ferry at the pier. Elias did not bother to look back to see if the old man was following.

Had Alexander seen the crown? Elias struggled to run and shove the crown in his backpack at the same time.

A moaning horn cut through the wind. Last call! Elias checked his watch.

"Lil, pick up the pace! Day camp is ready to leave!"

The ferry captain waved his gold-braided cap to urge the children to hurry. Aunt Kat stood at the top of the ramp checking off the return of people on their registration papers, while attempting to hold down her skirt that was being whipped around in the blustery wind.

Elias and Lily ran up the ramp, out of breath.

"I didn't think you'd make it." Annika hugged Lily. "Where's your pretty pink bag?"

"Oh no! Marina's in there! I must have left her at Apollo's palm tree." Lily's eyes brimmed with tears as she dashed back down the ramp shouting to Annika and Jon. "Tell Aunt Kat to hold the boat. I'm going back for my bag."

Another gust lifted the registration papers out of Aunt Kat's hands; some fell on the waves and sloshed against the pier. She knelt to gather them, and other day campers squatted to help. Elias figured it would take them a few minutes to sort it out, so he followed Lily.

When they got to Apollo's palm tree, there was no sign of the pink sequined *Dazzle It!* bag anywhere.

"I'm sure I left it here at the base. Right here!" They stared at the spot, wishing it would appear. It did not.

"Lil, maybe you dropped it someplace else. Let's go, before that creepy archeologist finds us."

Reluctantly, his sister turned away with him but when they reached the pier, Elias and Lily stood side by side in disbelief.

The ferry was chugging away. Its foamy wake left a watery trail on the churning gray-blue waves, until it faded into the misty blue horizon and could not be seen any longer.

PART THREE

More precious than gold,
sweeter than honey

Psalm 19:10

Scary mosaic of a mask, in the House of the Masks

25

A GREEK TRAGEDY

I can't believe Aunt Kat let Day Camp leave without us!" Lily, filled with rage, paced up and down the pier like a trapped baby tiger. "Annika and Jon were supposed to tell her to wait. What happened?"

"We've got bigger problems now, Lil," said Elias. "I still have Apollo's crown, but I can't climb again in this wind. It's gotten too strong. Besides, if we stay out of sight for a while that old thief Alexander will think we made it onto the ferry. I can try again when the wind calms down."

"You think the arch-o-gist is the ant—the ant-thingy-thief?" Lily's tongue stumbled over the words. "Maybe he stole my bag, too!"

"Who else could it be?" Preoccupied with multiple dilemmas, Elias did not bother correcting his sister's poor pronunciation. "Lil, the archaeologist knows a ton of stuff about this place, and he's always snooping around pretending he can barely walk. You saw how fast he moved when he saw me up on the tree, didn't you? I don't trust him. You know what? Maybe I shouldn't leave the crown up there anyway. He'll climb halfway up and snag it with his walking stick and take it for himself."

"What should we do instead?"

"I don't know. Maybe this is a blessing in disguise. It will take some time for Aunt Kat to realize we're not on the ferry and come back for us. Gives us time to decide what to do with the crown before we get back on the boat. All we need is a place to hide until we're sure the old guy isn't nosing around. But where?"

"How about the Grotto of Herakles? A cave makes a good hiding place, don't you think?"

"Lily! You're a genius!"

Whirlwinds of dust rose from the dry north side of Mount Kynthos. The pair shook their heads.

"I don't know, Elias. We might get blown off the mountainside."

"Yes, it's too open. Even if we don't get blown off, we could be seen. But you reminded me of something else—when we picnicked up at the Grotto I looked at the view, and there was one ancient house with a roof intact. It wasn't far from the *amphitheater*. From the house, we'll have a clear view to the sea to watch for the ferry coming back."

"Good idea. Let's go."

The wind blew at their backs, giving them wings all the way to the theater district. When they stopped to catch their breath at the far side of the massive semi-circle of ancient stone seats they found the house marked by a chiseled signpost:

HOUSE
OF THE MASKS

"I can't run another step!" Lily was breathing hard and nervously fingering her windblown curls. "Inside the house we won't get blown to pieces. It's perfect—but one problem. How do we get in?"

Most of the ancient houses had nothing but the sky for a roof and air for windows and doors. The House of the Masks, however, had solid-looking doors that blocked the openings.

"Just my luck! Not much of a plan if we can't get inside." But when he checked the door handle, he hissed, "*Yesss!*" The heavy door was slightly ajar, as if the last ancient occupant had left in a hurry.

They ducked inside, but their happiness at getting out of the wind was short-lived. One small glassless window allowed them to keep an eye out to the sea, but it also let in little light and a lot of wind.

Elias stood to the side of the window, as he'd seen police officers do on TV, and scanned the view every few seconds.

Lily wandered into a different room of the house, but came back instantly. "This place is creepy." She glanced over her shoulder and moved further away from the door, but froze when she nearly stepped on a mosaic covering the floor. A figure held a spear and rode a fierce wildcat. "Let's hide somewhere else."

"What's wrong with the House of the Masks?" Elias went around the mosaic and into the other room, but he came back faster than his sister did. He gave an uneasy laugh. "I'm not laughing at you. Here—let me show you."

"I'm not going back in there." Lily folded her arms across her chest and stood rooted as a statue.

"They are mosaics—just puzzle pictures, like in the other houses. Did you see the mosaic with the red face? Doesn't that face look like Mom when she's sunburned?" They both burst into laughter; his joke worked to break the tension, and Elias got Lily to follow him back to the other room.

Horrible faces leered at them from the floor. Big staring eyes. Red mouths. These mosaic tile 'carpets' had a very different feel from the pretty dolphins and wave patterns in other Delos houses.

"This house is so close to the theater, the actors may have lived here. Ancient Greek actors wore masks just like these faces—so people at the back of the theater could see the actor's emotions. See? Mrs. Struggles told us about it in school this year. Greeks wrote tragedies—plays with mean characters and sad stories. They did not live happily ever after, like in our movies. To tell the sad and scary stories, the masks had to show those emotions."

Lily refused to spend another second in that room. "I wish I had my bag. Brushing Marina's hair makes me feel better. She would help get my mind off the masks."

The light was so dim he was once again grateful for the comforting glow of his birthday watch. A streak of lightning ripped the storm-darkened sky, and the raindrops appeared to catch fire.

Elias remembered their other Delian discovery. He dug around in his backpack for the bright yellow Aqua Scribe. He switched on a power button and the screen glowed like a mini computer. It worked!

X's marked spots on a map, but he did not recognize the locations as real places. He scrolled down with the attached stylus and found long columns listing letters, objects and numbers.

"Look at this," said Elias. "There are names on the Aqua Scribe. 'Kat T., amphora vase with goddess Athena, 250 *euros*, Mykonos.'" Elias read off the data on the screen.

"Hey! 'Kat T.' could mean Katerina Tantalos!"

"I guess it is possible... she said she likes old Greek art, didn't she? And she likes to be called 'Kat'," said Elias.

"Why would her name be on the Aqua Scribe?" asked Lily.

"Lots of Greeks have similar names. That doesn't mean it's our Aunt Kat."

The House of Masks cast a dark and gloomy spell over his mood, and Elias set aside the Aqua Scribe. How long had they been hiding? Staring out the window, he watched a streak of sunlight break through the clouds.

"Do you remember the marble bench, Lil? Where I found the crown? Maybe the crown needs to go back there, under that bench. I won't get rich or famous or buy Dad a new spear gun or win any soccer championships. I won't have any friends, but at least pirates won't find it and sell it off. That would be something, wouldn't it?" Elias was thirsty, but his bottle did not have much water left. His stomach growled. "We didn't eat our lunch yet. I'm starving."

They peeled more figs and nibbled at the crispy pastry edges of the *spanakopita*, and discussed whether or not Annika and Jon would send someone back to rescue them, and how soon their rescuers might arrive. The food made them thirsty. They drank sparingly from their water bottles because they had no idea how long they would need to make it stretch. It struck Elias with a wave of worry that the island's only water sources were a water-free Sacred Lake and the undrinkable murk located in the Fountain of the Minoans.

The idea of dying of thirst on dried-up Delos made him extra thirsty, and extra nervous. He wanted a fireball, but he stopped himself from digging in his backpack for one. It would only make his mouth burn and make him thirstier.

Elias checked the view to the sea from the glassless window, thinking how googles of gallons of undrinkable salt water were out there. No sign of the ferry.

Lily's head fell on his shoulder, fast asleep, as usual. The fact that she did not snore this time (giving away their hiding place to anyone within a hundred meters) seemed like a gift from above.

Snuggling with his sister was not something he would choose to do (under *any* circumstance) but Lily's warmth and closeness made him relax—as much as it was possible to get comfortable on an ancient cold stone floor.

"I'll close my eyes for a moment, too... the ferry's horn will wake me up."

A daydream took over before he finished murmuring the words. In that fuzzy place between reality and sleep, a memory drifted to him from childhood...

It was a time—the only time—he'd gotten close to a girl who wasn't his mother or sister. It was summer after first grade, and he remembered goofing around the playground after a kiddie soccer practice. He was with someone... a girl... Kennedy. Their mothers were chatting, not paying attention, so he challenged her to a race to the bigger kids' skate park, which was luckily empty. He beat her there, but she dared him to climb up the steep slope of the skate board ramp.

They reached the top together. Swinging their legs over to sit on the narrow ledge, he remembered he was about to yell, "I'm king of the mountain!" when Kennedy did something that he immediately vowed to forget happened, and he had indeed pushed the moment to the furthest depths of his brain:

Kennedy threw both arms around his neck, leaned close and kissed him full on the lips.

It was not clear what happened next. He had been so surprised by Kennedy's kiss all he could remember was sliding down the ramp and pulling on his Mom's sleeve, demanding to leave that instant.

Slippery, like that skate board ramp, the (weirdly pleasant) memory of being kissed (and by the only person who stayed nice to him in fifth grade) skidded into a bad dream. Kennedy showed up on the pier, but became Ms. Katerina Tantalos, who tossed her papers in the air. They became a whirling white storm. Elias grabbed at the papers and saw they were pages ripped from a calendar. Days, weeks, months and years whizzed backward out of control. Delos was obscured in time. The ferry and Kennedy/Aunt Kat disappeared into a paper blizzard. A powerful flash of lightning zigzagged through the storm, and the white world dripped away, paper snow turning into rain. Christos, the fisherman from Mykonos, sat in his colorful caicque next to Petros the Pelican. Elias waved hello, but the fisherman transformed before his eyes into Zeus, king of the gods, master of lightning and father of Apollo.

Zeus turned his terrifying face to him and said, "You stole the snow from my son."

Bravely, Elias tried to reason with Zeus. "King... god... sir... I didn't take the snow from Apollo. It never snows in summer."

Zeus' face turned back into that of the fisherman, Christos. An old-fashioned lyre sat on his lap instead of the usual pile of fishing nets, and he plucked the strings to make music for Petros. The fisherman smiled at Elias and waved. Elias smiled and returned the wave, feeling a rush of relief.

The pelican opened his bill to catch a fish but the voice of Zeus emerged: "You stole Apollo's snow."

Elias felt a sharp kick. *Ouch!*... the kick felt real, but Elias was so sleepy he fell back into the bad dream just as Aunt Kat's red purse was bursting into flames, and nightmares became his only reality.

26

PINDAR'S PROBLEM

The ships! Delian ships are burning! Get up, you lousy slave!" A deep voice near my ear booms and the oversized face leers over me, the man's mouth stretched in a hideous sneer. Thin white curtains flutter over the open window and I breathe deeply of the fresh, salty sea air, trying to awaken.

Eyes bulge red and a tongue lolls to the corner of the wide black mouth.

A man's hand reaches up and pulls off his face. Not his actual face, it is but an actor's mask, nothing to fear. So why is the tone of his voice one of such urgency? And why am I sleeping when my growling stomach tells me it is time to prepare supper?

The music of a lyre twangs in the background, but abruptly stops.

"You, slave! Elias, you will look at me when I speak to you!" The man holding the mask points a finger at me. Looking down, I find my shorts and T-shirt have changed to a coarse brown robe. My feet are bare, with tough calloused soles. When did I change? Why is this man treating me so roughly? I did not deserve such treatment.

"Run to the agora and get me some olives."

I stare, confused. Another sharp kick pushes me to sit up. I rub my backside, fully awake.

"Slave, I said RUN!"

I scramble to my oddly-bare feet and stumble through the city streets. The streets and houses confuse me more than my new garb (as does the fact that I am calling my clothes "garb", but no time to dwell on that now). On both sides of the narrow lanes the houses that were ruined piles of stones are built tall on white plastered foundations. What happened to the low stone walls? The broken mosaics? It is the same island, the same view. Yet these buildings are not in pieces. Flowers decorate whitewashed walls and spill out of clay pots, like in Mykonos Town. Where are the famil-iar ruins I know so well?

Ah… here is the theater. Something I recognize. Rows of marble seats in the hillside, the seats of stone not old and broken up, but overall it is the same. It helps me get my bearings, but I never make it to the agora.

Directly in front of the Temple of Apollo, near the grandest of the three temples to the god, men in the costumes of soldiers engage in swordplay. I struggle to remember if the current drama in the theater has a battle scene? Did the actors in my house rehearse this last night? These actors are getting too carried away. The blood spilled on the pavement looks sticky and dark and real. I will report this raucous behavior to my master!

I see another group of men go up to a merchant's table and turn it on end, spilling baskets of produce. One chases a merchant until the seller falls: a flash of metal blade and fresh blood splatters onto the fallen fruit. Screams of shoppers fill the air.

These are no actors!

Outside the elegant columns of the grand temple, I scramble to get away from the all-too-real battle. Keeping a sharp eye on the soldiers, I fail to pay attention to my feet—and run smack into a boy not much older than myself, coming down the Temple steps.

This boy is dressed like a soldier, young as me, with one exception: upon his head he wears a gold leaf crown! A bulging sack hangs heavily from one hand, his helmet held awkwardly in the other. We crash head-on and fall to the ground in a heap, where we rub our bashed noses and stare at one another. His gold leaf crown falls to the pavement between us.

It is the strangest moment of my life. Somehow in the fuzzy logic of dreams, I know about that particular crown—know it very well—and I somehow know the raider boy, too, but inside me—the slave boy who is also somehow me—has never before seen as magnificent a thing up close.

To this slave part of myself, a piece of gold has but one meaning: the price of freedom!

The other boy and I stare at the gold crown lying between us, but I am quicker. I grab it from the ground, sling it on my arm like a bracelet, and run as if the entire raiding army is bearing down upon me.

The raider boy shouts after me, but I have a good head start. I glance over my shoulder. Pindar (for who else could it be, the Elias-modern-boy side of myself understands?) struggles to pick up the heavy treasure sack and re-fill his helmet from the objects spilled in our crash.

The load slows him down.

From a corner of my eye I see him, frustrated at the priceless treasure getting away from him; Pindar sets down his load and swipes at the head of a nearby statue with a sword. The stone head rolls down the street into the fresh blood.

I run until there is a good distance between myself and the soldiers raiding my city. I can't breathe, so I flop onto a wide, curved marble bench. Safe for the moment. This section of the city remains at peace, but I fear it will not last but a minute.

On impulse, I bend down and see a dark crevice under the marble bench. I shove the crown inside it as far as I can reach. The gold crown—and the freedom it promises—can wait until first light of morning. Lyre music floats on the air, mingling with mouth-watering grilled meats from the nearest houses. Perhaps the smoky smells of good food mask the fires building in the harbor on the other end of the island, because people are enjoying dinner, unaware of the raid. Yet off in the distance, back in the direction of the agora, I hear the first faint screams and the clashing of swords. A grin spreads across my face even though my world is being ripped apart. Sweeter than honey, the slave boy side of me tastes freedom on the air! My chest bursts with happiness. I feel generous: I will buy freedom for my sister as well.

Freedom! Freedom! Freedom!

I take off running faster than a goat scales Mount Kynthos, the calloused soles of my feet stirring up dust on the narrow alleys back to the Actors' House. I must warn my master and the other actors to hide in the rooms of the cave in the side of the mountain for safety.

Escape will not be easy.

Goodbye, Delos!

Another sharp kick. Elias jerked awake. Lily was standing at the open window, tapping at his side with her foot and yelling for him to wake up and come quick. He shook his head to clear it; the lyre was still twanging low notes that were moving in a light breeze... wait! It wasn't the lyre in his dream. It was a rougher, rumbling sound... it was a boat's engine! For what seemed like hours, they had not heard any noise except for the howling *meltemi*.

Elias leaped to his feet.

Lily jumped for joy at the familiar sound, but stopped to stare out the open window as if she were looking out for the first time. "Wait—I don't see any boats."

"Don't get your hopes up, Lily. It doesn't sound like the ferry. Could it be *Sargos?* Our boat should be fixed by now. Mom and Dad will come after us when they find out we didn't come off the ferry." He made his voice sound reassuring and confident, even though deep down he was not at all sure how soon their parents would be able to rescue them.

"But how will they find us? We've been hiding inside this house," said Lily.

"You're right. I don't think we're being followed anymore, and the wind has settled down. Let's go outside," he agreed.

They walked far enough to look down the slope to the pier; no boats were tied up there, and he could see none approaching. The wind was still pushing waves across the sea, even though he could tell the worst of the storm was over.

"That's odd. I don't hear the boat now, but I'm *sure* a boat engine was close by a minute ago," muttered Elias. "You heard the rumble of an engine, too, right?"

"Yes, I did. Listen, I have an idea," said Lily. "Let's go down by the beach where I found the Aqua Scribe. The tourist might be out there looking for it. We can give it back, and they'll be so happy we'll get a ride to Mykonos in their boat!"

Lily was stabbing at wild ideas, but Elias was ready to listen to anything. In his dream he had so recently (recently as in two thousand years ago, he was surprised to think) placed the Crown of Apollo under the curved marble bench, but here it was, heavy and cold in his backpack. All he wanted was to put it back where he found it and go back to their home-sweet-boat as soon as possible.

"I think we need to split up," he suggested. "I'll run to the marble bench and put the crown back. In the meantime, you go to the beach. See if you can flag down anybody in a boat. It sounded like *Sargos'* engine. If it is Mom and Dad, or Annika and Jon's parents, have them wait for me at the pier. I'll look for you there. Good plan?"

Lily nodded, ready for action too. "Let's do it."

There was no sign of the old archaeologist as his feet sped over the stony paths of ancient Delos. The marble bench glistened smooth and white and cool under the hot sun, but Elias hardly noticed as he threw himself on the ground next to the spot where (it seemed eons ago) he had reached for the tail of a lizard and struck gold.

The impact of what he was about to do settled on him as he unzipped his backpack. In another day, he would fly across the ocean to go home. How long would the crown stay under the bench this time? The slave in his dream had wished for morning to come to buy his freedom. Had he made it? The slave wanted the Crown of Apollo to wait in its hiding place until morning. And it had, staying in that spot until the next morning. And the next, *and* the next—for a hundred years of mornings. Plus two thousand more...

Mornings had come and gone for two thousand years! Would Apollo's Crown of Victory be lost forever?

The gold leaves glittered in its circle as brightly as they must have done the day a craftsman made each precious leaf. A tear slid down Elias' cheek when he knelt and slid it as far into the crevice under the marble bench as he could reach. He had failed the crown, somehow, but he did not know how else to make things right.

Elias swung his backpack over his shoulder—much lighter now—and did not look back. No greater wish swirled in his mind than to see his family. His feet moved faster without the weight of the gold on his back.

The pier was empty. The sunlight played on the calmer waters after the wind storm. No Lily. No *Sargos*. No tourist with a boat. No Sunny Days Camp ferry.

Elias ran past crumbling stone ruins, walls of old warehouses that lined the waterfront. The pebble beach near the House of the Masks was not far, but he could not see any sign of his sister—there, or anywhere. The beach was empty, the tall boulders holding their post at the far end like guards.

Where was Lily? If she wasn't on the pier, why didn't she wait for him on the beach?

Out at sea, not a single boat bobbed anywhere on the horizon, near or far.

The storm had kept boaters away from the sea that afternoon, but he was certain a boat engine had awakened him. They both had heard a boat. Where was it?

Elias kicked at some pebbles. The stones skittered across the beach and plunked in the water. Wracking his brains for a plan of what to do next, he picked up a handful of pebbles and threw them as hard as he could, and felt helpless as he watched them move with the surf towards shore.

Funny. Rocks don't float.

He waded up to his knees and scooped them into his hands. These weren't rocks at all—they were beads. Chunky beads of plastic in rainbow colors and more shades of pink than should be allowed.

27

GROTTO OF HERAKLES

U sing both hands, Elias groped after the floating colors as if finding them all would bring back his sister. Single beads bobbed on the sea, and then he found two bracelets, whole and unbroken, floating by. Elias shoved them all in his pockets, always finding more scattered on the surface. What had happened? Did Lily get too hot and decide to go swimming, and they simply fell off?

Not her. No way, despite her recent dips in the sea to cool off, Elias knew she would never go in the sea willingly without a life jacket. Period.

But if she *had* gone swimming, where was she?

Elias stared at the ripples on the water. He wished his sister's head would pop up and laugh at him. The water was not deep here, up to his knees. How did some of her bracelets get broken?

At the far end of the beach, giant boulders stuck out into the sea. Could she have swum around that point? It was impossible to think Lily went swimming here alone without a life jacket, but it was too frightening to think about alternatives. The archaeologist? Old, and strict, yes. But cruel? Elias did not think so, but how could he be sure?

He needed luck now, but he had learned that lesson the hard way: Luck blew this way and that way, not caring a mite if it was doing what you wanted. Just like the *meltemi*.

Smarts. That's what he needed right now. Lily would have the right thing to say and do, usually did (he had to admit to himself)—but she wasn't here. Nobody to count on but himself. Wrong-Way Tantalos. If Kincaid and Brandon could see him now, they'd be laughing their heads off for the wrong-way mess he'd made out of his summer vacation.

Can I do anything right? Anything at all?

Panicking, Elias threw his backpack onto the pebble beach and did a shallow surface dive. The clear water had good visibility, now that the storm was beginning to subside, and Elias kept his eyes peeled for any sign of Lily and her short mop of blonde curls.

Elias held his breath longer than he ever had before, searching in every direction until he felt his lungs would burst. Over and over, he pushed off the bottom, gasped at another mouthful of air and went back under. His eyes stung from the salt water.

Finally, exhausted, Elias dragged himself up the pebble beach and shuddered with relief and anxiety. She was not under the water, but he was no closer to finding her. What if somebody bad was nearby? What if she was hurt?

Not daring to yell her name, he put on his backpack and waded back into the sea, knee-deep, to search more intently for clues. Nothing but more beads and bracelets. He listened for any sounds. Did she simply fall asleep someplace? She was like that, able to sleep anywhere, and stay asleep through a hurricane.

Wait! Lily's snore *was* breaking the island's eerie silence! But where on earth was it coming from? The rumbling sounded as if it were coming from near the tall granite boulders... from *inside* the island. Did Delos swallow Lily whole? But no—this sound was too loud to be snoring.

For no reason he could fathom, the image of his mother's face floated into his mind. Mom's face, glowing in the chapel's candlelight, so thankful for their safety that day when they snuck away during the *siesta*. Thankful for *both* her children's safety, he knew that deep in his soul. *You are my treasures*, Mom had said. It didn't matter if he won or lost any game, or if he was a bad luck magnet or the lucky owner of the coolest ancient good luck charm. She loved him no matter what, like God did.

Looking up at the sky now, blue and bright with afternoon warmth, he wished he knew how to pray a really good prayer. The only words his brain kept repeating were *'please'* and *'help me'*. *Must be some better way to do it*, he thought—to say one that would *work*—but he couldn't think what. Prayers did not work like good luck charms. Prayers were for talking to God.

He lowered his head and closed his eyes. He asked God to keep his sister safe, and to help him find her, and then an image of the gold crown swam across his mind. Elias added, "Sorry, God. I wanted to keep it for myself. Please forgive me. That was wrong."

When Elias opened his eyes a sense of calm filled him up on the inside, and then out on the water he realised that the colorful plastic beads floating on the surface were making a kind of watery pink trail. He had not noticed it before, and a surge of new hope flooded through him, bringing fresh energy.

Elias splashed after the beads, stuffing them into his bathing suit pockets as he found more. The bead trail disappeared around the tall boulders at the end of the pebble beach. Swimming around them, he was unprepared for the shock.

A cave! The boulders were protecting its entrance.

The loud rumble, came from within the cave. The muffled sound of a boat's engine.

From the side, the cave entrance appeared to be a narrow slit in the rock, but closer inspection proved it was wide enough for a small boat to pass through. The boulders were situated like a gate, concealing a view of the wide entrance from passing boaters.

The water was chest-deep once he got into the cave. *Lily would never come in here,* he tried to tell himself. Water scared her too much.

Desperate for answers, Elias moved through the water as soundlessly as he could, and with every gentle slapping of the water he cringed further into the shadows cast by the sun behind the boulders.

A figure was crouched at the back wall of the cave. Lily! She was squatting on her heels, hugging her knees. Her big brown eyes were huge with terror. Anger surged inside him. Who had made her come through the waves to this cave when she was obviously afraid of the water?

As he forced his eyes to see into the darkness to get a better look at his sister, he realized that her eyes were glued to a sight off to her left. From where he was standing Elias could not see what she was looking at, since the watery cave made a curve to the right.

The boat engine noise was coming from that direction, but the rumble cut off abruptly. Elias began to sort out voices. Two slightly familiar, but one he had never heard before.

"What now, Theo? It's time to move out this load," said a voice Elias recognized.

"Yannis—what about the girl? Why'd Thanos have to bring her?" He sounded nervous.

"Don't you worry about it, Theo—we're paying you to drive the boat, not worry about the kid," said the voice of Yannis. "*Or* the stuff. You leave all that up to us."

Thanos and Yannis. Where had Elias heard those names?

The SCUBA shop!

Elias had no idea who Theo was, but it sounded to him like these three guys were up to no good.

"That *meltemi* whipped up the sea floor good," said Thanos. "We should make one more dive while daylight holds out. We don't want to miss out on anything special down there that might have shifted upwards in the sand. And I've got to find the Aqua Scribe—all our buyers are listed on there. This junk isn't worth a cent if we don't have buyers!"

So the Aqua Scribe belonged to these *pirates!* Elias strained his ears.

"You said the *meltemi* was a good chance to get the stuff out of here," argued Theo, "while there aren't any other boats around to see us. I vote we get out now. Leave the girl."

"Gear up," said Yannis. "If there's trouble, we can dive for a quick underwater exit. I'll make sure that meddling girl doesn't slip away and rat us out before we're ready to get far away from here."

"You take orders from *me*, remember? The girl was snooping; she saw us. What else could I do?" Elias distinctly heard a wetsuit being firmly zipped up.

Lily suddenly glanced in her brother's direction and gave a start of surprise. She shook her head back and forth only once, very subtly, signaling "no," and making a small hand motion for him to go back before he was caught too. Then she continued staring off to her left.

"Hey kid, do as you're told and you'll get that ride you wanted to Mykonos after all," Yannis said to Lily. Elias heard a sneer in the man's voice. "We'll be just outside the entrance. We *will* see you if you try to escape. I promise you this: We *will* find you and make you *very* sorry!"

The boat engine revved and echoed loudly around the limestone cave walls. It was moving out. Taking a deep breath, Elias submerged while the boat passed him. When he surfaced, he looked for writing on the stern. Sure enough: *WunderSea Adventures*.

The SCUBA divers were raiding the Mediterranean archaeological sites!

Elias waded around the bend in the cave to reach Lily. The back part of the cave had a dry floor about the size of his bedroom back home; the waist-high water ended at a natural ledge, almost like a stone dock. He threw a leg onto the ledge and pulled himself up. Sunlight came in from the cave entrance, but the sun's rays did not reach a high mound—a great pile—in a shadowy corner of the cave.

He could not pay any more attention to the pile because something grabbed him around the middle and squeezed his belly. It was his sister.

"I wanted you to find me, but I didn't want you to get trapped, too!" Lily hugged him, but her brown eyes flashed anger mixed with the fear.

"You fought back," he complimented Lily. "I'm sorry your bracelets got broken. But thanks for leaving the bead trail. That was smart!"

"Thanks! That meanie old Yannis broke one of the bracelets when he grabbed my arm, but that gave me the idea! Like the fairy tale—Hansel and Gretel. He's a grumpy old gingerbread witch, that guy—*wow*," breathed Lily, interrupting herself.

Elias followed her stare. Treasures heaped upon treasures, the wealth of ancient Delos filled the end of the cave around his sister: crates loaded with small, perfect statuettes, like a pile of marble dolls. Another overflowing with heads from larger statues, and beautiful vases of all shapes and sizes, many of them red clay with elegant men and women painted on in black. A full-sized statue of a man stood to one side, as if left there to supervise the stash, his fingers plucking a harp. The body and harp had been carved from one solid piece of white marble.

"This must be Apollo!" Lily ran her fingers on a leafy circle carved right onto its head. "See the crown? But why does he play a harp if he is god of the sun?"

"Apollo loved the laurel tree so much he made it into crowns, but he was god of music, too! It must be Apollo. You're right. Just look at this stuff!" Brother and sister forgot their danger in the splendid company of gold and marble antiquities.

"Now *this* is a bracelet!" Lily picked up a gold brace-let shaped like a snake, with a green emerald for its eye. She wrapped it around her forearm with a sigh of longing. "It fits perfectly!" Lily took it off and put it back in the crate.

A pair of clay horses looked rigged. Elias dug through the crate seeking a chariot just like the one Pindar had found for Philippa.

"Hey," said Lily as they looked around; "I found a way out of here." She pointed to the back wall of the cave at the far end. "A back exit, I'm sure of it."

"You've got to be kidding, Lil. We can't go in there," he said. "We'll just trap ourselves even worse and... all right, I'll say it. It's dark in there, and I am afraid of the dark." Elias felt good, admitting the weakness. *Strong.* It wasn't bad to be afraid of something. It was simply a *fact* of being Elias.

Lily rested both her hands on his shoulders. "Trust me?" she said.

In spite of their danger, Elias laughed. It felt oddly wonderful to laugh with his sister, like a bubbling fountain of relief, but he held a finger to his lips to be quiet. "OK," he agreed, but with far more enthusiasm than he felt inside.

"The day I went with the day camp, remember?" she said. "We explored a cave on an island near Mykonos that went on—Aunt Kat said for eighty meters! I'll tell you more, but not now—come on! It's our only chance!"

They put down the treasures in their hands and were turning to make their way across the cave when they heard a sound outside the tunnel. The thieves' boat!

"Lily, they're coming back!"

The pair ducked around the back of the mound to hide. He felt stupid; how much time had they wasted looking at treasures when they should have been seeking a way out?

The boat puttered in and pulled up to the rock ledge. Thanos hopped out and tied a line around a heavy-looking marble statue. "Wasted trip. I couldn't find my scribe, and no more antiquities. At least we've found the good stuff."

That was it! If Elias could keep the thieves on the island until help came, the treasure would stay, too.

Only one thing would keep the thieves on Delos longer. *More treasure.* One more piece, if it was the best.

Elias began to stand up. Lily tugged at his pant leg.

"What are you doing?" she asked in an urgent whisper.

"Trust me?" he whispered back.

Lily stared up at him with her big brown eyes and slowly nodded.

Elias stood up and bravely waved the light from his watch to catch their attention. It worked; all three of the men stared at him. "You haven't found the best treasure of them all. *I* did. Let Lily go and you can have it."

To cover how scared he felt inside, Elias spoke loudly; his voice ricocheted around the cave walls. When they realised they had been found out by nobody but a young boy, Thanos and Theo laughed heartlessly.

"And who is going to rescue *you*, kid? There aren't any more treasures here. We got everything good already."

"I've seen what you've got here. It's all right, I guess." Elias made a show of picking a fingernail, as if not at all impressed with the vast number of ancient treasures in the *WunderSea* lair. "Not as great as the gold crown *I* found." Elias taunted them to keep their interest. Theo cut off the boat's engine to listen. "A crown of gold laurel leaves. Worthy of Apollo. On Delos. Right now, in fact!"

"You're making that up. You think we're going to believe a couple of kids?" scoffed Thanos.

"I don't know," Yannis disagreed. "How would he be able to describe a crown like that if he hadn't seen it? Hand over your backpack, kid."

Elias panicked. The Aqua Scribe was in there—it was the only proof he had that the SCUBA divers were the island thieves. He couldn't let them look in the backpack.

Shaking his head Elias said, "What you are looking

for isn't in there. I put Apollo's crown back where I found it. Under a seat. A marble seat. Go get it yourselves if you want it. Just let us go."

While the three men argued and debated their next move, Lily tugged on Elias again.

"What? You can't give away the crown to pirates!"

Yannis sauntered over and interrupted their scheme, wagging a finger an inch away from Elias' face. "No funny business from you two. Where exactly is this marble seat?"

Elias played dumb, making a show of trying to remember. "Hmm... there's marble everywhere you look on Delos..."

Thanos had reached a decision. "Theo, keep the boat running. Yannis, finish loading and keep an eye on the kids until I find the crown. We've got to leave as soon as I get back."

Thanos turned to Elias and Lily. "We'll let you go AFTER we find the crown. And hey, if you're lying, kid..."

Yannis began to argue that he hadn't signed on to be a babysitter, and while the men were distracted Lily grabbed her brother's hand and pulled him after her. With no time to think, Elias's reflex action was to pull his arm away.

It smacked against the stone wall. His watch face shattered and the light went out, but he kept following Lily, moving deeper into the cave while they had the chance; there was precious little time to be afraid of the dark while Yannis argued with Theo about helping him load the boat and babysit two kids.

This was their last chance to make a move, Elias was sure, but as they inched along the shadows he despaired. What back entrance was Lily talking about? He saw nothing.

Lily dashed into the darkest recess at the back

of the cave, pulling Elias after her. She led the way through a low passageway cut into the rock.

They heard shouts behind them.

"Forget the kids—let's go up on the island to look for that marble seat!" Thanos sounded excited.

"You're crazy—they've have seen too much! I'm following the kids."

Elias panicked. Yannis was coming after them! "Lily, hurry!" he whispered.

"Suit yourself. I'm going after the crown."

The sounds of splashing reached Elias' ears; Thanos and Yannis were splitting up.

The passageway became so narrow they had to turn sideways and hold their breath to squeeze through it. A few steps later it got so low they had to get down and crawl on their hands and knees. It would be difficult for a grown man—even a determined one—to follow them through these tight spots.

Elias desperately missed his glowing watch. He crawled close behind Lily, finding comfort in her small, perky form; it was dawning on him that he had teased her so much for being afraid of things he loved, that he had never truly appreciated her spunk and bravery. He marveled at it now, crawling through the passage, where it was darker than outer space would be; at least there were stars up there, and openness—this was blacker than black could be. The rocky walls closed in on him.

Just when Elias thought he would never be able to stand up or breathe properly again, the passageway opened up and they could stand upright. A glimmer of sunlight greeted them like a friend, shining through cracks high up, like slits of skylights in the rock. It was still broad daylight outside. Elias started to breathe normally and relax, but he wanted to get out of there as soon as possible.

But which way was OUT?

His eyes adjusted to the dim light; it did not reveal much except they seemed to be in a cavern space large enough to fit his whole house back home. Stalactites hung from the ceiling. Elias stopped only once, when he noticed a cluster of bats' eyes glowing from a crevice high in the stone wall, but he forced himself to move past them.

They found that the passageway continued on the opposite end of the cavern, but it immediately became narrow and difficult once again.

Now that they were out of immediate danger, Lily kept up a stream of chatter that somehow helped keep Elias' mind off the dark.

"That day when day camp went to see caves, Aunt Kat showed us how a cave's passages can go on for hundreds of feet. She said they were sometimes carved out by underground rivers, or the rock was tunneled out by people. Ancient Greeks used caves like this for storage space or meeting places."

They encountered rough steps carved into the rock. Elias tripped and put a hand on the cave wall to steady himself, but his palm slipped on the moistness. The air smelled stale, and it gave him a queasy feeling in his stomach. Cracks with shafts of light and fresh air were becoming fewer and farther between.

Lily counted each step out loud. When she got to one hundred she began over again with one. By the time she reached ninety-nine for the fourth or fifth time, the passage had stopped rising. It leveled out, and the air smelled fresher.

"I think we're getting somewhere, Lily!" Elias said with relief.

The walls of the cave were now dry, and the passage became wider. It came to an end at the back of a long, wide space with a strange circle of dim light at the far end.

"I know where we are! Lily, we're in that cave on the side of the mountain!"

Elias ran to the mouth of the cave, gulping huge mouthfuls of the fresh evening air.

Between huge slabs of granite he could see that the sun was much lower than when he had followed Lily's bead trail. It was late afternoon, the sun a fiery orange ball in the sky. Would they end up spending the night alone on Delos with thieves?

"Is that Dad I see climbing the mountain?" Lily's voice cracked with stress and the shreds of faded hope. Long shadows made it difficult to pick out anything specific from that distance.

"Probably a shadow," Elias said. "Just wishful thinking." In the quiet early evening air that was still sunny but calmer and cooler, his voice seemed to broadcast their presence over the entire island.

"Well—I got *my* wish," came a wheezing voice from far-too-short a distance down the mountain.

The small pier at Delos, as seen from the ruins

28

FIELD TRIP

Alexander! He heard us, but maybe he didn't see us. Hide!" Elias hissed. "Let's go back in the cave!"

"It's too late!" Lily whisper-shouted back. "The pirates might be coming after us. We can't go back that way!"

Casting his eyes around the barren landscape on the mountainside, there was not even a large bush to hide behind. Only one place held promise. In plain sight in front of the Grotto of Herakles was the stone cup, fit for a giant.

"Big enough for both of us. I'll give you a boost."

Lily stuck her foot in his palm and he lifted her high enough for her to put a leg over the edge and climb down, where Lily squatted. She wrapped her arms and legs into a small ball. "There's space for you, too."

It was a tight squeeze, but Elias threw a leg on the lip and vaulted inside. Squashed beside his sister, he ducked his head to keep it lower than the upper edge. "With any luck he'll stop looking."

They were both breathing hard from their arduous hike up the tunnel and from the rush to hide, but it was too late. Elias and Lily heard the swish of a walking stick through dry weeds, and a wheezing voice closing in on them. Lily and Elias looked at each other and braced themselves for the trouble that was sure to come.

"Well, well, well... if it isn't the mosaic-maker. And the palm-climber!" The archaeologist Alexander leaned over the altar of Herakles with a serious face. And urgent voice. "You've explored the Grotto enough. And I don't believe the ancient Delians would have appreciated children playing Hide and Seek in their altar to Herakles. Come. With. Me. Now!"

The old man gave them one of his stretched-out crinkly smiles that Elias could never tell if it meant friendliness or not. Elias guessed not.

Alexander stepped back to lean on his walking stick, his chest working loudly from climbing Mount Kynthos. He waited.

Trapped again. The only way down the mountain was past the meddling archaeologist. How could this be happening? Outsmart thieving pirates only to land in more trouble? Impossible!

Anger and confusion made Elias feel bold, daring. Pulling himself out of the ancient altar, he gave Lily a hand out. Strangely, he felt not a mite scared.

"Go on," Elias said. With a bold stare he hoped was as cold as he felt, he glared at Alexander eye to eye. "Your *friends* are down there in that cave, ready to get away with all the treasures of Delos. Aren't you going to be late to help them?" He knew he was sounding rude, but this guy had some explaining to do!

"*My* friends... *your* friends are down there, if that

is what you mean, you impertinent thief." It was the archaeologist's turn to appear confused.

Lily had her hands on her hips. It had not escaped her attention that the man wore a sparkling pink *Dazzle It!* bag slung over his shoulder. "My brother means *the other thieves like you.*"

"You kids had better come with me," he said, sounding to Elias like a mind reader. "It is against Greek law to spend the night on Delos for anyone except the archaeologists who work on the ruins. And it is most certainly against the law to remove the smallest object that comes from antiquity!" Flushed in the face, he turned toward Lily. "Did you say *'other* thieves'?"

"Yes, *your* thieving friends are down there at the hidden cave with all the stuff!" Elias repeated. He stamped his foot.

"What are your names?" The old man leaned against his walking stick for support and breathed heavily; the walk up the mountain had winded him. He studied the two children, waiting for their answer.

Elias and Lily answered him truthfully, unsure what to make of the awkward situation. Had they caught a thief? Or, had the thief caught them?

"Well, Elias Tantalos and Mademoiselle Lily, I have found you at last. You know already that I am Alexander, an archaeologist. I am responsible for developing an Open Air Museum on Delos. I work with the French Archaeological School of Athens that has been excavating these ruins for the past one hundred years. *My* friends—and I can assure you they are not thieves—are on holiday this month. What are you two doing on the sacred island near nightfall and unsupervised?"

"Are you *sure* you're not Apollo?" asked Lily. She could not stop asking questions. "Have you been digging up ruins here for a hundred years? And what does this cave have to do with Hercules?"

He nodded to Lily. "No, Apollo was a myth, a story invented by people who wanted to feel closer to a universe that was largely unexplained two thousand years ago. And doesn't everyone have a desire to be closer to their God? That much has changed very little over the ages. As for working here one hundred years, I am not *that* old—not yet. Different teams of archaeologists have been entrusted with this important site over the last century."

His cheeks stayed stretched in his awkward smile; his blue eyes twinkled at them. "But I am flattered; Apollo was a handsome god of many beautiful things—light, harmony, reason. And, Mademoiselle Lily, a 'grotto' is another word for 'cave'. Ancient Delians dug out this cave for a place to honor the hero Herakles and his deeds of great strength. Many gods were honored at different places all around Delos."

Alexander surprised them by swinging the *Dazzle It!* bag off his right shoulder and handing it to Lily.

"I believe this is yours. As for *friends,* you might be surprised to know that two of *yours* are on the island. Do you know a Mademoiselle Annika and Monsieur Jon? They also missed the ferry. I found them searching for you and have asked them to wait for you and for the return of the ferry at my small apartment at the museum. I am trying to get through to Mykonos police to tell the ferry to return, but the *meltemi* whipped up trouble for my telephone connection. And I do not have my own boat. I rely on the ferry to go back and forth for food and supplies."

"Why did you walk all the way up here?" asked Lily, curious.

"Yeah, why?" Elias demanded. He was not going to be a pushover just because Alexander had a good story and acted like he wasn't angry at them anymore.

"Your friends and I were getting anxious to find you. I came up here for the wide view, to see where you might be hiding, in case you were afraid of being in trouble. Assuming for the moment that you had a good explanation for what you were doing, suppose you tell me about this cave. And... did you say *thieves?* You might tell me all about them, too, while we go down and find your friends at the museum."

Leading them down the mountain, Alexander poked the broken chunks of granite with his walking stick, and seemed to know the wobbly steps to avoid. On the way, Elias left almost nothing out: the SCUBA divers, finding the Aqua Scribe, the cave with antiquities big enough to hide the thieves' boat.

Elias told Alexander about everything, except the crown. He left out the part that he wanted to keep it for himself.

The old man became more and more concerned the longer Elias talked. "You kids were very brave down there in the cave. The police will be very interested in that Aqua Scribe with its list of the divers' findings and buyers," said the caretaker, touching a small gadget next to his ear.

"My hearing is not what it used to be. This hearing aid buzzes, so I keep it off when I am on Delos alone. I turn it on to talk with tourists and museum guests during the day. In evenings, I retire to my comfortable chair and read; I am afraid I have not heard the thieves' boat coming to the island." Alexander exhaled a long, heavy sigh. "This is what I have long feared. I work very hard from morning to nightfall to keep people away from the priceless antiquities you see all around you on my island. It never occurred to me I would need to worry about treasure under the sea as well as on the land. Those men will be gone by now, I am afraid. Their boat will have carried the treasures of Delos far away."

Elias took a deep breath. The time had come to tell. "I don't think so, sir. The pirates have not left Delos. Not yet. I'm sure of it."

"What makes you so sure, Elias?"

"I... um... I told them about something I found... something they want."

A movement in the shadows of the ancient city spread out below them interrupted Elias. The *real* thieves were getting closer to the *agora* and the marble bench. The two men, still dressed in their SCUBA gear, were searching the ruins of the Ancient Theater. *Good.* There were thousands of seats to check. That ought to slow them up for a while!

"We have to beat them to it!"

"To what, young man?"

"I'll explain on the way. I left it near the *agora.*"

In spite of Elias' urgings to go to the *agora* without delay, Alexander insisted on a stop at the museum to reassure Annika and Jon they were found and safe. A low modern building was built into the base of Mount Kynthos. How had Elias not noticed it before?

This was no time for a field trip! Elias kicked at a stone, which rolled to a stop at the base of a headless statue, this one dressed like a soldier. The statue had a stone sword hanging—helplessly—at his motion-less side. Elias wished he had an entire army of soldier statues who could come to life and help them. Together, they could round up the thieves; Elias was sure of it.

As soon as Alexander unlocked the museum door, Elias rushed past him and called out. "Annika! Jon! We're here!"

Nobody answered. Alexander said, "They might be looking around. Check the exhibit hall, please, while

I look in my office."

Elias fumed at the delay, worried his friends had fallen into the bad guys' hands—and equally worried about the crown. What if the thieves found the correct marble bench before he could get there? They would end up with Apollo's gold laurel leaf crown *and* all the other treasures of Delos!

He hurried into the museum's main show room. Lining one wall was a row of white marble heads. A fantastic thought came to him: Museums were usually filled to the brim with old weapons of war. Swords, spears, cannons. They'd have all they would need.

VOTIVE OFFERINGS TO ARTEMIS GODDESS OF THE HUNT AND PROTECTOR OF YOUNG GIRLS

Lily noticed a display case full of ancient clay dolls about the same size as Marina—offerings to Artemis. "We're wasting time here. Where could our friends be?"

"Look for weapons," Elias told her. "We'll fight the thieves if they're holding Annika and Jon."

One glance around the showroom made it clear: Long-ago residents of Delos liked art and food and music and religion a whole lot more than war. How could they fight off criminals with clay dolls? The ancient Delians had not been good fighters. Invaders, pirates and looters had reduced the once proud city to a pile of rubble throughout its long course of history. No weapons here.

In desperation, Elias checked out a funny-looking ancient barbecue grill. Not even a fire poker. How could he, Elias Tantalos, expect to save the treasures of Delos without a single weapon?

Standing proudly in the middle of the room was a statue of a young woman with an arm raised. The unsmiling, serious face caught Elias' attention. This had to be Artemis. The hunting goddess. Her short robes swung out from her sides in stiff motion as if frozen in time. The goddess was in the act of hunting a deer; the animal was carved from another block of solid marble.

It would be more helpful if Artemis held a spear we could borrow, Elias wished. But the statue was broken; the goddess did not have a spear. She didn't have a hand.

Alexander le Meilleur hobbled into the room. "Your friends are not here. Let's go out."

"If the goddess Artemis were real, she would be ready to fight the thieves. Don't you agree?"

Elias remembered the dream when Artemis had hunted *him* for stealing from her twin brother, Apollo. "Yes, sir, Artemis would definitely be on our side. But the goddess is missing her spear, and I don't see any swords or arrows around here, either."

"I don't think spears will be necessary, Elias," said the archaeologist gently. "My job is to keep you and your friends safe until you can be picked up, not to fight off criminals ourselves. That is far too dangerous."

The caretaker locked the museum doors behind them but grimaced to see a curtain fluttering in an open window next to the door. "I had locked the children here to keep them safe, but that window latch is broken. Seems your friends were desperate to get to you and climbed out. We must find them quickly."

Quickly? Every movement the old man made seemed painfully slow.

"Could we *please* go to the marble bench while we're looking for Annika and Jon?" He hoped the thieves were not as familiar with Delos *above* the ground as they were with the sea floor around it.

From the museum's vantage point on a rise at the base of Mt. Kynthos, no boats could be seen. Elias could not see any sign of the ferry, and he felt equally sure that the thieves were still around. Thanos and Yannis would search under every slab of marble that could pass for a seat until they located the crown.

Alexander nodded, and allowed Elias to take the lead. The boy's legs ached to run, but with great difficulty he held back out of courtesy for the older man, who picked out each step carefully with his cane.

At the great marble bench at last, Elias threw himself on his knees and reached into the deep crevice, praying hard that the crown was still there. His fingers curled around cold metal. *Yesss!* Elias got back on his feet and with two hands, presented the gold crown of leaves to the archaeologist.

Monsieur le Meilleur rested his cane on the end of the bench, then caught his breath with excitement when he saw what Elias was holding. The man's icy blue eyes warmed and sparkled with astonishment. "But this is—*c'est fantastique!*"

Alexander spoke his native French language while joyfully taking the crown from Elias' hands. The sun was a round orange ball sinking lower on the horizon, and a mellow glow seemed to come from the golden leaves. There was no sign of Annika and Jon.

"It shines magnificently in the sun," commented the old archaeologist. "Why, it must be every bit as beautiful as the day it was created. Nothing like this has ever been found on the sacred island before."

Elias fully appreciated in that moment that Alexander was not just an old man, but a passionate archaeologist who was looking at the discovery of a lifetime.

"Where did you find this amazing thing? And what was it doing in your possession?" the old man adjusted the hearing aid behind his ear to not miss a single word.

"I—I was trying to give it back. That is why I climbed the palm tree... to return it to... to Apollo. I wanted to give it back." The words sounded lame and stupid even to his own ears—Apollo was nothing but a myth, and this priceless object was not his to keep. Elias would not blame Alexander if he hauled him off to the police the instant they arrived.

The old man muttered to himself, turning the crown around in his hands to view it from every angle. His blue eyes twinkled with excitement.

"*Magnifique...* laurel leaves of Apollo... unbelievable... in gold, perfect in every way... probably made by the Macedons, master goldsmiths of northern Greece... worthy of a god!"

He didn't seem angry. The opposite, in fact. Gleeful.

"I have been an archaeologist at Delos for fifty of my seventy-eight years. Many wonderful things have been unearthed here by me and my colleagues— and yet, my friend, there is not another gold crown of laurel exactly like this in the entire world—*oh!* I hear someone coming, crunching on the path. Your friends returning to us, I hope!"

A pair of long legs in black SCUBA diving suits leaped over the back of the marble bench, and landed one on each side of Alexander.

"Oh, my goodness—"

Thanos grabbed the cane resting against the bench and—*crack!* He whacked the archaeologist over the head with his own walking stick, and threw the cane across the ancient street. It rattled against a stone wall and fell into the wildflowers.

Alexander moaned and slumped onto the hard

bench, while a small cloud of dust rose from the ground where the Crown of Apollo lay.

Unclaimed.

The thieves and Elias and Lily—pounced.

29

UNEXPECTED VISITORS

Like a bunch of slippery eels, the long black SCUBA-suited arms and legs thrashed over the children. Yannis, Thanos, Elias and Lily grasped at the golden prize lying in the dust. At the bottom of the mass of humanity was an unfortunate Lily. Elias tried not to squish his sister, while trying not to get squashed himself.

"It. Will. Be. MINE!" Thanos shouted between grunts.

Yannis pinned Elias' arms down to the ground; pebbles and pottery shards bit into his skin. "I've got the kid," said Yannis. "Thanos—GET THE CROWN!"

Elias kicked at the thieves with his feet.

"*Oof*—watch it, kid!" Yannis tightened his hold.

Lily's small fingers managed to wrap around one gold leaf. "Got it!"

Elias heard the squeaky whisper in his ear, but the moment of glee changed to horror when he saw Thanos' hand reach for Lily's arm. The thief stretched for her with one hand, while his other frantically scratched at the ground for the crown.

Lily wriggled from Thanos' hold and squirmed out of the man's reach. Elias felt her small body twist and turn to free herself from under the mass of bodies and, incredibly, he saw her hop to her feet and run halfway across the *agora* before Yannis or Thanos became fully aware that the crown was making an unexpected getaway.

"GO, LILY, GO!—RUN, FASTER THAN HIGHWAY!" shouted Elias, seeing the gold leaf crown glimmer in the sunlight as she ran off with the Crown of Victory.

Alexander moaned and tried to sit up, but he slumped back down on the bench, cradling his head in his palms.

Filled with anger that they had hurt the kind old archaeologist, Elias wrenched his arms away and pushed with both hands against the thieves with all his might, and miraculously succeeded while the men tried to sort themselves out. Elias scrambled to the old man's side.

"Alexander, are you all right?" Elias did not know how to help but he prayed the old man was not going to be dead.

"Don't worry about me... go save that crown!" the old man wheezed, then collapsed in a coughing fit.

Quicker than the Delos lizards could scale ruins, both thieves became aware that the treasure had slipped out of reach. "The crown!" the men grunted, as they untangled themselves from each other and got to their feet.

Where did Lily go?

Elias scanned the area and saw his sister's curly blonde hair whip behind the bushes of the Sacred Lake.

I should have gotten to the crown first, he scolded

himself. *I can run faster than Lily. We're doomed.*

"I'll come back for you," Elias called over his shoulder to Alexander.

His racing feet passed an enormous terracotta vase. He concentrated on sending a brain-wave message to his sister: *jump in a vase, jump in a vase, jump in...* He repeated the message over and over with every beat of his pounding heart, praying that Lily would find a good hiding place.

Behind him, the winding paths of the bushy Sacred Lake were slowing down the thieves. About a hundred meters ahead at the palm tree, Lily was racing past the birthplace of Apollo and Artemis. It was clear to Elias that his sister had not gotten any of his brainwave messages. She was obviously not trying to find a hiding place. What was she doing? She could not outrun the thieves for very long.

He stood on the stone bench that circled the palm tree to see which path she had taken. He spotted Lily's hair flying down one of them. He leaped off and chased her out of the Sacred Lake.

Lily ran straight down an open avenue and did not stop until she neared the large, square pit that Elias remembered was the Fountain of the Minoans. Lily squatted on the ground and was fiddling with the zipper of her sparkling bag.

What was she messing around for? "HIDE!" he screamed. "They're almost here!"

The thieves had emerged from the Sacred Lake and were quickly closing the gap.

Lily waved something in the air that glimmered with a streak of gold. "LOOK HERE! IF YOU WANT IT, COME AND GET IT!"

Elias could not believe his eyes and ears. She was *teasing* the thieves. On purpose! He struggled to get to her in time, but he was too late. *Can I do nothing right?*

Something glowing yellow in the setting sun shot through the sky in a graceful, high arc and landed with a splash. Lily took a few steps and peered into the deep well of the ancient Delians, putting her hands on her hips in a satisfied kind of way.

Elias blinked unbelievingly as he heard the splash rising from its depths.

Thanos and Yannis screamed, "THE CROWN!" From a distance, the thieves saw what Lily had done.

Elias caught up to his sister just as she was zipping the *Dazzle It!* bag shut. "Come on—we don't want to be standing right here when they catch up!" They threw themselves behind a fallen column a short distance up the slope.

Lily's brave defiance ebbed. The pair watched in paralyzed fear as the thieves rushed to the edge of the well.

Thanos and Yannis stared into the murky depths of the algae-covered waters of the Fountain of the Minoans.

Elias sat up, his elbows resting on the fallen chunk of column. He had a clear view down to the thieves, whose backs were bending over the pit looking for the crown.

An image of Artemis, goddess of the hunt, floated into his mind. He remembered her standing, tall and fierce, on top of the Ferris Wheel in his nightmare, riding it down to stop him—a thief. Elias raised his eyes to the mountaintop, renewing his prayer for help. This would be a terrific time for Artemis to swoop down from Mount Kynthos with her bow drawn!

Help was nowhere to be seen. Elias felt his entire body droop. The hard marble column bit into his elbows, and he rubbed the sore spots.

His brown eyes grew wide.

"Lily—this column! We can roll it down the slope

and it'll knock the thieves into the well! Help me get it going!" Elias and Lily knelt on the weeds and pushed at the round section of marble. It didn't budge.

"Push harder! We can do it!" But nothing would budge that block of rock.

Higher on the hillside, dry weeds crackled. As one, Elias and Lily turned to stare up the slope of Mount Kynthos.

Something *was* there, camouflaged against a background of weeds. Not the goddess Artemis, but a big, dark lizard sitting in an end-of-the-day ray of sun, still as a statue, the yellow dashes visible on his back.

Highway's head turned toward him. It might have been a trick of the light, but Elias swore later that the lizard winked at him.

The shouts of children pierced the air. Annika and Jon ran into view, glad to have found Elias and Lily at last, not noticing they were running straight into trouble.

Highway lived up to his name and darted away from them, quick as a flash of lightning. Running straight down the hill, the lizard ran along the edge of the fountain. Yannis was still leaning over the well when the dark lizard darted right in front of his feet. Startled, the thief tumbled over with a splash and a groan.

The water level was shallow this time of year, especially during the dry and hot days of August—only up to Yannis' knees—but the lowest step was several feet above Yannis' reach. Stuck in the murky water at the bottom of the Fountain of the Minoans, Yannis could not escape the pit without help.

"Give me a hand out of here, Thanos!" everyone heard.

The only reply Thanos gave him was, "THE CROWN,

I NEED THE CROWN!"

A frustrated scream echoed out of the ancient Fountain of the Minoans, and something was flung ungraciously out of the pit. A muddied, golden-haired doll lay in the weeds near his feet.

"Here's Marina, Lil! But the crown—?" Elias began.

Lily laughed, but oddly it sounded fake. "She looks more like Medusa now, Elias." Lily kept up the forced laughter while her hand moved down, covering her pink sequined bag in a protective gesture.

Unfortunately, understanding came to Elias and Thanos at the same moment. *The crown was in the girl's bag!*

Thanos' black eyes flashed with anger. "Game over, kids. Hand over the crown. *NOW*." He spoke in a voice thick with threat. "You wouldn't want anybody to get hurt, now, would you?"

Another wail came from Yannis in the pit. Thanos responded, "I'll get you later. Right now this little girl is going to give me the crown. Aren't you?"

Lily slowly unzipped her bag. "I'm sorry, Elias. I tried."

"It's okay.. You're doing the right thing. Here, I'll give it to him. Would you please go with Annika and Jon to help Alexander and get him safely to the museum? Find his phone and try calling for help."

At the first glint of gold coming out of her bag, Thanos pushed past Elias and snatched it from Lily. Her big brown eyes threw Elias a last desperate look before he nodded. Lily ran off, with Annika and Jon at her heels.

A wild look of glee lit up the thief's face. He held the gold leaves up to the sun as if he could not believe his eyes. *He'd won!*

Like men in a traditional Greek dance, Thanos held his arms out wide, the crown in one hand. He twirled around slowly, kicking back his heels high and singing: "It's MI–I–I–INE!"

Feeling more defeated than ever, Elias sank onto the ground, too sad to move. *Isn't it just like life,* he thought later, *to come up with the perfect answer to prayer just when you least expect it—and least deserve it?* This was exactly one of those times.

The shiny gold crown had attracted a new visitor to Delos.

30

SARGOS

Petros skimmed low across a sea that was as calm as glass and blue as the sky. His sharp eyes searched for the fisherman Christos, who was rarely this late coming back to the harbor to share his load of fish. So the pelican of Mykonos set out to find the colorful stripes of Christos' *caicque*.

Something glinted brightly in the warm, setting sun over a small island not far away. Petros ventured off the sea, flew inland, and plucked the shiny crown neatly from the hand of the thief!

With a toss of his long beak, the pelican threw back his head and the crown landed around his neck. He seemed pleased with himself, as he always did whenever there was an audience.

"The crown—" Elias and Thanos gasped, both acutely aware that the pelican could fly away with the treasure at any moment.

Elias recovered first. "Go, Petros, go!"

The pelican appeared to understand, waddled a few

steps, and took off in flight, traveling low. He touched down again just on the far side of the *agora*. The bird could not seem to resist being the center of attention in a crowd, even if this crowd was small and made up of criminals.

Petros left the ancient agora and waddled down the Avenue of the Lions as if he didn't have a care in the world, the priceless gold leaves of Apollo wagging around his neck like an expensive necklace. The sight spurred everyone to seek the prize once more.

Thanos, who was not taking his eyes off the bird for an instant, went for it but tripped on a chunk of white marble in his way; he picked himself up and kept going after Petros.

Elias took a short cut to the Avenue through the bushy paths of the Sacred Lake. He arrived first and clearly saw the thief gaining on the bird. There was nothing Elias could do to save the legendary crown now.

Sticking his hands in his pockets, he wished earnestly for *Sargos* and home. He felt something strange in his pocket... *beads from Lily's bracelets he had picked up in the sea!* With a new idea, Elias pressed himself next to a bush hidden from view, his heart pounding like it wanted to jump out of his chest. This had to work!

Thanos barreled down the Avenue of the Lions after the bird, who began veering directly toward Elias!

Half-hidden in the bushes, Elias was astounded. The pelican was almost within his reach! All he needed to do was reach out at the right moment and he could catch Petros—and the crown—but if he was successful he would need to deal with the thief...

In a split second decision, Elias held true to his original plan and threw fistfuls of beads on the ground directly in front of Thanos' running feet.

The thief tripped a second time, falling harder and slamming his head onto the stone base of a lion. He rolled over, moaned and lay silent.

Elias heard a rush of wind and saw Petros flapping his wings hard, ready to take flight. He held his breath and watched in awe as the bird, with the priceless treasure around its neck, lifted off the ground and became smaller and smaller in the sky, until it was out of sight.

Thanos did not move or make a sound. Bravely, Elias inspected the unconscious thief. The man's chest rose and fell quietly. *Breathing.* Elias was glad the man did not move, but was equally and strangely glad, somehow, about the breathing part—but now was not the time to sort out his feelings.

First he must find his sister.

He did not have far to look. Lily, Annika and Jon came into view from the opposite end of the Avenue, their eyes wide with amazement at the sight of Elias standing over the conquered crook.

Elias gave his sister a spontaneous hug. "You were fantastic back there at the Minoan Fountain."

"Thanks!" said Lily, hugging him back. She nodded to the unconscious Thanos and said, "Not bad yourself, Elias!

"Where's Alexander? Is he all right?" He hoped so.

Jon shook his head. "It's a mystery. He wasn't at the marble bench. The museum was locked up with no sign of him there, either."

"What should we do about *this* guy?" Annika asked. "Should we leave him here?"

Elias had been wondering the same thing, and he had an idea. "Lily, isn't the House of the Dolphins near here?"

"Yes, I think so. What does that have to do with anything?"

"I'll tell you on the way. Come on, everyone. Follow me, fast!"

By now, the sun had fully set, but a full moon was rising high in the sky and cast a light over the ruins of Delos nearly as bright as day, so the nighttime did not slow down the children at all. They dashed past the signpost marking the House of Dolphins, and stood next to the roped-off area preserving the beautiful mosaic tile pictures of the swimming dolphins.

"Be very careful not to step on the mosaics," said Elias. "And we'll apologize to Alexander for borrowing these ropes, but if we each carry a rope we'll have enough to tie up Thanos well enough not to bother anyone else—at least not tonight!"

A few minutes later, the kids came back to the motionless lion standing guard over its charge. Elias gave the honor to Lily. "You're better at knots than I am—why don't you finish up here? With your great knotting skills, I don't think this thief will be going anywhere soon!"

He helped Lily wrap the tourist-rope several times around the lion statue and the thief, securing the immobile Thanos to its base. With great care, his sister slowly looped the rope into a well-practiced boater's knot. Elias watched each step to see how she managed to do it so well and promised himself he'd practice, if he ever got so lucky as to take another boating vacation.

When she finished, Lily reached up as high as her arm could stretch and patted the stone lion's snout. "Good lion. Guard this guy for us for a while, will you?" she said.

Brother and sister collapsed, laughing in relief. They were joined by Annika and Jon, and they laughed and laughed and could not stop for a long, long time. The fear and stress of the day slid off Elias' shoulders, and a feeling sweet as honey filled up his insides. Not one of them remembered until it was too late that a third thief—Theo—remained at large.

More than anything in the world, Elias wanted to go back to his ultimate boating vacation that was busy in a lazy way, and not one filled with secret crowns and dark, claustrophobic caves, and thieves whacking old men with sticks. In short, he wanted *Sargos* and a safe harbor.

Without any discussion, Elias headed for the one place that would make him feel closer to his parents and their home-sweet-boat: the pier. Under the full moonlight, Lily, Annika and Jon followed like sleep-walkers.

Even though he no longer possessed the Crown of Apollo, Elias knew he had been trying to do the right thing, and it felt good. Elias did not know it then, but prayer and good choices would continue to help that feeling grow stronger than any bad luck magnet.

At the pier, *Sargos* was bobbing gently on the water as if nothing in the world was wrong. It seemed to Elias he had fallen into a good dream, one from which he had no desire to wake up.

Mom and Aunt Kat screamed hello and jumped up and down, waving their hands high when they saw the children approach. Dad stood behind them, holding the boat's line and grinning ear to ear. All the children were hugging and being hugged, Annika and Jon no less than the others. Everybody eagerly told their side of the story, and the group stood on the pier talking excitedly.

The bow on the empty *Sargos* dipped and rose with the waves. Elias' head jerked away from the group to scan the sea. In the light of the full moon he saw something that plunged him straight back into a nightmare that seemed it would never end.

A motorboat with double engines emerged from around the south end of the island. *WunderSea Adventures* rumbled past the pier. The boat sat low in the water, loaded down with a pile of heavy-looking marble statues.

Powerful waves from its wake rocked *Sargos* like a cradle. But there was no comfort for Elias.

"We have a problem," Elias announced to the happy, laughing group, and his voice grew serious. "There's another one! One more thief! *WunderSea Adventures* is getting away with a full load of priceless antiquities!"

How could he have forgotten there were *three* of them? Theo, the driver, must have given up waiting for the other two men and was breaking away with the priceless treasures of Delos—all for himself.

"He's getting away! Making a run for it—with *everything!* Mom, Dad—quick! We've got to catch up!" Elias leaped onto the bow, needing to take action. Mom caught on immediately, and jumped on board. She held out a hand for Lily, Annika and Jon to climb aboard while Elias could only mutter "Catch up!" over and over and over.

Dad quickly untied *Sargos* and cast off, but Elias was in a panic. After everything they had been through, how could the treasures end up in the wrong hands? It was just not fair!

"Slow down, son. You're safe now, don't worry," Dad put a hand on Elias' shoulders, trying to calm him down.

"No, that's not it," he shuddered, trying to explain through the rush of emotion he was feeling: they were safe, yes—but the antiquities were not!

"The thief is getting away. With everything!" Elias pointed to the wake of *WunderSea Adventures,* getting farther away by the second.

"We'll never catch up to a boat like that, but we can call ahead for help and maybe trap him between us," said Dad. "What do you say, kids?"

Elias, Lily, Annika and Jon jumped up and down and screamed into the wind as Dad phoned Officer Maria. *Sargos* followed the trail of white ripples on the dark sea, the leftover wake from the boat moving far ahead.

Elias took a last look at Delos. The bright moonlight cast the ruined columns and stone walls in eerie stripes of shadows and light. He wondered if he would ever see it again.

"*GO SARGOS GO! GO SARGOS GO!*" Lily, Annika and Jon screamed chants to encourage the old boat, and Elias joined in. "*GO SARGOS GO!*"

Mom and Aunt Kat were anxious to explain their delay and took turns shouting their story over the engine noise. The *meltemi* had fought against the ferry the entire distance, and despite setting out early it took hours to return to Mykonos Harbor, where Aunt Kat and the day campers were horrified to learn that two sets of parents remained empty-handed. She had seen all four of the children board the ferry, but had missed their premature exit.

In spite of her protest, the ferry's captain had refused to return to Delos until the storm subsided. Aunt Kat called the archaeological center on Delos but could not reach its caretaker; she left a message to look for four children who were stranded on the island until the ferry could return.

Repairs finished, Mom and Dad had decided to take *Sargos* to Delos and bring back all the children. Aunt Kat, who knew Delos well and felt responsible, insisted on coming. They assured Annika and Jon's parents they would return the children safely.

The *meltemi* proved too strong for the small power-boat, and the winds blew them far off course. Pushed too far to the south, they had sheltered in a protected harbor on another island until the storm lessened.

"We're gaining on him!" Elias interrupted, jumping up and down. *WunderSea Adventures* had slowed and was just ahead!

In the end, *WunderSea Adventures* had been caught up in the greed of its driver. Theo had not taken the time to secure the antiquities properly—one high wave reached its watery fingers into the boat, and the sea hungrily swallowed a small marble statue in one gulp. As Theo cut the engine to tie down the rest of his load, Sargos caught up close enough to see the panic on his face—just as several boats came roaring in from north, south, east and west. *Sargos* and *WunderSea Adventures* were completely surrounded.

31

THE ONE THAT ALMOST GOT AWAY

In a furious surge of white water that glistened in the brilliant moonlight, a fleet of five police launches, painted blue with white stripes and each bearing a flapping Greek flag, circled around *Sargos* and *WunderSea Adventures.* They made a close constantly moving ring around the two central boats, and every eye on deck seemed focused on *Sargos.* Elias leaned over the side and waved to get the officers' attention. He needed to tell someone to go to Delos and find Alexander!

The men and women on the other boats wore uniforms resembling Officer Maria's. One of the officers picked up a megaphone. *"AKINHTOI!"* The speaker followed with its English translation. *"FREEZE!* STAY WHERE YOU ARE. NOBODY IS TO LEAVE THE AREA."

Elias knew immediately who it was: Officer Maria— only she sounded much less friendly now than she had the day she'd asked for the boaters' help!

The police launches maintained a pattern of slowly circling the other two vessels. Officer Maria's boat broke out of the pattern and motored closer to *Sargos*, while another approached *WunderSea Adventures*. The three remaining police boats continued circling watchfully.

Dad had cut the engine on *Sargos* to indicate their full cooperation with the authorities, but immediately turned a concerned face to Elias.

"What exactly happened over there?"

"Um..." Elias tried to think fast. The only one who knew about the Crown of Apollo was Alexander. Had he reported Elias to the police? Is that why the police were here? He might think he was a hero, catching the crooks, but in reality? He might be in a LOT of trouble. Any explanation would come back to his theft of the Crown of Apollo. And worse: how he'd lost it forever.

The police launch came within a few yards of *Sargos*; Officer Maria tossed Dad a rope. They slowly pulled their boats close together until their sides nearly touched. As soon as they were close enough, she stepped over the starboard side onto the already-crowded *Sargos*.

Everyone's attention was fastened on the officer, but a sudden movement on board the *WunderSea Adventures* distracted Elias. Another police boat was attempting to close in on Theo, who was *not* being as cooperative. The thief realized he was being caught red-handed, and Elias watched in horror as Theo grabbed whatever ancient treasure was closest to his reach and dumped it overboard into the depths of the sea, getting rid of the evidence.

Elias gasped as a marble head plunked over the rail. A small clay pot followed, and then a handful of terracotta figurines floated briefly before disappearing from sight under the waves.

"The antiquities! He's getting rid of everything!"

Theo had his hands on a red and black *hydria* with two handles, but as the officer shouted at him Theo set it down at the stern and grabbed for his SCUBA gear. Since he was already wearing a wetsuit, all he had to do was hoist an oxygen tank onto his back and fix a mask over his eyes and he'd be gone!

"He's going to jump! Stop him!" Elias panicked. Theo was ready to break away.

Officer Maria recognized them and asked at once if everyone was all right. As she tried to sort out the details of what had happened, Elias tried to stay out of her line of vision, keeping his eyes instead on what was happening in the other boat.

Police officers attempted to board *WunderSea Adventures*, but it was so filled with antiquities and SCUBA equipment they could not detain Theo in time. Elias watched Theo point back to Delos, where he could see Mount Kynthos like a low dark mound. Sound moved clearly over the water and he heard every word of Theo's protest.

"You've got the wrong guy! I'm just the driver— the *real* thieves are—there!—they're still there! On Delos—and that boy on the other boat—don't let him get away!" He waved both arms wildly in the direction of the island and at *Sargos*. Then he adjusted his mask, shoved the mouthpiece between his lips and climbed over the stern. He paused long enough to grab a handful of ancient jewelry, small pieces that glittered gold and emerald green.

WunderSea Adventures tipped steeply to one side as the officers made a giant leap for Theo. To slow them down, Theo kicked at the two-handled vase; the dark red pottery tumbled into the sea, the black scene that was painted around it silvered by the bright rays of moonlight

The ancient *hydria* floated upright, and for several seconds time seemed to stand still. Elias was tired of waiting for somebody to do *something*. He had watched Apollo's crown fly away on the neck of a bird, and now watching Theo drip treasures through his fingers like sand on a beach was too much to take. In the Aegean Sea, the rare object would be gone forever, thousands of feet deep!

One of the bowl's handles dipped below the surface and the vase began to slowly fill with water. Elias made a bold decision.

On the crowded deck of *Sargos,* Lily was first to feel the splash. "Man overboard!" she yelled.

Dad stopped talking to Officer Maria while Mom and Aunt Kat did a quick scan of all the children's faces.

"It's Elias—he's missing!"

Everyone panicked at once.

"How could he fall in?" asked Jon.

"Where is he?" Mom's worried eyes searched the dark water for signs of Elias. "It's hard to see!"

"He should've come up by now if he just fell off," said Annika, her blue eyes determined. "Wouldn't he? He's a good swimmer, yes?"

"Yes," answered Dad, a grim look crossing his face. After a few more frantic seconds in which the dark surface of the water remained unbroken, Dad counted out loud. "Fifteen... eighteen... twenty-two."

One of the other officers on Officer Maria's boat, who did not know the family, was suspicious. "How do you know this boy isn't trying to get away with something? If he is such a good swimmer, he may try to swim over to Delos to hide something for himself."

"My brother just saved my life giving up the best treasure of all, so don't go calling him a thief!" Lily had her hands on her hips, and the officer took a step backward on his boat deck.

"Okay, little lady. It's my job to follow up all the leads. I'm just asking questions."

Dad interrupted, counting aloud again. "Thirty-five, forty... I'm going in!" He stripped off his T-shirt.

At that moment hundreds of bubbles appeared. Elias burst from the water, tearing the mask and snorkel from his face. He took a huge gulp of air. "At least... saved... one."

Elias tried to explain as an officer reached over the side to retrieve the vase from his grip. It was heavy, and the officer emptied water from the jar while Mom lowered the ladder and gave him a hand back into the boat.

"How did so many of you know to come out here?" Elias asked Officer Maria, while he squeezed water from each leg of his swim trunks.

"We got a call from your father, and before that from the Delos caretaker. Seems he had a run-in with some pirates. Knocked him out pretty good. He came to and became very worried about you children, but being hurt he could not find you quickly. We called the police from Syros, too, and everyone got here as fast as we could."

"Where did the thieves find so many antiquities?" another officer wanted to know.

It reminded Elias of something. *The underwater map on the Aqua Scribe!* He threw his backpack on the bench and dug it out to show the officer. "One of the thieves talked about losing something. Lily found this in the water just outside the cave where they hid all this stuff. Here—there's evidence on it. I saw a list of ancient stuff, and buyers. Take it!"

"Excellent! This will help us a lot. Thank you. Looks like we have the proof we'll need to book these guys, and their buyers, too. These thieves have been causing trouble all over the Aegean Sea. Setting up business as a cover-up for their illegal SCUBA activities. Moving to new locations before local authorities could catch on. Clever. Who would guess some kids could outwit a sophisticated crime scheme?"

Aunt Kat gasped. "Oh, no! My vase of Athena! I thought that boat driver looked familiar, but I didn't recognize him in the wetsuit—he sold it to me! I had no idea it was authentic. It seemed to be a very good reproduction."

She explained that she would bring her piece of antiquity to the police station first thing in the morning and promised to tell everything she knew about the sellers and her transaction with them.

Elias asked Officer Maria to be sure to check on Alexander at the museum. The officer promised, and then raised her eyebrows when Elias told her to look for the thieves in some other very unusual places— but he was not further questioned.

On hearing their skills were needed to round up the other thieves on Delos, the police officers snapped to business and did not waste any more time with *Sargos*. A pair of their boats sped off for the island, while another officer told Elias' parents they were allowed to take the children back to Mykonos. Annika and Jon's parents had already been notified by cell phone that everything was all right, but the family was anxious to be reunited.

It was their last night on Mykonos, but everyone was tired from the ordeals of the day. For dinner, they chose the *taverna* closest to the dock and their waiting beds on *Sargos*.

Officer Maria stopped by their table with a final request. Could Mr. Elias Tantalos please report with his family to the police station first thing in the morning?

Even though he was starving from his long and uncomfortable day on Delos, the delicious Greek food in his mouth tasted like cardboard and his stomach knotted with worry. He had never been summoned to a police station before.

Did the Greeks arrest kids?

32

THE POLICE CALL

The last morning of vacation dawned bright, with all traces of the *meltemi* dissipated into a light breeze, nothing more. Feeling just as tired as when he had gone to bed, Elias opened his eyes to the low cabin ceiling. He was brimming with worries about meeting the police.

Assuming he did not wind up in Greek kids' jail, it would be a calm day to take *Sargos* back to the small port town near Athens. His family would catch an airplane to Connecticut the next morning. He groaned about the idea of heading back to normal life, but he realized with surprise that his thoughts had been so filled with the island crime mystery that returning to school no longer held such a grip of terror over him.

The immediate worry of what the police were going to do to him was a much bigger concern. He had stopped the antiquity thieves and helped save most of the treasures that were on Theo's boat, but it did not change the fact that he had taken the priceless

Crown of Apollo into his own possession and kept it a secret. And he had wanted to keep it for himself. Like the thieves. The secret was out for good, now. Alexander would've told the police all about that crown, and his taking it from Delos.

In spite of his worries about what the police were going to do to him, a startling burst of joy tingled through him from his head to his toes: The secret of the crown would never drag down his mood or give him that guilty stomachache again.

He woke Lily out of her snoring sleep, got dressed, and leaped out of the boat to see if Jon was up yet. Now that the terrifying day was past, he felt a weird urge to laugh. Saved his sister, with the crown, only to lose it—for eternity—to a dumb bird! That was a fact! Nothing could change that.

Certainly the grown-ups—even the police—would agree that losing a crown was better than losing a sister. Wouldn't they? It was a better ending this way. Wasn't it? Why, in spite of the joy of doing the right thing, did he still feel so crummy? He needed to tell the truth, but that was the hardest thing to do!

When Lily emerged from the cabin she joined Elias and Jon, already on the dock. Lily too had woken up a bit worried about the visit to the police station. "Will Aunt Kat be in trouble?" she wanted to know. "Did she do anything wrong?"

"I don't think so, she promised to cooperate..."

"Hey! Wait for me!" Annika climbed out of their boat and joined her brother and the Tantalos family as they walked down the dock.

Elias had never noticed in all their days in Mykonos Harbor that behind the small blue-domed chapel, beside the police station, was the Mykonos Municipality Office. Tucked in between a *taverna* and the ferry pier, cheerful blue-and-white striped Greek flags, attached to its rooftop, flapped in the breeze.

Walking down the dock with his sister and friends, and their parents just behind them, Elias could scarcely see the Municipality Office's front door. A crowd had gathered in front of it, and there was a flurry of activity related to a large television camera and newspaper reporters with microphones. Everyone seemed to be asking each other what was going on.

"There they are!" someone said over the buzzing crowd. As soon as he stepped off the dock, lights flashed bright red and blue until Elias could not see anything but purple spots dancing in front of his eyes. He reached into his pocket automatically for a fireball, as he usually did when he felt uneasy about a situation; a plastic wrapper crinkled, but Elias slipped his hand out of the pocket without it.

A neatly dressed reporter in a colorful suit had a microphone in her hand, which she thrust in his face. The reporter—and the crowd—waited for him to say something, but Elias just stared at the rings on her fingers. It certainly did not *feel* like he was getting into trouble. Why were the police waiting to meet him here with a reporter? Great. Would his troubles go viral? Yet, the mood of the crowd was curious and excited, not angry.

"Elias and Lily Tantalos! Annika and Jon Johnson! Everyone wants to know how you managed to stop this crime ring?" Everyone on Mykonos suddenly knew their names. "How did you four kids succeed in catching these thieves, when they have eluded the island police all summer?"

The reporter handed Lily the microphone, but Lily took a step closer to Elias' side, acting uncharacteristically shy under all this attention. She handed the mic to Elias, who tried to pass it off onto Annika and Jon, but they shook their heads, stepped to the side and smiled at him encouragingly. Eager faces in the crowd turned to see him, and he realized more reporters stood ready with various types of sound recorders, smartphones and tablets, a few even with pens held over notepads. Red lights on TV cameras turned on, waiting. Elias saw a group of kids holding out their cell phones, recording the scene.

He had no idea what to say. He stood there with his mouth gaping open, like a big fish.

Elias realized that Officer Maria was standing nearby; she had noticed his distress and gently took the microphone. "On behalf of the Municipality of Mykonos, the Greek government and archaeologists throughout the country, we would like to thank Elias, Lily, Annika and Jon for their brave efforts to stop the removal of many priceless antiquities from the island of Delos. Children, we cannot emphasize the importance of your contributions enough, not only to the Delos museum caretaker and the people of the Cycladic islands, but to the citizens of Greece."

The reporters launched into questions for the authorities. "I believe the crowd is eager to hear about the criminals responsible for attempting to take away the Delian treasures. Officer? What exactly happened over there?"

Officer Maria held up her hands to quiet them. "I am pleased to report that last evening, Mykonos Police found two of the thieves on Delos in very unusual places—one in an ancient well, and one tied to a stone lion. It is our understanding that these four children are responsible for trapping them until police could arrive on the scene. Solid information has come to our attention that will link them to many crimes of this nature all around the islands."

Lily elbowed Elias and whispered so the microphones wouldn't hear what she said. "Aunt Kat! She gave them good information—she'll be okay!"

"And don't forget the Aqua Scribe you found, Lily. That had a lot of important information, too," Elias whispered back. They did a silent hi-five, and listened to the rest of Officer Maria's story.

"The two men, along with their boat driver, have been sent to Athens in custody of police on the very first ferry earlier this morning. Elias Tantalos acted well beyond his years in taking on the leadership role that led to the capture of these criminals!"

The crowd applauded harder while the reporter asked, "What will happen to *WunderSea Adventures?*"

"Needless to say," replied the officer, "*Wunder-Sea Adventures* will be closed down. We hope that a reputable SCUBA diving outfit can be found to run tourist diving trips around Mykonos legally. As everyone should know—" her eyes scanned the clapping crowd "—diving near Delos is *and has always been* off-limits due to the on-going archaeological work in and around the site of the ancient city, in preparation for its opening as an Open Air museum."

A commotion at the back of the crowd caused the officer to pause in her speech.

"Let the man through!" shouted a voice at the back, and the crowd parted like the red sea for Moses. Elias recognized the walking stick before the man.

"Alexander! You're okay!" Lily dashed to his side and helped the old man walk through the mass of people.

Out of place in this fashionable, youthful town, the archaeologist's walking stick thudded on the pavement instead of crunching on its usual bits of ancient pottery and marble. "Thank you, Mademoiselle Lily," he said, patting her arm and linking hers with his at the elbow to help steady his feet. He stretched his neck to stand tall between the four kids.

Cameras flashed some more. The old archaeologist rubbed a bump on his head, but he was smiling as Officer Maria handed him the microphone. "These children—Elias, Lily, Annika and Jon—deserve much applause, and a special thank you from the museum at Delos," he wheezed.

When the clapping settled down, Alexander motioned to four more police officers who each held a box. "To properly thank these four young people for their brave actions, I have a gift."

Out of each box, the other police officers plucked a green wreath—similar in every way to the Crown of Apollo except that these were made from real evergreen laurel leaves instead of gold—and placed the leafy crowns on the heads of Elias, Lily, Annika and Jon. Elias touched the laurel crown feeling like an ancient Olympic athlete after winning a gold medal.

"This won't fit in my jar," Lily said, beaming, "but it'll make a great souvenir to show my friends!"

Leaning down on his walking stick, Alexander's blue eyes twinkled. The archaeologist spoke just loud enough for Elias and Lily to hear. "A cheer of victory from our friend Apollo, you might say." Alexander wheezed. "Isn't that right?"

Elias smiled at his sister and their new friends. During the applause that followed the presentation of their laurel wreath crowns, Elias felt his ears flame red. Tears that had nothing to do with the shining TV lights pointed his way, stung his eyes. Nobody back home would see this; it would be broadcast on Greek TV, but it felt just right. It didn't matter. Nobody had said a word about the lost crown, or seemed angry at him for losing it. Quite the opposite. Everyone seemed to think they were heroes.

But would people call him a hero if they knew the *truth?*

33

PELICAN TALES

A reporter began asking questions from behind the big fuzzy black head on her microphone. Elias blinked his eyes and tried to concentrate on what was being said. "How did you kids manage by yourselves on a nearly deserted island—with criminals?"

She handed him the microphone and waited for his answers. Elias held it tightly so his hand wouldn't make it shake. "Delos turned out to be not so deserted after all. We made friends there who helped us. Alexander, of course, and we got help when it counted from our boat-neighbors, Annika and Jon. We couldn't have done it without a few special lizard friends, Highway and Sunny!"

Everyone in the audience laughed at that. Lily spoke up. "Don't forget my doll, too! Marina played a part!"

Elias smiled. "Yes, Marina got in on the action, too. But most of all, we had each other. We did it—"

and Lily, Annika and Jon chimed in with Elias on the last word "—together!"

Alexander took the microphone next. "This brave young man here, Elias Tantalos, deserves a lot of the credit." The archaeologist clapped a hand on Elias' shoulder. "He single-handedly rescued his sister from the criminals and cleverly led Lily and their friends into making those traps to keep the thieves from getting away. But this young man also helped me see that I have been wrong about something, and I would like to take this opportunity to make a very special public announcement."

Elias could not imagine. What had he had done to help Alexander? Wasn't the old man always irritated at him for so much as breathing on the ruins? He listened with as much curiosity as the crowd to find out what he had done. Would he be in more trouble?

"For many years, I have discouraged visitors to Delos and its museum, always with one excuse or another. I've taken my time carving the signposts and putting up ropes to protect the mosaic floors. Antiquities are so precious to me that perhaps I have held them too close. Elias and his sister, Lily, helped me see the ancient wonders anew through their young eyes. I would like everyone to know: the Open Air Museum of Delos will have its grand opening without delay!"

When the clapping had died down, everyone in the crowd turned expectant eyes to the front. Alexander handed the microphone back to Elias.

Elias gulped, and for no reason somehow remembered the gleam in the archaeologist's eyes the first time he saw the Crown of Apollo. In his mind he could still vividly see Apollo's gold laurel leaves flying far and away looped around Petros the pelican's neck. At that moment, the Crown of Apollo was likely to be eight hundred meters down at the bottom of the deep, blue sea.

A sinking sense of disappointment washed over him anew. Even though he was relieved that the Crown of Apollo no longer had its greedy grip on him, it had been a wonderful thing—and a treasure of the Greek people. It had been lost for two thousand years. It would never be seen again. For the rest of time, probably. Because of his mistake.

"I'm sorry," Elias said into the microphone. His voice crackled larger than life from the microphone speakers and bounced through the crowd, but he turned to speak from the heart directly to the archae-ologist. "This is all great, to have stopped those men from taking special old things from Greece, but... I don't deserve this crown." Elias slipped it off his head and held it loosely in the hand that wasn't holding the microphone.

"I—I don't deserve all this... attention. I had the greatest treasure of Delos—the Victory Crown of Apollo!" He swallowed, letting the words sink in, and the crowd gasped. "I tried to take it for myself, and keep it. I'm sorry. I tried to save it, but I couldn't..." Those last words tumbled over each other very fast. He stared at his toes, but slowly met Alexander's eyes to face Alexander's reaction. "I don't deserve this," he repeated.

The elderly gentleman reached for the evergreen crown in Elias' hands. Elias swallowed hard and stared back down at his toes.

He felt pressure on his head.

"That's where it belongs." Alexander's wrinkles creased up in a big smile as if the loss of the gold crown didn't matter to him in the slightest. "Elias, my friend, you gave up the crown and look what you accomplished by doing that! It takes a strong person to do what you did, and we are all very grateful. Of *course* you deserve the laurel crown."

Amid thunderous applause, the reporter must have seen Elias' eyes fill with tears, because she took the microphone from him and immediately faced the archaeologist and the three other kids.

"Does anyone have any more comments?"

"I DO!" shouted a husky voice at the back of the crowd.

What was this?

Elias recognized Christos the fisherman from Mykonos Harbor as the crowd parted to let him through, like they had done for the archaeologist. Christos' eyes twinkled at Elias just like the blue sea on a sunny day. In his hands, Christos carried an old wooden box. The reporter held the microphone to the fisherman's mouth so Christos could talk and hold the box at the same time.

"Hey ho! Hear this fisherman's tale! It was yesterday afternoon I got stuck out in my fishing boat off the coast of Mykonos in sight of Delos. Couldn't get the boat back round the island to the harbor because of that *meltemi* windstorm. And then, one of my best friends came out to sea looking for me and—hey ho! They say a dog is man's best friend, but I say it is my friend Petros the Mykonos Pelican! That big bird dropped a catch on my boat the likes of which my nets—and my *papou's* nets before me—had never seen. A payment, I would say, for always giving him the best of my catch. Would everyone like to see the gift brought to me by our special pelican friend?"

Shouts of "Yes!" responded to those words, and those standing nearest gasped when the fisherman opened the lid.

Elias could not believe his eyes. Nestled on a bed of folded newspaper was the Crown of Apollo. Its layers of gold laurel leaves formed a perfect circle. Lights flashed and the television cameras moved in for a close-up. Christos asked Elias to hold it up so the crowd could see.

His hands trembled as they reached into Christos' rustic old wooden box and picked up the wonderful antiquity. It somehow looked brand new, despite thousands of years and its recent adventures. Each gold leaf glittered in the morning sunshine. The crowd leaned in and oohed and aahed, amazed that the legendary object had sprung to life before their eyes.

Lily tapped the fisherman's arm for attention. "May I have a turn?" Christos was happy to oblige and handed Lily the microphone.

"Petros is a hero! Everybody clap for Petros!" Lily happily joined the cheering crowd jumping and clapping until the camera lights were finally turned off.

POWER BOAT SIMILAR TO THE 'SARGOS', COMING INTO
MYKONOS HARBOUR

34

EVERLASTING LAUREL

W hat I'd like to know is how the crown got under that marble bench in the first place?" Elias directed his question to Alexander. His vivid dream about putting it under the bench himself lingered on; it wasn't possible that it was real—but if he didn't, who did?

The archaeologist's wrinkles stretched out in his funny broad smile, the sparkle in his eyes fixed on the Crown of Apollo, and replied in his wheezy accent: "The Mediterranean Sea and its smaller seas were the highways of the past. Greece was far too mountainous for ancient Greeks to do much traveling by land. Many valuable things passed through the Aegean Sea right here, with Delos at its sacred heart.

"The crown was likely made for someone very wealthy, possibly a king, meant to give as an offering to the Temple of Apollo to ensure their side winning a war. Like everything else, the crown probably got knocked out of place during one of the destructive invasions. It is possible that someone hid the crown under the bench on purpose, intending to go back for it but got attacked himself, or got sold as a slave and taken away from the island to a foreign land, unable to return for the crown. We will never know for sure."

Elias had not told anyone about his dream in the House of the Masks, but he had special reason to hope. If a slave had tried to hide it, perhaps it meant he had managed to escape to freedom. *Without* the help of Apollo's Crown of Victory.

"What will happen to the crown now? Will it stay on Delos?" Elias asked. He hated the idea of parting with it, now that it was found.

"The crown will have to go to Athens for a while to be inspected by archaeologists at the National Museum. If it is what I expect, a work of the Macedonian goldsmiths, the crown will be presented to one of the museums in northern Greece in the city of Thessaloniki," said Alexander.

Annika and Jon's parents waved from the back of the crowd.

"We have to go," Jon said. "Come on, Annika. 'Bye Elias, 'bye Lily! Have a great school year!"

A new school year! He had forgotten.

Elias watched his new friend walk away, disappearing in the thinning crowd. Too bad Jon was going back to Sweden. Summer would be over and Elias would go into sixth grade. With a little jolt of shock, he realized that, while the idea of middle school still made him squirm a bit, it no longer terrified him.

Crown or no crown, he was determined to make sixth grade his best year yet, not the worst. *Catching thieves must be a whole lot harder and scarier than the facing my (former) best friends again!* Elias realized he was looking forward to the challenge. He would tell Kincaid and Brandon exactly how they made him feel last school year.

Elias had a sudden inspiration. "Lily, can I see your bag?"

In the brilliant Greek sunshine, Lily's *Dazzle It!* bag sparkled in its usual place over her shoulder, but seemed somehow less spectacular next to the simple, wonderful leafy laurel crown. "Uh, sure. How come?"

"Tell you in a minute. Hey, Jon—wait up!"

It did not take long. Elias came back through the crowd with the bedazzled bag over his shoulder. In his hand were the feathery pen, and the pink sparkly notebook with a cell phone number and email address scribbled on it. "Whatever happens when I get home, I've got a pen pal for sure!"

"But, Elias—" Lily grabbed his T-shirt sleeve and pulled his face down close to hers. "What are you going to do when Kincaid and Brandon try to break off your head to be the soccer ball?"

The all-too-recent memory of outwitting scuba-diving crooks floated into his mind. Elias shuddered, but smiled. "It's funny, Lil, but Kincaid and Brandon don't scare me anymore. Maybe I'll tell them I know some *real* pirates and they'd better watch their step. Maybe I'll practice extra hard with Kennedy and they'll see I mean to have another try at that championship. Maybe I'll tell them I stuffed my head this summer learning so many new things that it won't roll right."

Elias and Lily shared a good laugh. "I doubt I'll ever be good friends with them, like before, but we *are* teammates. We'll have to learn to play together to be a winning team, won't we?"

Lily nodded and smiled, happiness sparkling in her eyes like the sunlight on the sea.

Another pair of eyes flashed across Elias' memory. Kennedy's eyes. Green and... *sunshine-y.* He wanted to see those eyes again.

"You know what, Lily?" His cheeks stretched into a grin as wide and goofy as Alexander's, but he didn't care. "I have a feeling that middle school might be *very* interesting!"

"That's the spirit!" said Mom, who had been watching the TV interviews from the side of the crowd. She stepped forward to wrap Elias and Lily together in a hug, into which Dad joined, squeezing them tight. "You can be very proud of yourselves. I was thinking, Elias, that a cell phone of your own might be in order when we get home. In case of emergencies, you know."

Mom beamed with a smile that shone brighter than the gold laurel leaves of Apollo. "Next summer, though, can we keep our vacation nice and lazy and boring? Where the only emergency is running out of sunscreen?"

"No promises!" Elias and Lily said in harmony. "We like adventure!"

Dad broke the hug with the only bad news of the day. "Time to say good-bye to Mykonos and Delos, kids. *Sargos* is waiting to take us back to Athens—you know we have to catch a flight home in the morning."

Elias and Lily groaned. "Can't we stay longer?"

"No, but I've heard that the sea in northern Greece will be fantastic for tubing around this time next summer. What do you say?"

"*YESSS!*" Elias and Lily held onto their evergreen crowns and jumped up and down with joy.

Still holding fast to their victor's laurels, the pair sprinted past the chapel toward the dock and its red, yellow and blue striped fishing boats, sleek white sailboats, and powerboats old and new, to where they came upon a large bird with its long bill tucked into its feathers, standing near the *caicques.*

Petros stopped his busy feather-preening, and the brother and sister paused to thank the pelican for the best summer vacation of their lives.

THE   END

Glossary of Terms

Note: In *The Lost Crown of Apollo*, all Greek language words are in italics.

Aegean Sea	part of the Mediterranean Sea southeast of mainland Greece
Agora	a busy marketplace and town center in ancient Greek cities where food and household items were bought and sold; meeting place for people
Ancient	something or someone from the long ago past
Antiquity	an object belonging to or dating from ancient times
Apollo	son of Zeus, god of music, song, harmony, light; twin of Artemis
Artemis	goddess of the hunt; goddess of childbearing women
Archaeologist	one whose job is to excavate and preserve material from the past
Athens	capital and largest city in Greece; location of the Parthenon
Atherina	a very small silverside fish, served fried crispy and salty

Caicque	a traditional, brightly colored boat used by Greek fishermen
Column	a tall pillar, usually made of marble, used in important buildings
Cycladic	a cluster of islands in the Aegean Sea that form a rough circle
Delos	in mythology, a floating island; birthplace of Apollo and Artemis. Delos does exist as an island at the heart of the Cycladic circle
Efkharisto	Greek word for thank you
Feta	a salty, white Greek cheese made of sheep or goat's milk
Football	soccer in European countries is referred to as football
Gods, goddesses	Mythical, supernatural beings worshipped by ancient Greeks
Neh	Greek word meaning yes
Greek Mythology	adventure stories of gods and goddesses in ancient Greece
Gyro	a pita sandwich made with grilled lamb and *tzatziki* sauce
Hera	the jealous wife of Zeus and queen of the gods and goddesses

Hydria	a type of Greek pottery with two handles used for carrying water
Kalimera	Greek: Good morning, welcome
Koukla	Greek word of endearment meaning "doll"
Leto	a Titan's daughter and the mother of twins, Apollo and Artemis
Marble	a stone building material regarded as beautiful
Mask	a fake face. In this book, showing emotions of actors in ancient Greek dramas
Mosaic	a picture made from small colored pieces of ceramics set in mortar
Olympus	highest mountain in Greece; home of gods and goddesses
Parthenon	famous temple of Athena on the Acropolis in Athens
Pedia	child or children
Philadelphia	brotherly love
Ruins	Remains of something destroyed in ancient civilizations
Sargos	The name of the Tantalos family's boat; also a small, fast fish native to the Mediterranean

Taverna	a casual restaurant with outdoor tables
Terracotta	a brownish-orange, waterproof, hard clay used in pottery
Tzatziki	a refreshing, creamy sauce with Greek yogurt, garlic and cucumbers
Yassas	Hello or goodbye when greeting several people, or the more formal, polite usage, especially when greeting someone you don't know, or an older person with respect. When in doubt, use *Yassas,* even for a 'thank you' if you can't pronounce *efkharisto.*
Yassou	Greek word used for both hello and goodbye. *Yassou* would be used between friends or equals, or to children.
Zeus	the supreme ruler of the gods and goddesses; head of Mount Olympus and known for controlling the sky, especially lightning bolts; father to many gods and goddesses

Make it! Discuss it! Look it Up!

With a teacher, parent, or friend, here are some great ways to have more fun adventures with ancient Greece.

Make it!
Make your own ancient Greek crafts

Make a mosaic puzzle picture with Lily

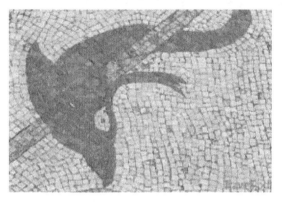

First, sketch a picture you have in mind on heavy card stock or piece of cardboard, something durable enough to hold the weight of the materials you are using. Don't put in too many details. The sketch lines will get covered up with your mosaic, so go for the big picture and add details with the mosaic pieces.

You can make a mosaic from shaped and colored pasta, small ceramic tiles, pebbles, newspaper or magazine cuttings, anything small in a variety of colors. Or make a paper mosaic: take scraps of construction paper in different colors and cut into smaller pieces, about the size of a coin. A larger size will make it easier to glue, and smaller sizes will make for more complex pictures with more details.

Begin with the smallest details. Use a glue stick (or stronger adhesive if needed for heavier materials like tile). Start by gluing down the smallest detail first. For example, if you make a picture of a sky, begin with the sun and clouds, and then fill in the bigger background.

Make Apollo's gold leaf Crown of Victory with Elias

Since ancient times, wreaths of laurel greens have been associated with victors of competitions. You, too, can feel like a winner from centuries past!

First, cut a long strip of stiff paper and have someone help you measure a length to fit comfortably but snugly around your head. Staple.

Cut leaf shapes from paper. You may trace a real leaf or make up your own shape. Green or gold, it is up to you! Glue or staple leaves to crown. If using glue, allow to dry thoroughly before wearing your crown.

Discuss it!

Use these questions as a starting point to discuss *The Lost Crown of Apollo.*

1. Have you ever felt like a bad luck magnet? Tell your story.

2. Why did Elias like fireballs so much?

3. Why did raiders like Pindar attack Delos?

4. What factors made ancient Delos so prosperous?

5. What is the job of archaeologists like Alexander LeMeilleur?

6. Compare the modern island of Mykonos to ancient Delos.

7. Why were the streets on Mykonos designed like a maze?

8. Would you like to live in ancient Greece? Why or why not?

9. Would you like to try snorkeling, SCUBA diving or spear fishing?

10. Did you ever find (or lose) something valuable?

11. What could you do to raise money?

12. Elias faced the choice between saving a treasure and saving his sister. Did he make the right choice? What would you have done?

13. Lily was not afraid of the dark, but she was afraid of swimming. Are you afraid of anything? What could you say to a friend who was afraid of something?

14. Have you ever gone to camp like Elias and Lily? What did you do there? If you haven't, would you like to go? Why or why not?

15. Why is it considered wrong to steal things from ancient Greece found lost in the sea for centuries? Why doesn't the old rule "Finders, Keepers" apply?

Look it up!

Fiction is a story invented by an author, but many details in *The Lost Crown of Apollo* came from real sources of ancient Greek history. Greece has a long history with much to discover.

Books and Regional Brochures used in the writing of The Lost Crown of Apollo

Zaphiropoulou, Fotini, Hon. Curator of Antiquities, *Delos Monuments and Museum*, Krene Editions, Athens, 2007

Hadjidakis, Panayotis J., Archeologist, *A Tour in the Archaeological Site of Delos*, brochure, sponsored by the Hellenic Republic, Ministry of Culture and the European Community, 2000-2006

Ministry of Culture, *Delos* brochure, Archaeological Receipts Fund, Athens, Greece, (written in both Greek and English), 2007

Michalopoulos, Aristidis, *Cyclades, A Complete Travel Guide*, Explorer Publ., Athens, Greece, 2004, pp. 111-133

Pearson, Anne, *What Do We Know About the Greeks?* Peter Bedrick Books, Simon & Schuster Young Books, 1992, p. 29, 35

Discover the Greek Islands, Editions D. Haitalis: Chrissalidos 30, 14343 Athens, Greece, pp. 86-89

Bulfinch, Thomas, *Bulfinch's Mythology*, Barnes and Noble Classics edition, NY, 2006, pp. 44, 150, 155, 241

Low, Alice, *Greek Gods and Heroes*, Simon and Schuster, NY, 1985, pp. 11-15, 49-50

ABOUT THE AUTHOR

In 4th grade, Suzanne wrote a story and bound it with a cardboard cover. She can't remember what the story was about, but she remembers what it felt like to hold her own book and from that moment, she dreamed about writing a real book that other kids can hold and read. She loves to travel and has visited 18 countries. Her favorite destinations include Greece (where her husband grew up) and Japan (where she once lived and taught English), and a lake in western New York called 'Chautauqua' (home of a great Christian camp, Mission Meadows).

Suzanne also travels through the pages of books. Her favorite childhood novels were *The Secret Garden,* by Francis Hodgson Burnett, and *Rasmus and the Vagabond,* by Astrid Lindgren. A member of the Society of Children's Book Writers and Illustrators (SCBWI), Suzanne grew up in the American Midwest with a brother and two sisters. (Her twin sister is a Sunpenny author, too!) Suzanne works at Sacred Heart University and lives with her husband and two daughters in Connecticut, where they share a backyard pond with a snapping turtle called Mel.

Suzanne loves to hear from readers! Please contact her at :

www.suzannecordatos.blogspot.co.uk

SUZANNE CORDATOS ON DELOS ISLAND

[BOTH PHOTOGRAPHS © BY ERICA CORDATOS]

SUNPENNY PUBLISHING GROUP

ROSE & CROWN, BLUE JEANS, BOATHOOKS, SUNBERRY, CHRISTLIGHT, and EPTA Books

MORE FROM SUNBERRY CHILDREN'S BOOKS:

If Horses Were Wishes, by Elizabeth Sellers
Sophie's Quest, by Sonja Anderson
The Skipper's Child, by Valerie Poore
Trouble Rides a Fast Horse, by Elizabeth Sellers

COMING SOON FROM SUNBERRY:
Sending Narda, by Jo Holloway
Sophie Topfeather, Superstar, by Sonja Anderson

MORE BOOKS FROM THE SUNPENNY GROUP:

A Flight Delayed, by KC Lemmer
A Little Book of Pleasures, by William Wood
A Whisper on the Mediterranean, by Tonia Parronchi
Blackbirds Baked in a Pie, by Eugene Barter
Blue Freedom, by Sandra Peut
Breaking the Circle, by Althea Barr
Bridge to Nowhere, by Stephanie Parker McKean
Bridge Beyond Betrayal, by Stephanie Parker McKean
Dance of Eagles, by JS Holloway
Daughter, You Can Make It! by Dag Heward-Mills
Don't Pass Me By, by Julie McGowan
Embracing Change, by Debbie Roome
Far Out, by Corinna Weyreter
Fish Soup, by Michelle Heatley
Going Astray, by Christine Moore